He bent his head and trailed his lips
over the side of her neck.

"Do you still have the Goblet?"

Oh, wow. Oh, wow. Oh, wow. She hadn't felt a man's kiss in so long. "Yes. Her name is Mona." She tilted her head and let him kiss her lower. Over her collarbone. Across her chest. *Oh, wow.* Her dress was way low cut. How low was he going to go? And in case the Otherworld judges were watching, it was all in the spirit of protecting Mona. She was interrogating a potential threat. And if she had to use her body to get answers, then that just showed what a dedicated Guardian she was. Right? Of course, right. *Ask a question about Mona to prove it.* Oh, good call. A question. She could think of one . . . um . . . "Are you after Mona?"

He slipped the spaghetti strap off her shoulder, his breath hot against her skin as he kissed where it had been. "Yes. I need to kill you and then steal her."

Oh, God. That was like the sexiest thing she'd ever heard. "I love a man who isn't afraid to tell the truth."

DATE ME, BABY, ONE MORE TIME

STEPHANIE ROWE

NEW YORK   BOSTON

Book design by Stratford Publishing Services
Cover design by Diane Luger
Cover art by Michael Storrings

Warner Forever is a registered trademark.

Warner Books
1271 Avenue of the Americas
New York, NY 10020

Printed in the United States of America

First Printing: May 2006

10   9   8   7   6   5   4   3   2

To my grandmother, Bonita Humphrey Black, who, at ninety-six years old, inspires me daily with her courage, her sense of humor, and her intelligence.

Acknowledgments

I am so fortunate to have an unbelievable team around me who supports me and pushes me to new heights every day. My incredible agent, Michelle Grajkowski, whose unwavering belief in me is a gift every author should have the opportunity to experience. My absolutely brilliant editor, Melanie Murray, who went to extraordinary lengths in her editing and her advice on this book. Her insight and support drove me to make the book so much better than it otherwise would have been. And my husband, whose contributions to my career are unending.

Date Me, Baby, One More Time

One

Today Derek LaValle was going to reverse the Curse, even if it meant saving the life of his blight-on-the-family-name cousin, Les LaValle.

Well, okay, most of the family would claim Les was blight number two. Derek was blight number one. Except when they wanted money from him. Then Derek was blight number one with an asterisk.

Derek's cell phone rang just as he was walking up the broken front steps of the dump Les lived in. It was his second-in-command, Becca Gibbs. "What's up?"

"The folks from McDonald's are here to talk to you about selling our pretzels in their stores." Her voice was slightly elevated; too much caffeine as usual. Becca was one high-strung woman. It made her a great business partner, though. She never slept and got more work done in an hour than most people did in a month. "The meeting's in five minutes and you're not here."

He glanced at his watch. Three minutes until his cuz bit the dust. "I don't have time to deal with them. Reschedule."

"Don't you realize what a huge opportunity this would be?" Her voice shot up a few more decibels. "You can't miss this meeting!"

"I need to deal with Les first." He swung the baseball bat loosely from his fingers as he rapped on the front door and rang the doorbell. "Les! Open up!"

"Derek! You blew off Dunkin' Donuts last week because you were in the library doing research on that goblet, and you missed the Starbucks meeting on Friday because you saw a woman with a dragon tattoo at lunch and got arrested for stalking her." She made a sound of aggravated distress. "These are incredible distribution opportunities and you need to take them seriously. McDonald's wants an exclusive, and we need to think about whether that makes sense for us, and we can't do it if you're off chasing some damned mumbo-jumbo myth!" She was practically snarling at him now, and he grinned. His business would have been neglected into bankruptcy if it wasn't for Becca.

"Go ahead and meet with them," he said. "They'll realize you're a hell of a lot more on top of things than I am, and they'll be thrilled to work with you instead of me." Hiring Becca five years ago had been his best business decision since deciding to open Vic's Pretzels. She was a business and marketing genius, and the stock price of Vic's Pretzels proved it. Gave him time to pursue more important things, like saving his cousin's life. Not that Becca agreed with his priorities.

Who did?

No one.

Of course, everyone who knew of his plans thought he was insane, so he supposed the fact they didn't support him was to be expected.

He tried the doorknob. Locked. "Les!" A quick glance at his watch told him he had only two and a half minutes now. Damn New York City traffic and his cousin for living so far out of the city. He felt his adrenaline kick in, and his heart began to pump.

But Becca wasn't finished. "These people want to meet with the inventor of Vic's No-Carb Pretzel, not his lieutenant. I will stall them for exactly thirty minutes and if you don't get your designer-clad heinie over here by then, I'm going to hand them the recipe and tell them to have at it." She slammed down the phone.

She'd sounded like she meant it. Crap. Time to save Les's butt and get back to the office.

Barely two minutes left. "Les!" He slung the baseball bat over his shoulder and sprinted around the side of the house. The gate to the backyard was locked, but he scaled it easily, an advantage of being over six feet tall. He vaulted up the rickety stairs to the back deck and nearly crashed into his cousin, who was sprawled in a lawn chair, absorbing the rays. "Damn, Les. Didn't you hear me?"

"Screw you." Les had his feet cooling in a murky plastic wading pool, his bulging stomach hanging over the waistband of his Speedo. "I'm not listening to any of your b.s."

"I don't care if you listen or not," Derek said. "I'm here to save your sorry behind anyway."

"I don't need saving. I take care of myself just fine." For the last six years, Les had been collecting disability for an "injury" to his back. He now spent all his time furthering his Internet poker addiction and bullying the neighborhood children into going to the store for him. The only time he wasn't at the computer was when he was too hungover to focus on the screen. Solution? Sun and beer for a couple hours to revive himself. "And if you keep running around insisting the LaValle men have been cursed, someone's going to pack you off in a straitjacket."

Derek shrugged. "Better insane than dead." His family had already tried to have him committed more than once. Having a vast disposable income came in handy for purchasing his freedom. "Every LaValle man for four generations has died at the moment he turned thirty-one years, forty-six weeks, four days, six hours, three minutes, and five seconds old." He looked at his watch and cursed. "That's in just over a minute for you."

He hoisted the bat to his shoulder and searched the yard for rabid pit bulls and homicidal yard implements that might develop a mind of their own. *I know you're out there, you murderous son of a bitch. I'm ready for you.*

Les took another slug of beer. "The LaValle men have had a run of bad luck. Nothing more."

"So everyone says." So his dad had claimed until the moment he'd become the victim of a wayward butter knife. Died right in front of fifteen-year-old Derek, while they'd been sampling a no-calorie waffle together.

"There's no Curse and I don't need you here to protect me against some crap you made up." Les folded his flabby arms over his saggy chest and glared at Derek.

No Curse? Not likely.

Not when you consider the way they'd died. One had been found impaled on his toothbrush. Another had choked to death on lemonade. How about the one who'd been kicked in the head by a newborn baby and suffered fatal brain damage? One unfortunate sod had actually shot himself in the head while cleaning his gun— although that could have been legit. The one that had been mauled to death by a pet hamster? Seemed a little fishy.

As if fate was grabbing whatever was available at that precise moment.

"I'm going to call my mom and tell her you're over here talking about the Curse again," Les whined. "And then I'm going to call the cops and—"

"Shut up and let me concentrate." If he could keep the Curse from succeeding with Les, he was hoping that would be enough to stop the chain before it hit him and his fraternal twin when they reached the right age. Which was in just over a week.

Forty-five seconds. "Maybe you should go inside," Derek suggested. "You could drown in that pool." His bat wasn't going to be much good if the water suddenly swelled up in a massive tsunami and swept Les away.

"You go inside. Get me another beer." Les belched and let his head drop back against the lounge chair. "Order a pizza while you're at it."

Derek looked up at the sky. No lightning bolt could come out of that blue sky, could it?

Ten seconds. He kicked an old pizza box off the deck. Not sure how cardboard could be deadly, but he wasn't taking any chances.

Les yawned. "I'm gonna take a nap."

Five seconds.

Les belched again and picked up a beer.

"Give me that bottle. I don't want glass near you." Before he could grab the bottle, Derek's watch alarm went off, and a huge rock came careening over the back fence, heading straight for Les's head.

Les screamed and dove out of his chair. Derek swung for the rock. It shattered his bat but ricocheted away from

Les and smashed through the living room window. "Believe me now, Les?"

No sound from Les.

Derek spun around. His cousin was lying on the deck, motionless, his neck twisted at an angle that was unnatural and very, very wrong.

Frustration ripped through him. "Dammit, Les. Why didn't you listen?"

No one listened. And everyone died.

Well, Derek wasn't going to die, and he wasn't going to let his brother die. He glared at the overgrown backyard. "You've just taken your last LaValle man, you hear me?"

He could have sworn he heard laughter on the wind.

Great. So he was burdened with a Curse that had a warped sense of humor.

Lucky him.

Four hours later, after dealing with cops and the ambulance and begging forgiveness from Becca for skipping out on the fast-food meeting, Derek banged open the door to his twin brother's office, making Quincy LaValle jump and spill coffee all over his desk.

"Damn you, Derek. Why do you always do that?"

"Because I like to pick on my little brother. Hello, Wendy." Derek nodded at the assistant filing in the corner as he moved a stack of papers off a chair, and dropped into the seat.

Then he looked again. Wendy Monroe had been working for Quincy for the last two years. Every time he'd seen her, she'd been wearing some gray outfit that barely showed she was a woman. No makeup. Glasses. She was the epitome of a nerdy intellectual and a perfect match for his math professor brother, if only Quincy would pull his head out of his books and realize it.

But today she was wearing a red sweater and her hair looked like it had been marked up with blond or something. What did women call that? Highlighted. Right. She looked like she'd gotten her hair highlighted. A monumental change for her. She actually looked like she had a personality. "You look nice today, Wendy."

She smiled at him and looked him in the eye. Another first. "Thank you, Mr. LaValle." She pulled open a drawer in Quincy's desk and pulled out a napkin, barely keeping her hip a proper distance form Quincy's arm.

"Derek," he corrected her, as usual.

"Of course." As she mopped up the coffee spill, her gaze flicked toward Quincy, and he was pretty sure he saw a light in her eyes he hadn't noticed before. Had she suddenly realized what every other woman on campus already knew? That his antisocial, absentminded brother was apparently a total chick magnet? That would account for the new sweater and colored hair. "Quincy? Do you need anything else?" she asked.

Quincy was already back at the computer typing away. He waved his hand vaguely in her direction. "All set. Have a good weekend."

She gave Derek a knowing smile. It was Monday at one in the afternoon. She still had a thirty-five-hour workweek until the weekend, but it was beneath Quin to keep track of things as mundane as the day of the week. "You have to teach class in forty-five minutes. I'll remind you."

Quincy looked up from the computer. "Really? Today? What class?"

"It's your freshman lecture."

"Oh. Right." He frowned and Wendy set a sheaf of papers in front of him. "These are the tests you're handing back to the students today. And on the top are your notes for your lecture."

Derek grinned as he watched Wendy take care of his brother with calm patience. The perfect woman for Quin. Maybe he ought to encourage Quincy to notice he had a female working in his office.

After they'd taken care of the Curse, of course. Until they beat it, relationships were pretty much doomed. Nothing like telling your date that you'll be dead by age thirty-one to scare her off. Somehow being beheaded by a green bean didn't seem to mesh with domestic visions of white picket fences and 2.3 kids, as their dad's unfortunate butter knife encounter had proven. Just think of the situation Derek would put his kids in if he had any: How do you explain to your friends at school that your dad was the victim of a wayward kitchen utensil that had been momentarily possessed by a supernatural force?

Wendy finished instructing Quincy on his plans for the afternoon, then stepped back from the desk. "Do you need my assistance for your meeting with Derek? If not, I'll keep filing in the corner."

Derek cleared his throat. "Um, would you mind giving us some privacy?"

"No problem at all." She flashed them a small smile and then hurried out of the room.

Derek set a tossed salad and a tuna sub on Quincy's desk. "Brought lunch."

Quincy grinned and began unwrapping the sandwich. "Great. I'm starving. I forgot to eat again."

"I figured that would be the case." The door clicked shut. "Les died."

Quincy looked up sharply. "When?"

"This morning."

Sharp lines tightened behind Quincy's glasses. "At what time?"

"Nine fifty-four and seventeen seconds. As I predicted." Maybe this would convince Quincy. It had to. Derek needed help to figure what was going on and how to stop it. Time was almost out, and eighteen years of solo pursuit hadn't gotten him any answers. He needed a partner, and since Quin was the only person who let Derek discuss the Curse without threatening to get him committed, Quin got the nod.

His brother frowned. "You were there?"

"Yep."

"What happened?"

Typical intellectual. He needed every fact before drawing a conclusion. Derek sighed and filled in his twin on the details, then fell silent.

"Huh."

"Huh? That's all you can say?"

"Well, what do you want me to say? Oh, sure, I believe all the LaValle men are cursed and you're going to die in a week and I'm going to die ten minutes after you?" Quincy shook his head. "I'm sorry, but I don't buy this paranormal spooky stuff. There has to be a logical explanation."

"Math is based on logic. Curses aren't. Forget what you know and open your mind."

Quincy pulled off his glasses and shot Derek a superior stare. "Math is real. Curses are myths. There has to be something else going on besides some fantastical intervention by fate."

Derek ground his teeth. "Listen to me, Quin. We have to find out how to stop it. One week and then we're dead. The leisurely approach is no longer an option."

"I'll do some research on the statistical odds of all these deaths happening at such similar times and—"

"Quincy!" Derek slammed his palms on the desk. "This isn't math! It's something more! You'll *die* if we don't fix this." Derek hadn't suffered all those black eyes and the broken nose defending his nerdy brother just to let him die from a rabid ballpoint pen or something equally ridiculous. A fatal carjacking in the city? Fine. That's fate. A damned ballpoint pen? He had his pride and he simply wouldn't be bested by a blasted writing utensil. "Don't ignore this, Quincy. I'm not crazy."

Quincy leaned back in his chair and gave Derek his tolerant professor look. "What would you have me do?"

"Let's find this Goblet of Eternal Youth. Find the Guardian."

"And then what? Kill the Guardian and steal the Goblet as the journal says must be done for the Curse to be broken? This is the twenty-first century. We can't go around killing anyone."

"What if it's the Guardian's life or ours? You think I should stand back and let us die?"

Quincy leaned forward. "Face it, Derek. There's no Goblet. There's no Curse. There is simply bad luck among the LaValle men. I'll write up a few equations and show that it's mathematically possible for all twenty-nine men to have died without any supernatural intervention."

"Fine." Derek stood up. "You do that."

"And then you'll let this go?"

"Sure." He turned away before Quincy could see the lie in his eyes.

Curse or not, Les was going to be the last LaValle man to die at age thirty-one.

He was going to find that Guardian and do what he had to do. But his gut dropped at the thought of killing anyone in cold blood, even to save his brother.

He hoped she tried to kill him first. Then he could behead her with a clean conscience. Murder in the first degree wasn't exactly befitting of a pretzel mogul. And what was the point of dodging the Curse if he had to spend the rest of his life in prison dodging . . . well . . . yeah. Probably best not to think about that.

First things first. Find the Guardian.

Deal with the rest later.

Two

Two hundred years at the same job is at least one hundred and ninety too many. Especially when it sucks.

Justine Bennett glared at the espresso machine sitting in the afternoon sunshine. "Enjoying yourself?"

The espresso machine, as usual, said nothing. Two hundred years ago Mona had been a jewel-encrusted goblet. Today, she was an espresso machine, thanks to her chameleonic ability to change form. A kitchen appliance who expressed absolutely no appreciation for the fact Justine had been chained to this life for two hundred years, protecting it from would-be evildoers in search of eternal youth.

"Pouting again?" An eleven-foot winged dragon wearing mascara and wine-colored lipstick wandered into the front room of their high-ceilinged loft. The dragon's name was Theresa Nichols, although she hadn't been in her human form in almost two hundred years, since she'd taken three sips from Mona. From rich, indolent siren to a four-footed horned monster with blue shiny scales. It was enough to make any girl cranky, and Theresa was no exception.

"I'm not pouting," Justine said. "I'm bored."

Theresa moved her horned tail aside and settled onto the

navy microfiber couch. Leather was a total no-go. Scales and clawed feet were hell on natural materials. Worse than a herd of destructive cats on speed. Certain synthetics, on the other hand, were impervious to snags and tears. Simply fabulous for the living comfort of dragons. "Me too. What do you say we go barhopping tonight?"

"Sure. You can freak out the entire city of New York, and I'll pick up a cute guy who'll drink from Mona and then I'll have to behead him. Sounds like a blast." Been there, done that. Lesson learned.

"Hey! If anyone deserves to be pouting, it's me. At least you have breasts and can get men to drool." Theresa blew a puff of black smoke, the dragon equivalent of a dramatic sigh. A few sparks dropped on the flame-resistant throw rug. Theresa had burned down their first six houses. It gets difficult to hide a dragon and remain under the societal radar when your house keeps burning down. Thankfully, fire-retardant products became available just as the NYFD began to keep an eye on Justine.

Not that it had been that bad. Some of the members of the fire department were quite sexy. Not that Justine was allowed to indulge. *Sigh.*

And none of the men, burly as they might be, were quite a match for an eleven-foot dragon who would very possibly incinerate them in the heat of passion. This meant the two roomies were celibate together, until and unless Theresa could find a cure for her four-footed form. "You have any luck today?" she asked.

Theresa shook her head. "The Internet is full of crap. With all those Web sites, you think at least one of them would have a legitimate spell for turning me back into human form." She scowled, which entailed flaring her cavernous nostrils and scrunching her gold-flecked eyes until they were barely open. "When I finally figure it out, I'm personally going to go out there and kick the butt of every fraud on this planet who claims to practice magic."

"Yeah, my day is going equally well."

Theresa held out a claw. "Let me see."

Justine passed over her sketch pad. "I'm supposed to come up with a creature that came from Mars and looks very sweet but is actually a deadly assassin. Blues, greens, and silver. Male. Maybe a military background. Can pass as human if he wants to, but is clearly an alien when he's in full kick-butt form." Justine's second job was as an animation designer for a major movie studio. They sent her specs and she created the creatures. First by hand, then she transferred the images to her computer and tightened up the 3-D image. It was one of the only jobs she could do and still stay at home with precious little Mona.

Unfortunately, being Mona's Guardian didn't come with a paycheck. Protecting all that's good in the world was supposed to be reward in itself. Yeah, who needs food and shelter?

Justine did, and supplying enough food to keep an unemployed dragon happy wasn't exactly cheap. At least their shelter was paying for itself, thanks to an excellent property manager named Graham Winthrop and centuries of Guardians who had made savvy real estate investments. Nothing like tenants to keep the income flowing in when they weren't making use of one of their safehouses. Their current lair was the top floor of a posh condo building filled with rich residents who guarded their privacy zealously. Perfect. Boring, but perfect.

"Draw me." Theresa pulled her lips back in a dragon

grin. "I'm bluish green and I kick ass. I could be your alien assassin."

"I already used you two years ago for the remake of *Puff the Magic Dragon.*" She glanced at the date on her watch. "That ad campaign was supposed to launch this week. Have you seen any of the commercials? We have to find a way to smuggle you in so you can see yourself on the big screen."

Theresa scowled. "You know I can't go. I'm a *dragon*, remember? No public appearances for me." She sighed with melodramatic self-pity. "Draw this new alien to look like me so I feel better. To give me a purpose in life. A reason to exist."

"I can't. This alien has to look harmless. That's not you."

Theresa tossed the sketch pad onto the wrought-iron coffee table (very fireproof) and flopped back on the couch. "I want to be adorable again. With pink cheeks and big boobs." She blew a smoke ring and watched it float up to the smoke elimination fan in the ceiling.

"I'd like to have sex. Or even a date. Dinner with a guy. *Anything,*" Justine countered. That damned Guardian Oath. *I swear to protect Desdemona's Temptation for all eternity until I die.*

It sounded simple enough. Until you got to the *rest* of it:

1. I swear never to trust anyone or make friends or emotional connections with anyone. To trust is to let down my guard and endanger Desdemona's Temptation.
2. I swear never to become intimate with any man. Temptations are distractions. Distractions are dangerous.

3. I swear I will never reveal any information about Desdemona's Temptation to anyone other than my designated successor, who will be chosen with the prior approval of the Council.
4. I swear to keep Desdemona's Temptation within my physical presence at all times, unless an emergency dictates leaving her with my designated successor.
5. I will kill to protect Desdemona's Temptation and I will die to keep her safe. I am married to Desdemona's Temptation for all eternity until my death.
6. In all areas not specifically covered by the Oath, I swear to follow the rules as outlined in the most current edition of the *Treatise on Guardianship*.

She hated that damned *Treatise*. It pretty much banned her from doing anything except eating and sleeping and cutting off people's heads.

And to think she didn't like her job. Go figure. "I'm still ticked off at my mom for roping me into being her successor. What kind of a life is this to foist upon your only child?"

Theresa rolled her eyes. "I'm so with you. Thanks to her, I have nightmares about the Council now. Hate them. They're seriously the most rigid, unforgiving, ruthless bastards I've ever met. I almost wish you'd die so I could be Guardian. First thing I'd do is incinerate them and rescind the ban prohibiting Guardians from having sex. And we should both disown your mom. After all, she was the one who talked me into being *your* successor, which made me agree when you asked, which resulted in me drinking from that stupid Goblet, which turned me into a full-time dragon, which then ruined me for all time."

"I know. What a sucky year that was. My mom dies, I become Guardian, you get stuck as a dragon, and we both never have a life again." Mutual bitch sessions were so cathartic.

"Seriously, why can't we disown her and kill off the Council? It could really be a lot of fun. I haven't gotten to kill anyone in ages and—"

A high-pitched ringing blasted through the condo and then the shimmery image of Iris Bennett, Justine's dearly departed mom, rose up from the black tile floor (tile is very spark-proof and black hides soot and ash—oh-so practical). She was wearing an embroidered black jacket, a pair of matching slacks, and a gorgeous pair of heels. Her hair was slightly blonder than it had been the last time Justine had seen her, and her nails were freshly mani-cured. "Are you girls talking about me again? You know I can hear you, don't you?" She gave the dragon a long look, and Theresa shrank back against the couch.

Justine grinned. "Hi, Mom. You look great. Since when does purgatory have such good shopping?"

Iris smoothed her outfit. "Actually, I'm here about the clothes, in a way. It's a bit of a problem." She floated across the floor and hovered in the middle of the coffee table. Literally, in the middle. Her legs disappeared into the wrought iron. It was then Justine noticed the stress lines around her mom's eyes.

"Mom? What's wrong?"

Iris moved to the edge and sat on . . . er, rather, in . . . the coffee table, folding her ankles elegantly. She hadn't lost her old school manners. "It's about hell."

Justine felt her heart tighten. "What about it? I thought you were firmly entrenched in purgatory."

"That's not entirely true." Iris sighed. "When I died, the Council told me that the mistake that got me killed was enough to send me straight to hell."

"Really?" For the two hundred years since her death, her mom had been visiting from the Afterlife, which was where all creatures with a soul went when they died. The bad ones went to hell, the good ones to heaven, and ones like her mom got stuck in purgatory while their future was sorted out. In all that time, her mom had never spilled any details about what had happened the night she died, other than to admit she'd made a mistake and was still paying for it. She said it was a burden her daughter didn't need to carry. "Then, why have you been in purgatory? A clerical oversight?"

Iris shook her head. "You."

"Me, what?"

"You're the reason I'm there." She reached out and trailed her hand through Justine's hair. "I get credit for being the mom of a great kid."

"Seriously?" Theresa asked. "You mean just because you got knocked up by some random guy, you avoid hell?"

"Classy, Theresa," Justine said. Iris had never told Justine who her dad was; she had many secrets.

Theresa blew sparks at Justine. "You're way too uptight."

"And you're way too crass." She turned her attention back to Iris. "So? Since I'm so great, why aren't you in heaven?"

Iris's eyebrows knitted, and a tendon in her neck twitched. "Well, my fate has been in limbo while they wait for your true nature to emerge."

"My true nature? What does that mean?"

"It means it hasn't been determined whether you're destined for heaven or hell."

"What?"

Theresa let out a puff of black smoke. "Are you kidding? Justine's about as pure and bland as tofu on a diet. She's not hell-bound."

"Tofu's a little harsh"—she scowled at her roommate—"but Theresa's basically right. I'm so good that my life has been the ultimate in boredom since I was made Guardian."

"Amen to that. Our life couldn't get more excruciatingly dull. No one to kill, no sex, not enough food to binge on . . ."

"Enough, Theresa," Iris said. "Justine needs to face a Qualifying Incident, and then they'll know whether her dark side's going to prevail. If she suppresses it, then both of us will be destined for heaven." She patted through Justine's knee. "Don't be upset because I didn't tell you all this earlier. I didn't want to put any pressure on you."

Well, that was nice and everything, but . . . "Why are you telling me now? What's changed?"

Iris pursed her lips. "I had a chat with Melvin."

"Melvin?" Justine raised an eyebrow at Theresa to see if she'd heard of Melvin. The annoyed snort of smoke indicated that Theresa was as clueless as Justine was.

"He's the new boss in my neighborhood." Iris rolled her eyes. "That's what he calls them now: neighborhoods. Thinks it makes us sound more secular."

"Is he hot?" Theresa asked.

Justine shoved a fire-resistant pillow in the dragon's mouth and gave her a quelling glare before turning to her mom. "What did Melvin say?"

The pillow shot past Justine's head, a trail of ash in its path.

Iris didn't even blink at the stuffed projectile. "He has much higher clearance with heaven than his predecessor and got the inside scoop. Apparently, Satan has spent the last two hundred years trying to get access to me."

Justine shivered at the mention of the leader of the Underworld. "Why? Why would Satan want you?"

"What kind of access does Satan want? Wooing, dating, shagging, that kind of thing?" Theresa asked, then let out a low whistle when Iris nodded.

Oh. Justine was starting to feel sick. "Satan wants to . . . have sex with you?"

"He also wants me to be the queen of his domain."

"What?"

Iris nodded. "After submitting seventy-eight unsuccessful petitions, he finally picked the right Afterlife official to bribe. As of now, they are officially considering his petition to have me expedited to hell."

"Don't even tell me they're going to let him?" She glanced at Theresa, and the dragon's golden eyes were wide and unblinking as she listened to Iris, her nostrils flaring in agitation.

"Well, at this point, it's basically a political decision," Iris said. "It's always good to keep Satan happy. Plus, there are a few Afterlife officials who would love to have a reason to send me to hell. Not quite over my little incident. And since your true self hasn't emerged, well, nothing is really stopping them."

True self, where are you? "So how long until they decide?"

"Melvin was lobbying for two hundred years, but Satan got them down to two weeks."

"Two weeks? Are you serious?" Her face began to tighten in that "I might freak out really soon" mode, alleviated only when Theresa gave her a reassuring tail flick. Surely, a dragon and a Guardian could handle this situation, right? *Urk.*

"Apparently, he has excellent bribing skills," Iris said. "He even got them to permit him to come into purgatory to try to win me over while the petition is pending. If he can convince me to go with him of my own free will, then the petition won't even matter." She gestured to her outfit. "The clothes are part of his attempt to win me over."

"He's a rat bastard," Theresa announced. "Justine and I will go to hell, assassinate him, and call it a day."

Iris raised an amused brow. "I appreciate the sentiment, Theresa, but if you and Justine murder the leader of hell, that might send me to hell anyway. Remember the Qualifying Incident?"

"We'll find another way to save you," Justine said. "I'll find a Qualifying Incident and prove to them you deserve better than to spend eternity as Satan's harem girl."

"How are you going to find one? It's too iffy. Our best option is to take him out," Theresa said between puffs of smoke and snarkles of fire. "Please? Can we kill him?"

Iris kneeled in front of Justine and rested her hands in the middle of Justine's thighs. "Listen to me, baby. I made the choices that put me in this position. If that's my fate, then that's my fate." She paused to take a deep breath. Then another one. She lifted her chin, nodded firmly, and managed a too-bright smile. "Things could be worse."

"Worse than being Satan's concubine for all of eternity?"

Justine cleared her throat to get the panicked squeal out of it. "What's worse than that?"

Theresa tapped her chin thoughtfully. "Do you think it's true he's the best lover in the Afterlife? Because if it's true, and he'll buy you nice clothes, well, it's something to consider. I bet he'd let you kill anyone you wanted."

"I've heard he's very good in bed," Iris agreed, then she looked at Justine. " 'Worse' would be spending eternity in one of Satan's torture chambers. If I have to go to hell, going as his one and only is the way to do it."

"Well, that's true, but—"

"But you don't have that option, sweetie. If you fail the Qualifying Incident, you'll end up in hell, and it won't be as Satan's honey. You could have a really bad time."

"A bad time . . ." *Understatement of the millennia, anyone?* If you went to hell as one of the commoners, you didn't get designer clothes and unlimited orgasms. You got tortured, disemboweled, and other such lovely things. "Why are you warning me now? Why not two hundred years ago?"

"Melvin's greasing some palms to try to get some of the officials to manufacture a Qualifying Incident for you before Satan's petition goes through. If I can get to heaven before a decision is made, we're all set."

The tension in her shoulders eased. "Okay, so that's good, right?"

"Only if you make the right choice," Theresa said. "If you don't, your mom's screwed. Literally. And you'll be damned for all eternity. That's some serious pressure riding on you, girlfriend."

She glared at Theresa. "Thank you for that editorial."

Theresa puckered her lips. "Anytime, sweetie. You know I'll be by your side."

Iris cleared her throat. "If Melvin succeeds, you could face one soon, but if Satan finds out what's going on, he might try to influence you to choose the dark path so he gets me. Be aware of the pressure to make the wrong choice. Don't give in to your dark side."

Justine blinked. "I would never give in."

Iris smiled. "That's my girl. Keep telling yourself that." She looked at Theresa. "You need to help her, Theresa. It won't be easy, I know it."

"I'm all over it. If Satan interferes, I'll fry his ass while Justine does what she needs to do. It'll work out just fine."

Iris frowned. "You have issues with violence. You do realize that, don't you?" The loud ringing sounded again, and Iris began to fade. "I have to go. I'll come back when I can." And then she was gone.

Well, crud.

Theresa whistled softly. "Damn, girlfriend. How does it feel to know that it's completely up to you whether or not your mom ends up Satan's sex toy for eternity?"

Justine glared at her roommate. "You're not helping."

"Not trying to. If she won't let us take Satan out, I have no idea how else to help you on this one."

Unfortunately, neither did Justine.

Three

———

Derek frowned at the journal in front of him, gazing at the images he'd looked at a thousand times, sketched by his ancestor, Carl LaValle.

He was studying a drawing of the dragon Carl had claimed was a friend of the Guardian. It was the sketches of the dragon that had convinced his family that Carl's journal contained nothing but the rantings of a lunatic. Everyone knew dragons didn't exist, right?

Next to the rendering of the dragon was one of hundreds of sketches of the Guardian herself. Even drawn in black and white on journal paper that was almost two hundred years old, Derek could still tell she was beautiful.

He frowned as his eye went back to the dragon. Hadn't he seen something that looked like it recently?

He was sure he had.

He set down the journal and searched for "dragon" on the Internet. All the usual sites popped up. He searched for pictures of the Guardian and the dragon every few months or so, hoping a picture of one of them would appear. Yeah, it was a long shot, but everything was a long shot at this point.

If Carl's journal was right, both the dragon and the Guardian would still be alive. The Goblet of Eternal

Youth was yet another reason why Derek's family had dismissed the journal's contents. Dragons, immortality, and curses? Only a lunatic would believe that crap.

He clicked on a new link that hadn't come up before. It was an article about a new movie, a *Puff the Magic Dragon* remake. He frowned as he clicked on the image, then his gut tightened.

The resemblance between Puff and the dragon in Carl's journal was uncanny. Even down to the earrings and ruby ring on her left claw. He enlarged it and looked closer, and his gut dropped. There it was: the tattoo on the underside of the dragon's neck. It was the same design as the tattoo on the dragon in the journal, an unusual symbol he'd never been able to match to anything. Until now.

A match could not be a coincidence.

His adrenaline spiking, he picked up his phone and called the movie studio.

Twenty minutes later, he was an investor in a new movie and had a name and address. For money, people would do anything, including violate the privacy of their independent contractor animation designer who just happened to be living in New York.

It had to be the Guardian, didn't it? What were the chances of an exact match between the new Puff and the dragon in the journal? According to the journal, the dragon never went out in public. Who else would know what the dragon looked like? Someone who'd seen the journal that hadn't left his family's possession since it was written, or someone who knew the dragon. Derek would lay bets that the animator was either the Guardian, the dragon, or a descendant of one of them. And in New York! After one hundred and eighty years, she was still living in the area.

He grabbed his keys and shoved back from his desk, his heart racing.

His hand was cold and clammy when his fingers touched the doorknob, which turned before he could grip it.

Becca shoved the door open and stopped when she saw him standing directly in front of her. She was wearing a sharp red suit that made her look like the tough negotiator she was. Her short black hair was sticking out at all angles, and her blue eyes narrowed. "Where are you going?"

"Out. I think I found that woman I've been searching for." Becca knew he was doing research on an ancient goblet and a historical myth, but she had no idea how it related to his personal life. He'd been tempted to clue her in so she could assist him, but he hadn't succumbed so far. She didn't exactly seem like the type to accept the truth. Much too literal and business-minded.

She folded her arms and blocked the door. "No way. The McDonald's team will be here in ten minutes. You're not leaving."

"You rescheduled?" Was she good or what?

"They accepted the death of your cousin as a legitimate excuse." She raised an eyebrow. "I assume you didn't kill him on purpose just to have a reason not to come back to the office?"

An edge in her tone caught his attention. "You think I killed him?"

She tilted her head. "I doubt it, but if it would mean you'd get more time to do research, it wouldn't surprise me."

Was he really that bad? Nah, she was giving him a hard time; he wasn't *that* obsessed. "Can you handle the meeting? I really need to go."

"Use the phone. I'm not letting you out of your office until the meeting is over." Becca folded her arms across her chest. "After the meeting, I will personally drive you to meet this woman and anyone else you want to visit."

He knew the look on her face. There was no way he was getting past her.

And she was right. This meeting was important. And the Guardian had been around for two hundred years. What did another couple hours matter? If he died, Vic's Pretzels needed to live on to support the LaValle clan for years to come. "Give me five minutes to call Quincy, and then I'll be out."

"I'm guarding the door."

He grinned. "I don't pay you enough, do I?"

She flashed him a genuine smile. "I'd do this job for free. I love it."

"You love bossing me around."

She shrugged. "Call me a control freak. I like being in charge of lots of money and powerful men and I like having the title of vice president." Anger flashed in her eyes. "You let me call the shots. I'd give anything for this kind of power in all areas of my life."

He frowned at the simmering rage on her face. "Everything okay with you, Becca?" He didn't know anything about Becca's personal life. She'd made it clear it was off limits, and he'd never worried about it.

"I'm fine," she snapped. "You have eight minutes left. Better make the call to your brother." She spun away and snarled at one of the regional directors when he tried to joke with her. "Eight minutes, LaValle. Be ready."

"Yes, ma'am." He shut the door and retreated back into his office.

Becca was right. He'd been neglecting Vic's Pretzels. And apparently her.

But in less than a week, he'd have stopped the Curse. Or he'd be dead. Either way, he wouldn't be worrying about it anymore, so that was good at least.

He jotted a note to himself to make sure his will was in order. Becca had to stay on as the head of Vic's or the business would go down, and his entire extended family would starve without the income from Vic's to support them.

Then he dialed Quin's office number. His brother answered on the eighth ring. "Quin here."

"I might have found her. At the very least, I've definitely got a strong link to her."

"Her? Her who?"

"The Guardian."

There was utter silence on the other end of the phone.

Finally, Quincy spoke again, stunned disbelief heavy in his voice. "You might have found the Guardian?"

"Yep. She lives in New York."

"New York? How do you know?"

Derek gave Quin the recap on the dragon sighting. When he was finished, Quincy sighed. "You didn't find the Guardian. You found the designer of an animated dragon."

"It's the same dragon. Trust me, I've been searching pictures of dragons for years. This is the first match I've found."

"Derek—"

"I need you to do me a favor."

Quin gave the long suffering moan of brotherly love. "What now?"

"Go visit this woman. I have meetings all afternoon

that Becca won't let me skip. Just go see her, feel her out. I don't want to wait until tonight on this. What if the production company calls her and tells her they gave out her name? I think it would benefit us to catch her by surprise."

"You want me to visit some random woman and ask her if she's the Guardian of the Goblet of Eternal Youth and has a best friend who's a dragon?"

"No, I'll do that. You just meet her and run some math equations on her. See if they compute." Quin might not believe in the Curse, but he was very perceptive. If there was something off about Justine Bennett, Quincy would know.

"Fine. I'll stop by after my next class. Name and address, please."

Derek rattled them off, his adrenaline pumping again. "Call me the minute you've talked to her. I'll take the call even if I'm in a meeting."

"Fine." Quin hung up on him just at Becca stuck her head back in the room.

"Got a couple minutes to go over strategy before the meeting?" she asked. She'd ditched her anger and was back to her usual efficient professionalism. Good. He was much more comfortable with this Becca.

"Yep." He pulled the McDonald's file in front of him.

Time to focus on business.

Yeah, that was going to be easy.

Theresa was hammering away at the keyboard and Justine was on her nineteenth rendition of her alien (all of them sucked, by the way; sort of difficult to concentrate when she kept thinking about Satan plying her mom with whipped cream and champagne) when a heavy knock echoed through the loft.

Justine tensed and Theresa was on her feet instantly, her horned tail switching dangerously close to the china cabinet. "Expecting company?"

"No." They didn't have friends. They were antisocial to neighbors. Justine telecommuted to work and used a post office box for correspondence. They owned the entire top floor of their building. And they gave their doorman a very big tip every holiday season to keep people away.

No one ever visited.

Ever.

Except the Council, when Justine had screwed up and they decided she needed punishment. *Urp.* She still wasn't over the six months of bamboo shoots under her fingernails and the daily chore of carving the entire Oath (including the fine print) on her thigh. Yes, it healed up in a few hours, but it still hurt when she was doing it—which was the point.

One hundred and eighty years later, and she was still on Guardian probation. Not that there was anything to worry about. She'd learned her lesson after the Carl incident and hadn't taken a misstep since. And she hadn't even endangered Mona that time. Imagine if she really screwed up?

No, let's not imagine. She'd never be stupid enough to mess up again, so there was no way the Council was on the other side of the door.

The elevator began to beep its irritation at not being allowed to leave.

And their visitor knocked again. How had anyone gotten past Xavier?

"I'm outta here. You better get it. Could be those hunky firefighters again." Theresa sighed dreamily as she pranced across the room and disappeared behind the solid door at the far end of the loft.

Justine waited until she heard Theresa slide the lock into place, then she walked up to the door. "Who is it?"

"Delivery from Vic's Pretzels."

Theresa stuck her head back into the room. "Let him in. I love those pretzels."

"Just be ready to incinerate him."

"Really? You'd let me have the honors? I love you." Theresa winked and shut the door again, no doubt standing with her ear pressed against it, listening for the go-ahead to toast their visitor.

Justine frowned as she turned toward the door. She bought a Vic's soft pretzel every day when she went out to check the mail. One for herself, and twenty-three for Theresa. They were awesome *and* no-carb. No one knew how Vic's had created a no-carb pretzel, but if you had bought stock in Vic's Pretzels five years ago, you'd be a millionaire today—probably solely because of Theresa's consumption of them. "I didn't know Vic's delivered," she called out.

"It's a new service," the man said.

"I didn't order pretzels." She flipped the cover on the door's spy hole, but all she could see was a box with the vic's pretzels logo on it.

"Someone did. They're already paid for."

Either they had a secret admirer or it was a setup to get into the apartment. She was betting on the latter.

A normal girl in New York City would never open the door in this circumstance. A normal girl would tell the man to leave them with the doorman and she'd pick them up later.

Except she wasn't a normal girl. If this man was a threat, she needed to know it and eliminate it.

She really hoped he wasn't cute. It always felt like such a waste to have to kill good-looking guys. Not that she'd done it that much, but once had been more than enough.

She sighed, flicked the lock, and opened the door.

And got a gun in her face.

Four

Nothing like having the tip of a gun pressed against your left nostril to make you really wish you had a different job. Justine eyed the man on the other end of the weapon. He was actually quite attractive. Surfer-boy blond hair, a pair of cut-off jeans, flip-flops, and a tank top that showed off a nice set of biceps.

So not the type you'd expect to whip out a gun in the middle of a sunny Tuesday afternoon while carrying a box of Vic's Pretzels.

She could only hope that she was being assaulted for her money or her hot bod, but she seriously doubted it. She was going to have to kill him, wasn't she? Was this the test her mom had been talking about?

Option 1: Don't kill him.

Result: By sparing his life, she proves she has a good side and Mom goes to heaven, but Justine violates her Oath to keep Mona safe and gets sent to the Chamber of Unspeakable Horrors for all eternity.

Option 2: Kill him.

Result: She fulfills her Oath and avoids the Chamber by protecting Mona, but Mom goes to hell because Justine took a life.

Damned if you do, damned if you don't. Literally. Stupid

Qualifying Incident. She was totally overthinking and doubting herself and had no idea what she was supposed to do. *Argh!*

Then again, maybe she was overreacting. Maybe it was a case of mistaken identity and she didn't have to off him. It was worth a try. "May I help you?"

"Hand over the wineglass."

Huh. So he *was* after Mona? How was that possible? She and Theresa had worked very hard not to be findable. Not even Satan had been able to track them down. The only people who could find them were her mom and the Council, because their portals were linked to wherever the Guardian was. So how in the world had this surfer dude found them? No one had tracked them down since Carl. What trail had they left? What mistake had they made? This was not good. Really, not good.

But, on the plus side, at least it made her day interesting. After a hundred and eighty years of no action (well, except for the incident in the Amazon after Carl died), there was nothing like a hot surfer guy with a gun to suddenly make the day much brighter. If every day had this kind of eye candy and threats to Mona's safety, maybe she wouldn't be so bored all the time.

A girl could hope.

She eyed him carefully, taking a moment to enjoy his biceps before focusing on the bigger issue at hand. She needed to find out how he'd found her, and then clean up the mess. "Please, do come on in."

She stepped back and he followed, keeping the gun pressed against her face.

He kicked the door shut behind him. "Where is it?"

"Are you going to kill me after I give it to you?"

"Yeah."

"So why would I give it to you, then?" She peered more closely at his face. His eyes had a weird blurry look. Sort of glazed. Drugs? But why would a druggie spend time chasing down Mona? "How did you find me? How did you learn about the crystal Goblet?" She wasn't about to tell him Mona was now an espresso machine. He was working with dated information but it wasn't up to her to point that out.

He frowned, his eyebrows crunching together in thought. "I don't know . . ." The gun started to drop, then he lifted it back up. "Hand over the wineglass."

"You already said that." She waved a hand in front of his face, but he didn't even blink. Interesting. "Let's make a deal. You leave without killing me or taking any of my kitchen supplies, and we'll call it even. As long as you tell me how you tracked us down."

"Hand over the wineglass."

Hmm . . . Not a lot of creative thinking going on in his mind.

He moved so quickly she almost didn't have time to react. His finger twitched on the trigger, she kicked his knee out from under him, the gun went off and a bullet singed her left ear. Then he was on the ground, the gun was in her hand, and her knee was in his chest. "Damn you," she grumbled. "All I want is some answers. Don't make me kill you." Now really wasn't the time to add a dead body to her list of Otherworld credentials, "Otherworld" being defined as all things magical and nonhuman, including such nasties as the Council and Satan.

"Hand over the wineglass."

"What are you, a robot or something?"

He shifted underneath her, and she ducked to the side just as he whipped a knife from behind his back and clipped her neck. So she smacked him in the temple with the gun and let him drop to the floor unconscious. A couple centuries of training did wonders for hand-to-hand combat, especially since men tended to underestimate her. A five-foot-four woman? What could she possibly do to a big strong man? "Kick your ass," she said to the lump on her floor. "That's what I could do to you." But he had gotten in a good whack with the knife. She was getting careless.

The door slid open and Theresa poked her head in. "Did he bring pretzels?"

Justine leaned back against the wall and held her hand to her neck. The blood trickled down her collarbone; there must be a decent-sized hole in her neck. Her quick healing capabilities didn't stop it from hurting like hell. "I need bandages before you eat."

Theresa tossed her the first-aid kit then pranced over to the unconscious guy. She blew a puff of ash over him, and watched it settle. "That's weird."

Justine winced as she taped two oversized gauze pads to her neck. *Crap*. It totally hurt. "What are you talking about?"

Theresa nudged the surfer dude with her right claw, which was sporting a fresh manicure of frosted silver nail polish. She snorted a load of soot over him. "See how the ash slows down right before it hits his skin? It's being stopped by something."

"Are you serious?" Justine crawled over to the guy and looked more carefully. She leaned closer, and caught a whiff of something delicious. It was the scent of man. Of skin. Of aftershave. She inhaled deeply. It had been too long.

"Getting off on our unconscious friend?" Theresa asked.

"Shut up." She ordered her nasal passages to shut down. "Blow the ash again. I want to watch."

She did, and this time Justine definitely saw the ash linger over the surfer boy's tanned flesh, though it dropped freely over her own skin. She frowned and peered closer. That's when she noticed the golden hue emanating from his skin. The ash was resting on top of the layer of gold. "Is that his aura?" Weird. She'd never seen an aura before. Wouldn't have thought it would be gold either. Maybe blue or yellow or red. Not gold, unless he was rich. But he looked like an eighteen-year-old beach bum, and most of those weren't rich. Of course, most of them weren't in New York City either.

"Is what his aura?" Theresa asked.

"That golden hue over him. You see it?"

Theresa crouched beside her and inspected the man. "He looks normal to me. Except the ash hovering two millimeters off his skin, of course."

"The soot is resting on something gold. It's like a glowing light. You don't see it?"

"Nope."

"Weird. You ever seen soot float like that?"

"Nope."

"Well, why would that happen?"

"No idea."

She sat back on her heels. "You're a two hundred and thirty-two year-old dragon. How can you not know how ash works?"

"For the first part of my life, I was letting hot men have their way with me, and I've spent the last two hundred years trying to get back in human form. I haven't exactly had time to be researching the properties of *ash*." Theresa's tail flicked sharply, a sure indicator that she was getting annoyed.

Theresa's bad moods usually meant a visit from the fire department, so Justine grabbed one of the many fire extinguishers stashed around the condo. She tossed it at Theresa. "Suck on this for a while, okay?"

Their captive groaned, and Theresa dropped a spark on the carpet next to his head, all complaints forgotten. "May I? It's been so long since I've gotten to kill anyone, I'm actually twitchy from the withdrawal. I swear I won't so much as singe the floor. Pretty please? It would be so fun. You have no idea what it's like to be constantly suppressing my instincts. I feel like my chest is going to explode all the time. *Please?*"

"Can't you forget about killing people for one minute and focus on the issue?"

"No, I can't. I'm a dragon and it's in my blood to incinerate and destroy."

Justine grimaced. The last thing she needed was a rampaging dragon. "Well, maybe just *threaten* to toast him when he wakes up. We need to find out why he's here."

"Then can I incinerate him? Fry his trespassing ass into oblivion?" Theresa warmed up, a symphony of toots, growls, and hisses as she worked the air around in whatever body part was responsible for generating fire.

"Maybe. We really need to try to avoid killing him." But they were really going to have to find an outlet for Theresa soon.

"You think refraining from deadly skirmishes will save your mom?"

"I'm hoping." Justine tensed as the man opened his

eyes and gazed at her. Such blue eyes. Too beautiful to be owned by a murderer who wanted to ruin the world by stealing Mona. "Who are you?"

He propped himself up on his elbow, his forehead furrowed. "I'm not sure." He peered at her. "Who are you?"

Justine frowned. His eyes had lost that glazed look. Now he just appeared confused. "I'm the one with the wineglass." She braced herself for his attack. "I need to know how you found us."

He shook his head like he was trying to clear it. "What wineglass?"

"The one you wanted to steal."

He snorted. "I'm a beer guy. Why would I want a wineglass?" He struggled to a seated position. "What happened?"

He hadn't noticed Theresa, who was pacing restlessly behind him. Justine gave her roomie a look.

Theresa widened her eyes and jerked her chin toward the surfer, flicking her tongue in frantic circles.

What was she trying to say? Even after all this time, Justine had difficulty reading dragon body language. *Um* . . .

The dragon finally blew a little puff of ash, and it dropped freely over the man's skin, with no impediment. That's when Justine noticed the golden hue was gone from his skin. He was just a normal guy now. He didn't even seem to notice the gray dusting as he staggered to his feet. "I gotta get home. I feel like shit."

He didn't look over his shoulder, or around the room, or at Justine, as he limped to the door. He yanked it open and nearly fell into the elevator. But he wasn't holding his head where Justine had clobbered him. He had his arms wrapped around his midsection, like his stomach was hurting. Or he was freezing cold. Or both.

Completely freaking weird. He hadn't even remembered his gun.

The elevator shut behind him, and she let it go. There would be no answers coming from that guy.

Justine locked the door behind him, then leaned her back against it. "What in the world just happened?"

"I didn't get to fry him. That's what happened. I'm going to have to go set fire to something else now that I'm all worked up. Are there any chairs you don't like?" Theresa scooped the box of pretzels off the floor. "At least he left these. It's always best to destroy things on a full stomach."

"Theresa!"

"What?" She blew on a pretzel to heat it up, her eyes going all glittery in anticipation of the snack she was about to get. "You don't want me to burn up a chair? Fine. A bed works for me. Whatever. Just pick something soon or I might set you on fire instead."

"Get a hold of your instincts, will you? There will be no burning today. I was talking about the surfer guy. What was that gold glow and ash thing all about?"

"I don't know. Why do you always expect me to know everything? You're the Guardian. That's your job. I'm just a useless roommate who lets you save the world." She popped the warm pretzel in her mouth. "That is one good pretzel. The first thing I'm going to do as a human is go find the man who created these snacks and give him an entire week to do with my body what he will. He's totally deserving."

Justine frowned as Theresa chomped the pretzels. First, her mom's visit. Now, someone had tracked down Mona? And he was glowing? What was going on?

All she knew was they'd been compromised. Which meant one thing. "It's time to move on."

Theresa stopped mid-chew. "What?"

"That guy found us. We have to bail. I'll call Graham and have him clear the tenants out of our Santa Fe property. We'll leave tonight."

"But I don't want to leave! I like New York and we've been here only five years."

"I'd like to stay too, but you know the drill. Mona's protection takes priority." She swept photos off a table. "Clear out the personal stuff. We'll have Graham take care of the rest." Dammit. She didn't want to leave. Life was finally getting interesting! Guns, biceps, and assailants? It was about time she got to do some Guardian stuff! How else was she going to get off Guardian probation, if she didn't get a chance to prove herself? As long as she was on probation, the Council had the right to spy on her unannounced and unrevealed. It drove her crazy wondering when they were around, watching every little thing she did, waiting for her to screw up so they could toss her in the Chamber of Unspeakable Horrors.

No, she wanted to stay so she could slay someone in the name of Guardianship and redeem herself.

Plus New York had great delivery services. If you're stuck in your apartment most of the time, you might as well live in a city that delivers anything you can imagine twenty-four hours a day. What could they get delivered in Santa Fe? Cactus pie and sand appetizers? In New York they could even order a man if they wanted to . . . Hmm . . . not a bad thought . . . no strings, a little action. If only that damned Council wasn't watching, bastards.

"New York is home," Theresa whined.

"I know." New York was the one place where they weren't the weirdest couple around, always a comfort when your only friend is a sexually deprived dragon considering breast implants, and you have eternally perky boobs that no man has fondled since long before electricity was invented.

And now that someone had found them in New York, who knew how long it would be until it was safe to return? Maybe never. Crap. Her first duty was to avoid the danger. Stand and fight was available only if flight didn't work.

Theresa stood up. "I'm not leaving."

"Fine. You can stay here." Her voice wobbled at the thought of leaving Theresa behind. "But I have to leave with Mona."

"But I can't be here alone. I need someone in human form to do errands for me. I need a personal servant and you're my only option!"

"Dammit, Theresa! What do you want me to do? I don't have a choice! I'm the Guardian, remember? Page eleven of the Guardian *Treatise* specifically says I must spirit the Goblet away in the event of any threat to her safety, which includes the appearance of idiot, gun-wielding treasure-seekers who have somehow found her." She slammed a picture down too hard and cringed as the glass shattered.

"Aren't you tired of running away? Don't you want a life?"

"Of course I do! So what? I tried once and we saw how well that worked out, didn't we?" It still irked her that she'd violated her Guardian Oath for a man who'd betrayed her. She'd been a total idiot and she wasn't going to make that mistake again, even if it meant bailing prematurely from the coolest city on the planet. She was going to follow the *Treatise* word for word even if she thought the damned book was outdated, uncreative, and basically useless.

"Well, I might have a solution."

Justine stared at her friend. "What are you talking about?"

"Well, I know this guy—"

"What guy? You never go out. How do you know a guy?"

"I met him on the Internet—"

"Are you kidding? One of your cyber lovers?" She sank down on the couch. "Did you tell him about us? Are you the reason that man came to our house today?"

"No, no, no. I haven't told him anything." Theresa sat down next to her and pulled the computer onto her lap. "I met him when I was researching dragons who had been deprived of their human form. He's really into all this stuff and we've been e-mailing each other and, well, I think he might have the answers we need."

Justine couldn't believe the soft look in Theresa's eyes as she typed away at the computer. "You fell in love with a guy you've never met?"

"It's not love. It's great cybersex. The dragon stuff is pillow talk."

"You like him!" Justine had never seen Theresa's gold eyes glitter like that. "It's not just sex."

"Sure it is. He's an amazing cyber-lover and I'm sexually deprived." Theresa cleared her throat and set a coaster on fire. "He lives in New York, but I told him we live in California, so don't freak at me."

Justine studied her friend. "You want to stay here because he's here."

"As if! It's not like I'll ever meet him, thanks to my scales. I just like the view from my bedroom. Nothing like cement to make a girl sleep well at night."

"You're lying." Justine grinned. "You're a romantic. You want to stay here so you can breathe the same air he's breathing."

"Ha. Not hardly." But Theresa kept her gaze firmly fixed on the computer screen. Avoiding eye contact, perhaps?

"Liar." This alone was reason not to leave New York. She was so going to have to track this guy down and meet him. Take pictures. Maybe invite him to the apartment for naked beer pong so Theresa could watch him over the security camera. Pretend they had a normal life instead of one governed by the Council and the *Treatise*. "Want me to stalk him for you?"

Theresa slanted a gaze at her. "Maybe. At least knock out the front teeth of any female he kisses."

"Done." Justine flopped back on the couch. "How fun would that be? We haven't done anything like that in centuries."

"And you want to go to Santa Fe? Who are you going stalk there? Rattlesnakes?"

Justine sighed. "I don't want to go to Santa Fe, but if we stay here and Mona gets stolen, we're both in serious trouble." And her mom would definitely have to go to hell and play strip poker with Satan. Her mom sucked at poker.

"Give me a chance to ask him about the gold auras. He knows this stuff." Theresa paused with her claws over the keyboard. "Please? Running away isn't the best answer anyway. You should know what you're dealing with and eradicate it, right? Isn't that the better solution?"

"Well, yes, but not at the risk of exposing Mona."

"A day. Give us a day."

Justine heard the plea in Theresa's voice and sighed. How could she say no? It had been too long since she'd had the chance to rag on Theresa about men. Life was *boring* and Santa Fe would be even worse. Plus, if someone needed to be beheaded, better to do it in New York. No one would even notice a headless body in a Dumpster in this city. She was pretty sure she could find a section of the *Treatise* that supported staying in town long enough to identify the enemy. "Fine. But you better be ready to incinerate first and ask questions later if anyone else shows up here, even if it's lover boy."

Theresa hugged her. "You're the best."

"Yeah, yeah. Go IM your sex toy. What's his name anyway?"

"Zeke. No last names."

"Of course not." She stood up. "Twenty-four hours, Theresa. And then we have to go."

"Promise." Theresa was already frantically typing. "He'll deliver. I know he will."

"I hope so."

If he didn't, she might have just sent her mom into the arms of the lover from hell.

Literally.

Or maybe this wasn't a Qualifying Incident set up by certain corrupt Afterlife officials. Maybe this was simply an ordinary threat to Mona. Or maybe . . . maybe facilitating her best friend's sexual needs was a selfless deed that would propel her mom to heaven.

Or maybe she was hosed either way.

Five

Derek stood on the marble floor of the lobby and eyed the huge black man staring him down. The name badge identified him as Xavier, but "Death" might have been a better fit. Sure, he was dressed in a gold-gilded doorman's outfit and wore shiny black shoes, but there was no doubt the man was lethal.

People didn't have that look in their eyes unless they'd tasted blood before and liked it. Derek remembered that expression in the eyes of his childhood karate class instructor just before he'd broken the nose of his least favorite student.

Personally, Derek preferred that no one get to taste his blood. Call him stingy, but he liked his red blood cells to be doing their job, not staining marble floors. His black belt wouldn't do any good if Xavier whipped out a gun and popped him between the eyes. Derek cleared his throat. "I'm here to see Justine Bennett."

Xavier gave him a long look, then broke into a smile that startled Derek with its warmth. "Thank you so much for stopping by, but Ms. Bennett has requested privacy." His voice was cultured, his tones amiable and soothing. "I'm sure you'd prefer to go have some coffee and read a newspaper instead, wouldn't you?"

Coffee. Now that Derek thought about it, coffee did

sound good. And what had happened on Wall Street today? A burning need to know *this instant* suddenly flared up inside him.

He began to rifle through his briefcase, searching for his *Wall Street Journal,* then he stopped himself. What was wrong with him? He was here to see Justine Bennett, not to surf headlines. He scowled at Xavier. "I need to see her. If you could buzz her, that would be great."

Xavier's smile broadened. "Of course, you'd much rather go home and watch television, wouldn't you? The Yankees are playing the Red Sox tonight. You wouldn't want to miss that, I'm sure."

Derek blinked. His feet turned toward the door even as he tried to form an argument in his mind.

He was six blocks away before he remembered he didn't like baseball, and even if he did, he wouldn't put baseball over tracking down the Guardian.

Weird. One little suggestion about the game and he was rushing to watch it?

Maybe his family was correct, and he was certifiable and making up all this shit.

But he didn't think so.

Either way, he needed to meet this animator and it was clear the doorman wasn't going to let him up.

No problem. He could work around Xavier.

On his way back to the condo building, Derek pulled a manila envelope out of his briefcase, dropped some papers in it, and wrote Justine's name on the outside. Sure, the papers had nothing to do with Justine, but the legalese would keep her confused long enough for him to do what he needed to do. He sealed it, straightened his suit, and marched back inside. "Good evening, Xavier." He stuck out his hand and pumped the doorman's hand vigorously. "I'm her new lawyer and I brought some papers for her to sign. Derek LaValle at your service."

Xavier lifted a brow. "Ms. Bennett doesn't see guests."

Derek tried to look insulted. "I'm her attorney, not a guest."

"You're hungry, aren't you? Pizza sounds good . . ."

Jesus. He was suddenly starving? He'd had dinner an hour ago, and now he could practically smell the oregano and baking pizza dough.

"You also need coffee. Expensive coffee. Somewhere on the other side of town."

Damn. Derek didn't even drink coffee, but suddenly he felt like if he didn't get a vanilla latte in less than a minute, he was going to lose his mind. It was all he could do to ignore the craving long enough to realize that there was no more doubt: Xavier was working him over.

And if Xavier really had this kind of power, who knew what other impossibilities could be true? Like dragons, Guardians, and Goblets?

He had to know. Had to get answers. He *had* to find a way to meet Justine Bennett, and *now*. His adrenaline racing, he gave Xavier a hard look. "I know what you're doing, and cut it out. I don't have time to go get coffee or eat pizza, so drop the magic shit. I need to get back to the office." He was pretty sure Xavier's left eye twitched in surprise. He took advantage by handing the man the envelope. "Just see that she gets these, all right? And tonight. I'll pick up the signed papers on my way to work in the morning. Around six?" He nodded before Xavier could argue. "Great. Thanks for your help." He frowned. "And tell me I'm not hungry or thirsty and I can work all night.

I have a lot to do, and if you screw it up by sending me home to watch the baseball game and OD on caffeine, I'm coming after you."

Xavier blinked.

"Undo the damage, Xavier. I'm so hungry I could eat your damned name tag."

Xavier frowned, his forehead furrowed deeply. "Fine. You're not hungry. You need to work. Go . . ."

"I can take it from there." Amazing. He was suddenly so full he couldn't even stand the thought of food. All because of a few words Xavier had spoken. What kind of situation was he getting involved with? He let his breath out softly, then realized Xavier was still staring at him.

"Justine doesn't know about me," Xavier said. "How do *you*?" Xavier's hands curled into fists. They were like sides of beef. Probably had metal spikes that came out of them or something. "How do you know?" Xavier repeated. His voice was soft, but instead of charming, it was deadly.

Great. Just great.

Derek forced himself to snort and roll his eyes, even as he eased into a ready stance and tried not to wonder if he was about to get a supernatural ass-kicking. "Give me a break, Xavier. I've been around this crap so long it takes someone a lot more subtle than you to fool me." Would this tactic work? He sure hoped so.

Xavier narrowed his eyes. "How long is 'so long'?"

"Too long." He gave Xavier an easy smile. "Don't worry. You're better than most." Most what? He had no clue. "Keep at it and you'll be great. But I need to get back to the office. Get Justine the papers, and don't worry, I won't tell her about you." God, he hoped he was making sense to Xavier, because he sure as hell had no idea what he was saying.

He made it to the revolving door when Xavier stopped him. "LaValle?"

Derek grimaced, then turned to face him. "Yes?"

"What are you?"

Not *who, what.* Best not to analyze the implications of that question. He didn't think his brain could handle it. And somehow, he didn't think "ordinary human" was the right answer. "Tonight, I'm just a lawyer."

"And other nights?"

"Guess." He left before Xavier could start listing things he didn't want to know about.

He was in way over his head.

Which meant he was right.

Hot damn. *He was right.*

The intercom buzzed as Justine was sharpening the blade of her favorite sword. After the surfer-boy incident earlier in the day, she'd decided she needed to prepare for battle. The diamonds on her sword always glittered so nicely after a slaying, it usually improved her mood. Diamonds were indeed a girl's best friend, even when on the butt of a sword that had just beheaded someone.

The intercom beeped again, and the red light was flashing insistently. "Another visitor? Did someone post a treasure map on the wall of a public restroom or something?"

Theresa didn't look up from the computer. "It's not my fault."

"Why would it be your fault?"

"It's not, so it's not. So there."

"Being in love is rotting your brain."

"You mean great cybersex is rotting my brain. There are worse ways to go."

"True." Justine set the blade on their granite-topped kitchen table (even Theresa couldn't burn that sucker) and walked over to the intercom. She punched the gray button. "Xavier?"

"Your lawyer left some papers for you."

"My lawyer?" She glanced at Theresa. "Are you cyber-boinking a lawyer?"

"Not that I know of."

Huh. Justine frowned at the speaker. "Are you sure it's not a bomb?"

"It's papers." Xavier sounded proper as always. The man had no personality, but he was very effective.

"Open it," she said.

She waited for the rustling of paper, then Xavier came back on. "It's a bunch of legal stuff. Contracts or something. About pretzels. Nothing lethal. Want me to bring them up?"

Pretzels, eh? Their assailant was too stupid if he thought they'd fall for the same line twice. "No. I'll come down." She disconnected. "I'm going to the lobby."

Theresa nodded and shifted on the couch, still typing furiously. "Yeah, whatever."

"Are you getting info on gold auras, or on orgasms?" Only twenty-two hours left before they had to break camp, unless Theresa could get answers.

"Okay, fine."

Justine set her hands on her hips. "It could be someone after Mona in the lobby. They might try to take me out and come up here. Or maybe Xavier has been possessed, and when I go down there, he's going to kill me."

"Mmm-hmm . . ."

"Theresa!"

The dragon finally looked up. The scales on her cheeks were shining and her eyes were glowing so bright they were almost bioluminescent. "Did you say something?"

"*What* are you doing on that computer? Is it even legal?"

Theresa's lips curved back in a grin. "Leave me alone, you cybersex virgin. I'm busy."

"I guess." Justine slipped a dagger in the back of her waistband and put another in a sheath between her shoulder blades. She tucked her favorite black-market handgun into her shoulder holster—no need to put the cops on alert by registering it. Then she put a denim jacket on, fluffed her hair, and freshened up her makeup. "Good enough to date, bad enough to kick some ass." Since Mona's benefits didn't include becoming ultra-strong or fast, her best bet was to appear harmless and take her assailants by surprise. It had worked so far and she always got a kick out of the look of astonishment right before she dropped some jerk on his butt.

Ah, the small pleasures in life.

"Have fun." Theresa sighed. "I want to be Guardian. You get to do all the killing."

"Killing in the name of eternal youth is overrated, and the only way you'll get to be Guardian is if I die."

Theresa rubbed her chin. "It's a thought . . ."

"Shut up and turn the intercom on. If it sounds like I'm about to be beheaded, come down and burn the place up."

"You got it, sister."

Justine punched the elevator button and waited, her foot tapping impatiently on the tile floor, her fingers twitching restlessly near her waistband dagger. She could be heading toward her death, something she hadn't had to worry about for the last one hundred and eighty years, since the Carl incident.

Which meant today was turning out to be the most interesting day she'd had in decades.

A clear indication that she really needed to get a life.

From his vantage point in the shadows outside the glass double doors of the building, Derek watched the elevator open, his body tense.

And then she stepped out into the lobby, and he nearly dropped the journal.

It was the Guardian.

Almost two centuries later, and she still looked exactly like the drawings in the journal.

Unbelievable.

Her hair was a shoulder-length light brown, sort of intentionally casual looking, as opposed to the old-fashioned style in the journal. She was wearing jeans and a pair of clogs, and her black V-neck T-shirt hugged a very fit body. She was the epitome of a modern New Yorker, but there was no doubt it was the same face as the one in the sketches.

It was her.

He watched as she chatted with Xavier, her forehead furrowed in concentration.

Time to move and approach her.

But he stood there for another moment. He simply couldn't believe it was true.

Was he going to have to kill her?

The papers made no sense. Well, they made sense, but they didn't seem to have anything to do with her. "It's a contract between Vic's Pretzels and McDonald's. Why would someone leave this for me?"

"Inside stock tip?" Xavier suggested. "Everyone around here knows you keep the Vic's on the corner in business."

"Maybe." She slid the papers back into the envelope and looked at her doorman. After the surfer episode, she'd grilled him about letting the kid up. Xavier had denied seeing the boy arrive, let alone permitting him access to the elevator, though he *had* seen him leave. Xavier was still meeting her eyes easily, so she didn't think he was lying. But neither of them had been able to figure out how the kid could have gotten in the elevator without Xavier seeing him. Things were getting weirder by the minute. "So, who left these papers?"

"I did."

She spun around, her hand going to the small of her back. A man in a business suit was standing inside the lobby doors, a briefcase in one hand. He looked just over six feet, short dark hair, and a stance that exuded readiness. He was absolutely gorgeous and made her mouth go dry, which meant the odds that she was going to have to kill him were quite high.

And he looked very, very familiar.

Xavier moved next to her. "Want me to get rid of him?"

"No. Not yet." She eased away from the doorman so he didn't cramp her movements. "Who are you?"

"Didn't my brother say I'd be coming by? I asked him to stop by earlier."

"Your brother?" This was the surfer dude's brother? "He wasn't real chatty."

The man sighed. "Yes, sometimes he's a bit distracted."

Her fingers closed around the knife. "Do I know you?"

It was his chin, she decided. She knew that chin. Nice angle, strong. Masculine. "You look familiar."

He lifted a brow. Nice eyebrows. "My brother looks like me."

"No, he doesn't." Not at all. "Not that I believe he was your brother. Paid assassin is more likely."

The man raised the other eyebrow. "Assassin?"

"Yes, and he wasn't a very good one either. Next time you should check references."

"If I ever hire an assassin, I'll be sure to keep your advice in mind." He took a few steps toward her, and she moved to her right, drifting to the middle of the lobby so she'd have room to maneuver. "At the moment, however, I just want to ask you some questions."

"Ask away." Seeing as how his "brother" had tried to kill her earlier today, she knew she ought to take him out first and skip the questions. But unlike Theresa, she didn't get a thrill out of killing people, and she was still hoping he'd turn out to be a vacuum cleaner salesman.

He moved opposite her, until they were both moving in a slow circle, like assailants looking for an opening.

Which she was.

Was he?

A spike of adrenaline washed over her. She hadn't had a good battle in forever. How fun would it be to have one now? Maybe she couldn't sleep with him, but she could knock him around a bit.

"You know any dragons?"

She stopped. "What?"

"Dragons. Know any?"

Who *was* this guy? "Xavier, I think you should leave."

"I think *he* should leave. I think he's tired and needs a nap," Xavier replied.

"Shut up!" The man glared at Xavier. "You say one more thing and I'm blowing your cover."

Justine eyed her doorman, who nodded and closed his mouth. "Um, what cover?" she asked Xavier.

"Nothing. You asked me to leave and I will." Xavier scowled at their visitor. "You hurt her, and you'll die."

The man didn't look impressed by the threat. "Go have some coffee."

Xavier growled, but he walked out the door, muttering what sounded like orders to go to sleep immediately.

She directed her attention back to the man, catching the tail end of a yawn. "Who are you?"

He yawned again. "The Curse. I need to know how to stop it."

"What curse?"

He staggered slightly and slapped his cheek, even as he yawned again. "Bastard." His epithet was mumbled, his eyes bleary.

"What's wrong with you?"

"Xavier." He blinked and stumbled over to the wall. He leaned against it, then slid down to the floor, his head collapsing against the wall with a thud. "The dragon. The Goblet. Need answers." His eyes closed for a moment, before he jerked them open again.

She let her fingers slide off the dagger. "What goblet?" Was he faking it? He didn't look like it. He looked like he was about to pass out.

"Eternal Youth." His eyes closed and his head slumped forward.

Shit. He knew what he was talking about. At least he

didn't know Mona was an espresso machine . . . or did
he? "What do you know about it?"

No answer.

She withdrew her gun and pointed it at him, then eased
over to him, nudging him with her toe.

No response.

Was he dead?

Keeping her gun out, she squatted next to him and felt
his pulse. Strong.

He was alive.

And he smelled divine.

She took a quick glance around, then leaned forward
and buried her nose in his neck. Closed her eyes and inhaled him. He smelled like man, like woods and sophisti-
cation, all tangled up together. Surfer Boy had smelled
good, but this guy smelled incredible.

"What's going on down there?" Theresa's voice bellowed out from the intercom.

She jumped and sat up. "He passed out."

"Who is he?"

"I don't know." She flipped open his suit jacket and felt
for a wallet, trying not to notice he had a very nice chest.
"Got a wallet."

"Is he hot?"

"I didn't notice."

"Liar! Take advantage of him while he's unconscious."

"Don't tempt me." She opened his wallet and pulled out
a driver's license. "Holy shit."

"What?"

She collapsed against the wall, staring at the words.

"What?"

"His name. It's Derek LaValle."

Silence for a moment. "You think he's related to Carl?"

Her heart thudding in her chest, she turned and studied Derek's profile. He had Carl's chin. "Yes." No wonder he'd looked familiar.

"Well, shit and damn. Is he as good-looking as Carl was?"

"Better." She clenched the license in her hand.

"Better? He must be gorgeous! Is he gay, like Carl was? Or is this guy fair game?"

"I have no idea."

"Well, did he check out your breasts before he passed out?"

"Theresa! I don't know! God, what am I supposed to do with him?"

"Bring him upstairs. We'll handcuff him to your bed and torture him sexually until he confesses all. If we blindfold him, do you think he'll realize I'm a dragon?"

"I think I should kill him." She stood up and pulled out her knife. "Carl betrayed me. This guy's 'brother' already tried to kill me today. There's no way this guy can be anything but a danger to us." But she stood there staring at Derek, who wasn't moving. She really didn't think killing in cold blood was the best approach, given her mom's situation. Plus he was so good-looking and smelled really delicious, and, well, would it be so bad to take a couple minutes to inhale him? Not long. Just a brief moment.

"Justine? Did you kill him? I don't hear any blood rushing around down there."

She shoved the dagger back in its sheath. "I'm bringing him up."

"Oh, goody. Can we torture him? Burn him up? Use him until we're all heavily sated and exhausted?"

"No, to everything except burning him up, and that's a maybe."

"Sweet. This will be so fun!"

Justine eased behind him and wrapped her arms under his arms and around his chest . . . Oh, wow. It felt so good to have him smashed up against her. Maybe Theresa was right. Maybe she should make him her love slave for the next few hundred years. . . . She dragged him into the elevator, got his feet clear of the door . . . but didn't let go.

Not yet. She wanted to enjoy this sensation for another minute. Granted, he was passed out and limp against her, but she could feel his muscles. He was a man, for God's sake, and he was in her arms. It had been so long. Was this why Theresa had turned to cybersex? But how could cybersex possibly make up for the feeling of a man's body against hers, the heat from his skin pressing against her and—

He twitched, spun around in her arms and flipped her beneath him, trapping her instantly under the weight of his body, on the floor of the elevator. Big enough for moving in couches, it was apparently also big enough for two adults to stretch out in a very intimate fashion.

He opened his gorgeous eyes and peered down at her, the slightest hint of smugness in his expression.

Oh, so that's how it was? Try to lull her into submission with his manly appeal and then take her out? Not so fast. She was a Guardian first and a woman second, and he was so going down. But damn, he smelled good.

Six

His first thought was that the sketches in the journal didn't do her justice.

His second thought was that her body felt extremely nice under his.

His third thought was that she had on a gun holster under her jacket.

He suddenly didn't feel so bad about pinning her to the floor of the elevator. "You planning to shoot someone?"

"You." She didn't sound contrite. Or worried. "Will you please attack me now?"

Adrenaline rushed through him as he stared down at her flushed cheeks and disheveled hair. "Attack you how?"

"Try to kill me."

"Oh." He'd thought of a much friendlier, more intimate kind of assault than killing her. *Yeesh*. Mind in the gutter? He was here to find out whether she was the woman he had to behead, not take advantage of the fact he was lying on top of her. "Why do you want me to kill you?"

She rolled her fantastically gorgeous green eyes and, for a moment, he forgot about everything except getting sucked up into them.

"I don't want you to kill me. I just want you to try, so I can slay you in self-defense."

"Ah." With that answer, it was time to disarm her. He shifted slightly and removed the gun from its holster. She didn't try to stop him. Not that she had a choice. He was pretty impressed with the position he'd gotten her in, actually. Might stay here for a while. Just until he was sure she wasn't going to kill him. Yeah, that was why he didn't want to move: self-preservation. "Thanks for the offer to battle to the death, but I'll pass for now."

She scowled. "You're not very accommodating."

"My apologies. My family would no doubt be disappointed in my unwillingness to help someone kill me."

She lifted a brow at that. "Really? Your family wants you dead?"

"Locked up at least."

She looked much more interested now. "Why?"

"Apparently, I'm insane."

She tilted her head, seeming not at all concerned that she was still pinned underneath him. Either she sensed he wasn't going to hurt her (yet), or she was entirely serious about her ability to kill him.

Maybe Xavier wasn't the only one with supernatural ass-kicking skills. He shifted his position again, a more secure setting that put his thigh in a very interesting place. He tried not to notice, but her sharp intake of breath and the sudden glow in her eyes made it impossible for him not to think about it. Or wonder what her lips tasted like. And . . .

She cleared her throat and took a deep breath. "Well, so, why are you insane?" Her voice was a little high pitched. A little frazzled.

He grinned. No problem. They could have a perfectly normal conversation while their legs were entwined and his pelvis was pressed against hers. Easy. *Ahem.* "I'm insane because I believe in curses, dragons, Guardians, and the Goblet of Eternal Youth."

Her face froze for a split second, before she gave him an easy smile. Too late. He'd seen her expression. She knew exactly what he was talking about.

"You really believe in that stuff?" she asked.

"Yep. You?"

"No. I'm a secular kind of gal."

At that point, the elevator door slid open, and he glanced instinctively into the room. The door to the apartment swung open, and the blue head of a dragon popped into the elevator, its eyes instantly widening. "Shit!" It punched the emergency STOP button in the elevator, then slammed the door shut. He heard something crash inside, followed by another curse.

Holy shit. There really was a dragon? And it talked? Jesus. He was never going to recover from this night.

Justine took one look at Derek's stunned expression and knew she was in trouble.

He'd seen Theresa, he knew what she was, and he wasn't about to believe it was a Halloween costume.

He looked down at her, his facing twitching with the effort of keeping his composure. She was pretty impressed he hadn't leapt to his feet and tried to bolt to safety. It wasn't every day one had their first look at a fire-breathing dragon. The man had backbone, and she was a sucker for tough men.

"Care to amend your claim of being a secular girl who doesn't believe in dragons?" he asked. Okay, so his voice was a little strained. It was sort of cute actually. Big man afraid of a lady dragon.

"No." *Yeah, great reply.* Where was her brain? Why couldn't she think of a smart retort? Just because she was having trouble thinking about anything other than the fact that there was a man between her legs didn't mean she had to completely abandon her Guardian skills.

He lifted a brow. "So, tell me this: Are you the Guardian or merely her offspring?"

She pressed her lips together. What was she supposed to tell him? It was a little late to pretend to be the sweet Catholic girl from down the street. Not that she was in a good bargaining position. He had her in a very secure hold. She tried to move her wrist and he grinned.

She had no chance.

Bastard.

Or not. He was the first man who'd gotten the jump on her in centuries. She sort of liked the fact that she might have to work to take him out. No woman wants a man she has to worry about hurting.

But still, this situation really wasn't optimal. If she could just get free. . . . She squirmed under him, and instantly felt something she hadn't felt in way too long. Something against her leg that sent a surge of hormones catapulting toward her nether regions. *Um, hello! Haven't seen you for a while.*

"Stop moving." Derek's voice was strained.

Yeah, that was a good idea. Otherwise she might find herself doing things that she wasn't supposed to be doing. With her mom's fate in her hands and the Council hovering, now wasn't the time to violate her Oath. Especially since Derek might be here to kill her.

Nothing like some heavy duty sexual attraction to make

a woman forget her life might be at risk. She cleared her throat. "Theresa! A little help here!"

Derek tensed as Theresa's voice echoed through the door. "Are you kidding? After two hundred years of celibacy, you want out from under that hunk of burning love? Forget it. You need to get laid and I'm not helping you until you do. Why do you think I hit the STOP button on the elevator? Take advantage of him."

Derek grinned and she felt him relax. How amazing to be so close to a man that she could gauge his moods by the tension in his body. God, it felt good. Too good. She needed to focus.

"Some kind of bodyguard you have," he said.

"Shut up. And it hasn't been two hundred years since I've had sex." Not that it was any of his business, but sometimes a girl had to protect her reputation. She gave him her most hostile glare. "What do you want?"

"Dinner."

She blinked. "What?" She'd been expecting him to say Mona, or propose a deal, or demand eternal youth. Not "dinner."

"Dinner. My treat. How about tomorrow night?"

"A date? You want a date?" A shiver of a very girlish emotion rushed through her.

He tilted his head. "Sure. Let's call it a date."

"I don't date." But it was oh-so-tempting.

"Then let's call it an exchange of information. I want to know about this Guardian thing, you want to know who I am. I'll buy, you eat, and we both talk. Deal?"

"Or you could bring him in here and we could torture him until he confesses," Theresa said through the door. "I could bite off his extremities one by one. Please? Bring him in?"

Derek grinned. "My vice president knows I'm here. If I miss work tomorrow, she'll have your head. And I'm not kidding. She has no mercy when it comes to business."

Did he really know the only way to kill her was to behead her? She needed to find out more about Derek LaValle, and the sooner the better. Despite what Theresa said, she couldn't kill him for wrestling her to the floor and getting her hormones in an uproar. "Fine. Dinner."

His smile broadened. "Great. I'll pick you up here at seven. Make sure Xavier knows I'm coming. I'd hate to pass out in my dinner."

"Thanks for the reminder." She lifted a brow. "How do you know Xavier? And what little secret do you two have going on?"

"Sorry. No answers until tomorrow night." His smile faded. "Now that I've wooed you into a dinner date, I'm thinking I'll take off now, but if I get up, you might kill me."

She grinned at his matter-of-fact tone. "I promise not to kill you until after dinner."

"And Theresa?"

Her voice came easily through the door. "Fine. I won't either. But I'm not happy about it."

He nodded. "Deal." He rolled off her, sweeping her dagger out of the back of her jeans as he went. "Insurance."

Refusing to wail in dismay at the loss of their intimate position, she jumped to her feet and faced him in the elevator that suddenly seemed very small. Cozy. She cleared her throat and nodded at the dagger hanging from his left hand. "I'm very hurt you don't trust my word and felt the need to take all my weapons."

"Except the one between your shoulder blades. I couldn't reach that one."

She blinked. God, she liked a man who could find all her weapons. Made her feel almost doted upon. Cherished.

He grinned at her surprised expression. "I'm psychic."

"Or you felt it when you grabbed me."

"Could be that too." He reached around her and flicked open the door to her apartment. "Your stop?"

She backed out of the elevator, keeping an eye on him. But he didn't try to barge into the loft. He simply gave her a nod. "Until tomorrow at seven. Dress up. We're going fancy."

The door slid shut before she could figure out how to respond to that request.

"Hot damn, girl. He's totally gorgeous."

She sighed and glanced at her blue-scaled friend. "You realize that means I'm definitely going to end up having to kill him?"

"Yeah. Bummer."

Major bummer.

Iris Bennett was in the middle of her Pilates workout in the living room of her house. And a very charming house it was: it fit in perfectly with the rest of the neighborhood. Nice yards, well-trimmed bushes, and a grocery store with decent produce. She'd gotten the upgrade to the higher-end residential area of purgatory after it had become clear she'd be there for a while. It wasn't heaven, but it wasn't bad either. She was at peace, enjoying the moment, when there was a flirty knock on her front door.

She knew that knock. It was the knock of a scum-sucking bastard. She released her pose and rolled to her feet, aggravation already building.

She used to think it was a cute knock. It used to make her heart flutter and her body tingle. Now? She picked up her fully loaded, double-barreled turbo squirt gun and stalked over to the door. She took a moment to get it positioned, then opened the door and blasted the vile jerk with both barrels.

"Iris!" Satan dove for cover behind a potted plant, steam sizzling off his gorgeous Italian-made suit. "Cease torturing the man of your wildest sex fantasies! You must stop!"

"Fat chance of that." She followed him behind the geraniums, unloading the water onto his lovely head. She grinned as his hair melted and crackled and flattened. "You need new hair gel. Your current brand isn't up to snuff." She squirted the final drops into his ear, then nodded with satisfaction as his ear started to slide down the side of his neck. "So good to see you, my dear."

Satan stood up, a cloud of steam rising from his deformed body and half-melted head. "I do not take any pleasure in these attacks."

"I know. That's why I do it." She tucked the gun under her arm. "Does it really hurt?"

"It is extreme pain that would destroy any man except Satan, the lord of the Underworld." He wiped his cuff across his forehead, leaving an indent from the buttons.

"Excellent. You look hellish. No woman will want you. So sad, too bad." Iris spun on her heels and marched back into her house. No need to shut the door behind her. He'd find his way in, like he always did. He only knocked because he was trying to delude her as to his true nature.

Hah. He'd fooled her once. Now? Forget it. It didn't matter how many erotic dreams she had about him. The man was pure evil, and she was now both smart enough to see that and strong enough to resist his allure.

In the past, she'd been his victim. Today, she was his equal, and she was armed.

She walked over to the sink and turned on the faucet for a refill.

Satan squished into the kitchen. "My love muffin, if you try to torture me with that instrument of death again, I will be forced to manhandle it from your grasp. I cannot permit you to humiliate Satan twice in five minutes. A man must keep his fierce and brutal reputation intact at all costs."

"Stop whining. I'm just readying myself for your next visit." She knew his limits. One round he'd tolerate because he was trying to woo her. If she tried another assault, he'd grab the gun, his hands would slip onto her breasts and her body would betray her and they'd wind up in a gyrating pile on the linoleum. She might know he was an ass who didn't deserve her, but even the best intentions were a poor match for Satan's kissing ability. "Where are my gifts? You know I tolerate your visits only because you bring me material items of great value and unmatched beauty."

He fished a dish towel out of the bottom drawer and began mopping his melted body up. "I left them in the limo. They would be ruined by the water. I was highly suspectful you might shoot me."

She grinned at his disgruntled tone as she popped the plug back in the gun. "You're such a smart guy. I always knew there was something to you besides being a manipulating, arrogant bastard." She set the gun on the counter and glanced at him.

Mistake. He was already regaining his human form, and some form it was. He was the drop-dead sexiest hunk of beefcake she'd ever seen, and he knew she thought so. *Contemptible pig.*

Satan gave her a smug grin and dropped the towel onto the counter. "I am pleased you noticed that I am manipulative and an arrogant bastard. Does being around a man of such stature make you long for naked flesh and moans of ecstasy?"

Yes. "Not at all."

"I can tell your resistance to my charm weakens." Satan trailed his fingers down the side of her neck. "Say, 'yes' this instant, before my love explodes."

She batted his hand away. "Say yes to moving south of the border and being your love slave for all eternity?"

"*I* will be *your* love slave. All you have to do is dominate me."

It wasn't the first time her hormones had been more than half-tempted by the idea. Everyone knew Satan was the best lover in the Afterlife. "You used me, tricked me, and nearly destroyed my legacy. It's going to take a lot of clothes to make up for that."

"I have much money. I am the richest being in the Afterlife, and I can buy any gift you yearn for. . . . Your breasts are looking lovely as usual." He wiggled his eyebrows at her. "I would love to lick them."

"Oh, please." She rolled her eyes. "That is so not how to woo a woman."

"Why not? Every woman wants to know a man thinks she's attractive, does she not?" He flicked the final bit of water out of his hair, making the short dark ends stick up.

"She wants to feel valued as a woman, not as a piece of ass to be bought and then nailed . . ." Her voice trailed off at the smug look on his face. "Dammit! You tricked me!"

"I am compelled to trick you so I can learn what will win you over." He beamed at her. "I will show you I value you as a woman, but I will still ogle your body. It is too ambrosial to ignore. Would you like to ogle mine?"

"No!"

He feigned a hurt look. "You wound me. I bargained for many souls to secure this body. I did it for you, my most dedicated career woman who I admire so deeply."

She poked him in the chest. "Did you just say it's my fault all those poor sods are stuck in the Underworld?"

"Yes. Isn't it wonderful?" He gave her a glowing smile. "You practically have family down there already."

"*Never* joke about my family in hell." She grabbed the gun and pointed it at his crotch. "Justine will *not* go to hell! Do you hear me?"

He yelped and held the dish towel in front of his family jewels. "I was not referring to your offspring! Put that away before I am forced to show you how ruthless and powerful I can be!"

She hoisted the gun over her shoulder. "Never mention my family in hell again, or I'll shoot your boys with *purified* water."

He lifted his chin and tossed the towel carelessly aside. "You would not hurt them."

"You're so certain?" She tightened her grip on the gun, and he grabbed the towel again.

"New topic," he said quickly. "I am here to share secret information with the woman for whom my loins throb."

"A spy? Who do you spy on?"

He snorted. "I do not spy. I am Satan and I do no actual work myself. One of my spies reported in, and I thought I could parlay the information into hot sex with you."

Iris frowned. "What's the secret information? That you have clean sheets on your bed and you need someone to mess them up?"

"No, nothing like that." He hesitated. "May I have the gun? I suspect there is a fairly significant likelihood that this news could upset you."

"Fine." She handed the gun over, her curiosity aroused. "You've never shared any political secrets before. What's going on?"

He drained the gun into the sink, then shut it in the cabinet with the plates. "The fiery sexual siren known as your daughter may be in danger. Someone who wishes to cause her harm has found her."

"Justine's in danger? I'll kill anyone who comes near her!" She bolted for the patio, which held her portal back to the mortal world, which was where humans lived out their mortal lives and Otherworld beings did their thing, whatever that might be. "I'll—"

Satan grabbed her arm and hauled her to a stop. "No. You cannot interfere. It is too dangerous."

"Dangerous? I'm already dead! What could possibly harm me?" She tried to yank free of his grasp, but he didn't release her.

Satan gave her the smug look so typical of a man who feels superior. "Actually, my naive butterfly, you are not really dead. Granted, you are quite dead according to the mortal world, but as you can see, you are very alive and throbbing with vitality and sexuality. Sadly, you could wind up really and truly dead. And that is not such a good state. Even I, ruler of the Underworld, would prefer to avoid it, and I am a macho man who can withstand any torture."

She scowled at him. "I won't let anything happen to Justine."

"And neither will I. I am Satan and I will resolve the situation with ease."

The conviction in his tone stopped her struggling. "Are you serious?"

"Very. I know she means much to you and if she were killed, you would be very sad, and I cannot allow that."

Something fluttered in her belly. "You care if I'm sad?"

"Of course. If you were sad, you would not want to have sex for many, many centuries. That is not something I can afford. A true man can go only so long without sex."

She paused in surprise. "You expect me to believe you don't have sex with other women?"

He met her gaze without flinching. "You are the only woman my tower of passion throbs for."

"Really?" *Ack!* What was she doing listening to his claims of monogamy? *Focus, Iris.* "What's the threat against Justine, how do you know about it and what are you planning to do? And if I can't do anything, why did you tell me?"

He nodded. "Smart questions. I admire intelligence. Would you like to sleep with me?"

"Satan!"

"I will continue to work on valuing you as a woman." He held up his lovely hand when she opened her mouth to yell at him again. "I have assigned one of my most prized Rivkas to manage the threat. I have not yet gotten the full report on the potential assailant—"

"Assailant?" Justine was trained to handle threats to Mona, but Iris knew from her own experience that some threats were too dangerous even for a Guardian to handle. And since Justine hadn't faced a true threat since Carl, who knew how rusty her skills were?

"No fear. My Rivka will interfere and cause the demise of the assailant, but I think you should warn your daughter to be careful. My Rivka is very good, but if word has leaked out that Desdemona's Temptation has been located, others may follow." He grimaced. "Others who are not so easily disposed of."

Iris set her hand on her hips. "Wait a sec. What do you mean, Mona has been located? By who?" She drew her shoulders back. "By you?"

He shook his head quickly. "I do not know where the Goblet is. Though I suspect my brilliant and talented minions would locate the Goblet with ease and joy, I have ordered them not to find out, and if they do, they are to forget the information immediately. If I knew where the Goblet was, I might find the temptation too great, and I know you would not have sex with me if I went after it while it was under your daughter's protection."

"Damn right, I wouldn't." Apparently, she'd better abstain from sex with Satan forever, if the only thing keeping Justine and Mona safe was his obsession with getting Iris into the sack. "I'll tell her to leave town."

"No. She will be followed. She must stay where my Rivka can protect her and end the threat before it multiplies."

"Multiplies? Not acceptable. I'm going to talk to Melvin. He'll arrange something."

Satan caught her hand, wrapped his elegant fingers

around her wrist. "Melvin cannot interfere. No one in the Afterlife is allowed to interfere in the mortal world. You know that."

She pressed her lips together, trying not to be comforted by the warmth of his touch. Satan was heartless, lying scum, not some sweet lover who would keep her safe. "So how come you're interfering?"

He looked surprised by her question. "Because I'm Satan. I do my best to break rules as often as possible."

Duh. "You know, the fact you're an unscrupulous son of a bitch might actually come in handy."

He beamed at her. "I'm so glad you realize that. I'm very handy. Are there any rules you'd like me to break for you? It would be my pleasure."

"Just save my daughter."

"Of course." He laid a quick kiss on her lips and dodged out of reach before she could get her knee into his precious manly regions. "I will go give orders to my Rivka to kill this Derek person who is after her. You will be impressed with my success and want to suck my—"

"Satan!"

"Too crass?"

"Get out!" That brief kiss had been much too tempting and she needed a moment to regroup before heading down to see Justine. She couldn't stop herself from watching his butt as he pranced out her front door, even when he flicked her a grin over his shoulder, delighted to catch her ogling.

Maybe she'd install a sprinkler system triggered by a motion detector before his next visit.

Yes, that was a very good plan. Or a moat of purified water. Brilliant. She'd call a contractor first thing in the morning.

Seven

"I can't believe you're dressing up for a man who's planning to kill you." Theresa was lying on Justine's bed, watching her prep for her dinner with Derek.

"I turned in my alien assassin design, so I celebrated my freedom by buying myself a new dress, like any modern woman would, and I'm going to dinner." Justine turned sideways to the mirror and sucked her belly in. "You think this will distract Derek enough that I can get some answers from him?"

"It better, or you're going to be busted for invoking the Emergency clause so you could go shopping without Mona." Theresa was using Justine's favorite T-shirt to polish Mona, who was perched on the bed next to the dragon. Theresa paused to inspect Justine's chest. "Try duct tape. You won't be able to get breast implants in the five minutes before Mr. I'm-Here-to-Murder-You arrives, and without more boob action, I seriously doubt he'll forget to kill you."

Justine wrinkled her nose at her not-so-buxom chest. "How do we know Derek is really a threat to me? Maybe my mom was referring to someone else. After all, it was Satan who told her. Since when did he become trustworthy? Maybe Derek is actually an anti-Satan agent and Satan wants us to eliminate him to clear his path toward Mona."

Theresa snorted, then stomped out the small fire on Justine's bedspread. "I think spending a little time between Derek's legs has made you forget about your job. You do realize that your self-imposed twenty-four hour deadline has passed and we're still here, all because Mr. Assassin offered to buy you dinner."

"You heard my mom. We have to stay here and solve this thing."

"Yeah, because Satan told her that. You just said he wasn't a trustworthy source of Guardian advice. Plus, she also said you have to off Derek and you aren't listening to that."

Justine gave her breasts a final lift skyward, scowling when they dropped right back down into place, then she turned away from the mirror. "For your information, I'm fully prepared to kill him if I need to. And I'm going to dinner to get information from him, not to lust after him." Theresa snorted again, and Justine grinned. "Well, I might lust after him a little."

"After two hundred years of celibacy, you have to be attracted to the man who, as we speak, is planning your demise?"

Justine shrugged. "He does it for me. What can I say?" She tested the edge of a collapsible dagger for sharpness, then slipped it inside her slim black purse. "And how goes it with Zeke? Has he come up with any info on gold aura stuff?"

Theresa shook her head. "He's on it, though. It's sort of awkward, because he needs more details to do a thorough study and, well, I didn't figure sharing the whole Goblet of Eternal Youth thing with him was appropriate."

"Amazing that you're still able to form a coherent

thought after all the cybersex." She checked her makeup in the mirror again. Still looked fine, but her nerves were totally strung out.

Yeah, it wasn't a date.

Yeah, she was merely ascertaining his nefarious intentions so she could off him without guilt.

Yeah, he was only using her for information.

It didn't change the fact that a very hot guy was buying her dinner. It might not be a traditional date, but a Guardian couldn't be choosy.

Their buzzer rang, and she jumped.

Theresa gave her a look, but she ignored the dragon and hit the intercom. "Hello?"

Xavier's voice boomed through the loft. "Your attorney is here again. He says you have a date. Shall I correct him?"

"We do have a date. I'll be right down." She disconnected, but couldn't quite wipe the grin off her face.

Theresa studied her. "Why the happy face? You're going to have to kill him."

"I guess it's that I know it won't be easy to kill him. He might even beat me." She shrugged. "It makes life interesting, you know?"

"You are warped, my friend."

"But of course." She checked the security of her thigh holster, then stood up. "Do I look okay?"

"If looks could kill . . ." Theresa cocked her head. "Have you considered that this might be a farce to get you out of here so someone can slip in and try to steal Mona?"

"Well, their loss. An immortal dragon is nothing to sneeze at."

Theresa pressed her lips together, and Justine's elation faded. "What's wrong? You should be thrilled at the possible opportunity to turn someone into a crispy critter." She frowned. "Fight with Zeke?"

The dragon didn't look happy. "I think Derek might be more of a threat than we're thinking. Your mom, well, she seemed really concerned. And I don't like Satan being involved. It just sounds off. And, well, to be honest, I'm not sure you'd be quick enough on the trigger if Derek came after you."

Justine frowned. She'd never really enjoyed that part of her job, but . . . well, should Derek really still be alive? No. "Fine. He won't survive the night, I promise."

Theresa looked relieved. "Great. Just make sure you sleep with him first."

"Good-bye."

When Justine Bennett walked out of the elevator, Derek decided he'd better end her life as soon as possible.

If he didn't, he'd probably get down on his hands and knees and beg her to make his last five days on this earth as heavenly as possible.

It was a crime to look the way she did in that dress.

She took one look at his face, and broke into an amused grin. "You're putty in my hands."

"Quite possibly." He ignored Xavier and held out his arm. "Shall we?"

She nodded, then frowned as she got closer. "What are the red marks on your neck?"

"Let's just say I'm glad you answered the intercom as quickly as you did. Xavier didn't take too kindly to me showing up again." He cocked a look at her as she slid her hand around his elbow. "Thanks for telling him I was coming."

She flipped him a saucy smile. "I wanted to test your manliness. See if you could get by him."

"It was all I could do to refrain from permanently disabling him." They both ignored Xavier's snort as Derek held the door for her.

"You're such a gentleman."

"I only hold the door for women who try to get me strangled before our first date."

"Does that happen often?"

"You'd be surprised." He let the door slide shut and rested his hand on her lower back to guide her toward his limo. "This dress is too fitted to hide the dagger back here." He rubbed his thumb over it. At least a six-inch blade. If she wasn't the Guardian, she was one highly prepared Girl Scout. A surge of awareness rushed through him. If she was by his side when the Curse hit, together they might have a chance.

"I'm wearing that knife because I thought you might want to go treasure hunting later. Figured I'd give you some goals."

He eyed her as his driver opened the limo door. "The dress would have to come off for either of us to get to that."

She gave him a wide-eyed look. "I know."

He cursed under his breath as she slid into the car. This was going to be some kind of night.

It was after they'd ordered, but before the appetizers arrived, when Justine brought it up. "Are you planning to kill me?"

He grinned. "What happened to the first-date small talk?"

She frowned at his smile and how it made her belly go

all jiggly. "I don't do small talk. Are you going to try to kill me or what?"

He raised one dark eyebrow, and his grin faded into something much more subtle, and much more male. "Not as long as you look that good in that dress."

Heat oozed through her body, and she shifted in her chair, her fingers tightening around the stem of her wineglass.

Focus, Justine.

She thudded her glass down on the linen tablecloth, nearly spilling the wine. "My mom said she heard you intend to end my life."

He regarded her over the rim of his glass. "Who's your mom?"

"She has connections."

"Is she the Guardian?"

A twinge of disappointment gutted her. She didn't want him to really be after Mona. "What do you know about the Guardian?"

He swirled the golden wine in his glass, watching it catch the light.

She leaned back in her chair and folded her arms over her chest, and let the silence sit between them.

"You look like you'd be difficult to kill," he observed.

"I am."

"So am I."

She watched his fingers lightly stroke the rim of the wineglass. Such a light touch. Delicate. Tender.

Ahem. She shook her head and dragged her gaze back up to his face. "Are you immortal?"

He grinned, a new light gleaming in his eyes. "Nope. You?"

She narrowed her eyes. "Nice try." As if she was going to announce she was; that was equivalent to admitting she was the Guardian.

"If you weren't immortal, or familiar with such things, it wouldn't have occurred to you to ask."

Crud. He was right. Where was her brain? Years of training down the toilet just because her body couldn't stop noticing he was a man. She leaned forward, picked up the butter knife and began rapping the handle on the table. "You're the one who brought up the Goblet of Eternal Youth yesterday before you passed out in my lobby." She frowned. "What was up with the nap anyway? I grilled Xavier on it and he gave me some stupid story about a strip club and your sex addiction, but I don't buy it."

He leaned forward and slipped the knife out of her hand. "I'm not supposed to tell you."

She picked up a fork and starting tapping *that* handle on the table. "So what? He's making up unfavorable stories about you. I'd think you'd want to clear the air."

"I do, but he still scares me. I don't want to mess with him. But I don't have a sex addiction." He made a move for the fork, then stopped when she gave him a warning look. "Let's make a deal. You want info. I want info. Neither of us is giving it up."

She stopped tapping the fork and cocked her head. "What kind of deal?"

"I can tell you're prepared to kill me. You suspect I'm planning to do the same to you. We got the tough stuff out in the open already. Why don't we share info and see how it goes? Otherwise, we can go straight out to the parking lot and see who will win." He leaned back, one hand resting casually on the table, the other arm draped over the back of his chair.

Only the restless drumming of his fingers gave him away.

She grinned at the energy emanating from him. "I do prefer to know all the details before I take action."

"Me too. Deal?"

She pursed her lips. Even if she told him things she wasn't supposed to, she could still exterminate him afterward. And then at least, she'd have answers. If he wasn't immortal, he wouldn't be able to best her. She felt a surge of disappointment at the thought she could kick his ass, then frowned at herself. It wasn't like she was going to date the man, so a pansy was good in this situation. She nodded briskly. "Fine. It's a deal."

"Don't sound so thrilled."

"No, it's fine." She picked up her glass. "To the exchange of info."

He took the glass from her hand. "Let's dance."

She jerked her hand away from him even as a tremor of awareness rolled through her body at the thought of him holding her. "What?"

"Dancing. You've heard of it?"

"Don't be a smart-ass." Derek might not be wielding a sword, but the man was heavily armed and using his entire arsenal, if the steam rising from her lower body was any indication. "There's no one else dancing." She waved an arm around the sparsely populated restaurant, where the tuxedo-clad waiters were hovering in the corner, waiting for a beckoning from their exquisitely dressed patrons.

He jerked his head toward the back of the room. "That

corner was made for dancing." His gaze flicked over her dress, and she felt her thighs clench. *Oy.*

She glanced at the small secluded area in the corner with a gorgeous inlaid wood floor and some floaty curtains. Only someone seated at their table would have the right angle to see past the curtains into the corner. It was private and secluded, perfect for a romantic interlude.

Or a hostile interrogation.

He stood up and held out his hand. "Shall we?"

She took a deep breath. Dancing would be the perfect opportunity to put her dress to work and question him. That's what she was here for, right? Right. *Dance with him.*

A flutter of excitement rippled through her. There was something about the combination of intense sexual attraction and the knowledge that he might pull a blade at any moment that was quite thrilling. She reached between her thighs, gave her gun a reassuring pat, then stood up. "Fine."

Justine let him take her hand and followed him as he wove between linen tablecloths and expensive crystal candlesticks. She watched him eyeball a waiter into turning up the music.

A man with power. Her fingers tightened around his, and she felt a shiver of anticipation.

They slipped between the curtains to the dance floor, and he slid his hands around her waist, his fingers curving around the dagger pressed against her lower back. "I love a woman who carries weapons," he murmured as he coaxed her against him.

Oh, hell. Why not? She flattened her hands on his chest, slid her fingers under the lapels of his jacket, trailed them up to the back of his neck. She felt his body tense as she pressed herself against him.

Her breath released in a long sigh and she let her eyes close for a moment. God, it felt so good to have a man hold her.

Not just any man. A man who might want to kill her, and freely admitted it. No deception, like there had been with Carl, just open honesty. A man who didn't even hold it against her that she might have to lop his head off at any moment. That was the kind of man you could take home to Mom.

And he smelled so unbelievably good.

She turned her head and pressed her face against the side of his neck and inhaled. He smelled like woods and spice and man. If she died right now, that might be all right with her.

"My turn," he said.

What? He wanted to bask in her fragrance? Sure.

"Are you the Guardian?"

Oh. That kind of turn. She sighed, then froze at his small groan as her breath eased over his neck. That was the response she'd been angling for when she bought the dress, but she hadn't quite prepared for the intense rush of having him respond to her sexuality. There was a certain level of smug, female satisfaction at making a man quiver, even if it was merely part of her job.

She blew on his skin again, grinned as he made a small noise of protest, then answered his question. "Yes. I've been the Guardian for the last couple centuries."

His hands skimmed her lower back, his fingers searing through the thin fabric of her dress. "Your turn."

She pressed her body against the hardness of his chest, not quite able to keep herself from doing it. Because she was a good interrogator, doing her best to distract him while she grilled him. *Right?* "Are you related to Carl LaValle?"

"Yes. He's my ancestor. What happened with him, anyway?" He rubbed his cheek against her hair, and she barely managed to stop herself from making a horribly embarrassing female coo of encouragement.

Total abstinence had almost convinced her she could survive without sex, but one minute of human contact . . . It would take her the next three centuries to get over the feeling of Derek's whiskers resting against her head.

Justine cleared her throat and pulled back slightly. "Carl befriended me shortly after I became Guardian. He was my best friend and convinced me to reject Theresa. I told him about Mona and appointed him my successor. Right after he took the Oath and the third drink, he tried to behead me." She shrugged. "So I beheaded him first. Theresa forgave me. I got put on probation. We moved to the Amazon where Mona turned into a piece of fruit and got abducted by monkeys. And yes, there are some very old monkeys in the Amazon now. When we finally got her back, we decided civilization was easier to control. And now we're back, we're bad, and we try our best to kill people first and ask questions later." She frowned as she realized he was now staring at her. "What?"

"You murdered my ancestor?" He looked slightly shocked.

"Self-defense. The guy was a prick and you should pretend you aren't related to him if you have any hope of getting home alive tonight." Not that he really had a chance. Not after she'd just told him about Mona's chameleon ability. Why had she done that? To make him into more of a danger, so she would be forced to remember she couldn't get cozy with him? *Yeah, that was it.*

Derek studied her. "I didn't think you were *actually* the type to kill."

She lifted her chin. "It's who I am. Got a problem with that?"

He tilted his head and traced the tendon in her neck with his middle finger, drawing an involuntary quiver from her. "I'll have to think about it."

She blinked at the fact that she dealt in death wasn't an automatic "See ya later, baby." Something leapt into her belly and settled there. Was it hope? Dammit. She had no right to hope. Even if Derek could handle her job (and that was a big if), he was planning to steal from her and send her into the Afterlife. And she had to return the favor, remember?

And even if by some miracle she didn't have to kill him, her Oath required her to have no loyalties except to her successor and to Mona, which is why Carl had kept their relationship platonic. She would never have considered breaking her Oath for a little slap and tickle, and Carl had realized it instantly and played the gay-confidant angle. At the moment, however, she was having serious trouble not thinking of rumpled sheets, sweaty bodies, and wandering lips. Yet another reason to kill Derek: If he coaxed her to violate her Guardian Oath, she would be in very, very big trouble.

He bent his head and trailed his lips over the side of her neck. "Do you still have the Goblet?"

Oh, wow. Oh, wow. Oh, wow. She hadn't felt a man's kiss in so long. "Yes. Her name is Mona." She tilted her head and let him kiss lower. Over her collarbone. Across her chest. *Oh, wow.* Her dress was way low cut. How low was he going to go? And in case the Otherworld judges were watching, it was all in the spirit of protecting Mona. She was interrogating a potential threat. And if she had to use her body to get answers, then that just showed what a dedicated Guardian she was. Right? Of course, right. *Ask a question about Mona to prove it.* Oh, good call. A question. She could think of one . . . um . . . "Are you after Mona?"

He slipped the spaghetti strap off her shoulder, his breath hot against her skin as he kissed where it had been. "Yes. I need to kill you and then steal her."

Oh, God. That was like the sexiest thing she'd ever heard. "I love a man who isn't afraid to tell the truth, even if it might interfere with his getting laid." She caught her breath as he trailed his index finger over her breastbone, his touch light and hot. "Why do you need to steal Mona?"

"That's two questions in a row, but I'll give you a break because you taste like heaven." He paused for a moment to suck on her throat. *Oh, God.* Maybe this was his weapon. Make her so weak she couldn't fight when the time came. Unfair. She had to turn it back on him. Regain control. "According to Carl's journal, it's the only way to break the Curse. No offense, but I've decided I'm willing to trade your life for that of generations of LaValle men."

She grabbed his face and kissed him, his breath mingling with hers as he took over the kiss, plunging to take possession of her soul. His arms locked behind her as he bent his head, his tongue hot and wet and . . . *oh, God.* She was going to explode right there on the dance floor, in a public place.

He didn't even break the kiss, his words falling into her

mouth with his breath and his essence. "Why'd you curse us? It really sucks."

She slipped her hand under his jacket, her fingers sliding between the buttons of his shirt. What was up with the undershirt? Didn't he know that it was more important for her to caress his bare chest than to be all proper with a damned undershirt? How else was she supposed to get him so turned on he couldn't think straight? Oh, *yeah. Right there. Kiss me lower.* "What curse?"

"You sound breathless," he murmured, his lips skimming the top edge of her very low-cut dress. "Out of shape?"

"Hah. I could kick your ass all day long and still have the energy to run a marathon." She scrunched her eyes shut against the torrent of sexual energy racing through her and tried to think about her job. "What curse?"

"The Curse that kills all the LaValle men at age thirty-one." His thigh slipped between hers, and she let out a little yelp, nearly dropping to the floor and dragging him with her. "I love a woman who's loaded between her thighs."

Please tell me he's talking about the gun. "I couldn't decide whether to shoot you or stab you, so I came prepared. I'm sort of a whimsical killer. Whatever weapon strikes my fancy at the time."

"God, you're hot." He moved his leg again, and she found his mouth, pouring years of abstinence into him as he flooded her with heat, with passion and raw sex. "You owe me an answer. Why did you curse us?"

"I don't know about any curse, I swear."

Derek broke the kiss, and she almost wailed with dismay. He frowned at her. "You're serious? You didn't curse us?"

She blinked and tried to pull back, attempting to unclench her fingers from the back of his neck. "Why would I curse you?"

"Because you were mad at Carl and beheading him showed you how much fun it would be to torture LaValle men for eternity?" His brow was furrowed, but his hands were still on her back, though the fervency of their exploration had faded somewhat.

She shook her head, endeavoring to focus again. There were too many hormones rushing through her for her to have any chance at rational thinking. "I don't even know how to curse anyone, and for your information, beheading Carl really wasn't all that fun."

He rubbed his thumb over her chin. "So, if you didn't do it, then you don't know how to undo it?"

"No." He was definitely using sex to distract her. She was morally offended, and as soon as he stopped talking, she was going to start kissing him again to weaken his defenses to her own interrogation.

"Then I'll have to kill you."

She took a deep breath. "Well, if you're going to try to kill me, then I'll have to kill you."

"Want to have sex first?"

A blast of heat rushed through her so hard she almost stumbled. "I'm not allowed to have sex. Guardian Oath thing."

He lifted a brow. "You have a sucky job."

"It has its perks." She wrapped her hands around his upper arms, trying to focus on her job instead of relishing the feel of his biceps flexing under her touch. "So, what's with the gym-rat body? Part of your plan to take me out?" Or did he know the only way to kill her was by beheading her?

"I've studied almost every kind of self-defense in an attempt to beat the Curse when it comes for me. I'm quite proficient when it comes to threats against my well-being." He slid his hands down to her butt and hauled her against him. "I could give you quite a battle, I think."

Her heart stuttered, and then burst to life. How could she pass up this opportunity? Not just sex, but sex with a gorgeous man who could possibly beat her in a fight to the death; one who knew all her secrets, and wanted her anyway. No long-term commitments, obviously. Just sex. Sex as part of her job, that is. She ran her hands over his chest, let herself absorb the feel of his muscles under her hands. She looked up, met his gaze, and spoke a truth that terrified her almost as much as it excited her. "If having sex with you was necessary for me to protect Mona, I don't think it would violate my Oath."

A slow grin spread over his face. "I have many secrets that I'll spill only in the heat of orgasm. As a good Guardian, it's your duty to find them all out. After all, that's why I'm propositioning you. To distract you so you accidentally tell me everything I need to know."

Her fingers dug into his chest on their own, laughing at her complete inability to stop them. "Then for the sake of Mona, I guess I'd better sacrifice myself." She felt hot, the room was spinning. She took a deep breath and lifted her chin. "But in the interest of being able to concentrate on the interrogation, I think we should agree that there will be no assassination attempts until we are both satisfied . . . that we've gotten all the info we need."

"Deal." The heat in his eyes was simmering.

"Mona's safety is very important to me. I feel I must begin the interrogation as soon as possible. Skip dinner?"

"Hell, yes. Your place or mine?"

"I have a roommate."

"Right, the dragon. My place." He grabbed her hand and tugged her out of the alcove. Had they been putting on a show? No one in the restaurant seemed to notice them, but who cared? She was going to have sex! And she didn't even have to lie or pretend she was some sweet thing! It was incredible. Sex with honesty, what a concept.

And she even had the *Treatise* angle covered.

She hoped.

Eight

He was a fool, but he didn't care. For the first time in his life, he had the chance to be with a woman who knew the truth about him and didn't think he was certifiable. He didn't have to hide what he believed in, and he didn't have to worry that she'd fall in love with him and then he'd die on her. It was such a relief.

He didn't even know if she'd keep her promise to not kill him until he was ready, and he didn't care. He'd spent his life preparing to fight off a violent death, and he'd be ready if she tried something.

Sort of made the thought of sex with her all the more interesting, actually. Instead of worrying that he had to protect her from his baggage, he had to protect himself from her.

A definite turn-on.

He glanced down at her as the doorman opened the door to let them out of the restaurant. Her cheeks were flushed, and she grinned at him. "Having second thoughts?"

"Not a chance."

"Derek!"

He slammed to a stop upon finding Becca standing next to his limo. His driver was slumped in the front seat, apparently taking a nap. At least he hoped that's all it was. Becca was wearing a jog bra, running shorts, and Nikes, and she looked even more strung out that usual. "Becks? What are you doing here?"

"I was in the middle of a workout, when I heard that you were out with the *Guardian*! Is this her?"

He felt Justine tense against him, and she stepped away, her hand sliding under the hem of her dress and toward her gun.

"Who are you?" Justine asked. She sounded calm and unconcerned, but he knew what she was wrapping her fingers around under that black silk.

"Justine, this is my vice president of Vic's Pretzels, Becca Gibbs. Becca, this is Justine Bennett, my date for the evening." He stressed "date," hoping Becca would take the hint. Tonight was not the night for a session on marketing strategy. Not that she was dressed for work. In fact, he'd never before seen her out of a suit. It sort of made her look human. He'd never considered her human before. She was his workaholic VP, and nothing else.

Justine glanced at him, her eyebrows arched in surprise. "You own Vic's Pretzels?"

"In name only. Becca's in charge."

"He invented the No-Carb Pretzel," Becca said. "You should see what he's working on now."

"Can I get your autograph for Theresa?" Justine asked.

He grinned at Justine. "Are you sure it's for her? Maybe you want a memento of our date?"

"Hey!" His VP scowled at him. "We need to talk."

"Tomorrow. I'm on a date." A date who still looked ravishing in her dress, the heat from his kisses still flushing her cheeks.

Becca shook her head. "This is really important."

Justine suddenly frowned at him. "Wait a sec. The guy who came after Mona yesterday was from Vic's. You sent that surfer to kill us? I was beginning to think you weren't the type to have someone else do your dirty work." She looked very disappointed, and the lust was starting to vanish from her face.

"I don't know any surfers." He looked at Becca. "Later, okay?" Having his vice president show up in the middle of a date was a major mood killer.

"No!" Becca glared at Justine. "She's a danger to you."

Oh, she has no idea. "Trust me, I've got a handle on the situation."

"Excuse me, Mr. LaValle, is this woman bothering you?" The doorman walked down the steps toward Derek. "I could call the police."

"No, it's fine." He slipped a twenty out of his wallet and handed it to the man. "Sorry if we're being loud. If you'll just excuse us—"

"You bet it's fine," Becca snapped. "I keep him in line, so back off." She snarled like a wild animal, and the poor man nearly fell up the stairs trying to get back inside.

Derek slowly turned to Becca, a cold feeling creeping up his spine. "Did you just *growl?*"

Justine stepped in front of him before Becca could answer, her hands on her hips as she scowled at Derek. "You said your brother came by earlier to see us. The only person who came by was a kid with a box of pretzels and a gun."

Becca moved closer, and her eyes were narrow slits. "Get away from her, Derek."

He held up his hand to stave off his vice president for another minute. "Justine, my brother is a math professor.

He's not a surfer, he would never try to kill you and I would never ask him to. I asked him to stop by, and he said he forgot. Typical." He stepped back as Becca shoved her way between them. "What's so important that it can't wait until tomorrow, Becca?"

"Hang on." Becca slapped her hand over his mouth and focused on Justine. "Goblet Girl, did you say someone tried to kill you, and it wasn't Derek or his brother?"

Justine narrowed her eyes. "What's it to you?"

"That means someone besides Derek has found you! I'm not prepared for that!" Becca flung her hands up and whirled away, rattling off something in a foreign language and gesticulating wildly.

Derek frowned as he watched her pace. He'd never seen her this crazed, this tense, this frazzled. In fact, she was always the epitome of professionalism. "Becca? What's wrong?"

Justine grabbed his arm, spinning him toward her. "Why does she know about me? Now I'll have to kill her, and it's your fault. And who else have you told? Because I'm going to have to take them out too." She gave him a hard shove and folded her arms across her chest. "Did it ever occur to you that I don't like killing people, and now you're making me go on a mass extermination spree? Is that thoughtful? Is that nice? What kind of date are you anyway?"

"I didn't tell anyone," Derek snapped. "Quincy knows, and that's it. If there's someone else after you, it's not because of me."

Becca turned back toward them, her hands in fists by her sides. "Okay, we need to go somewhere and talk. All three of us." She jerked her head at a couple strolling by, happily oblivious to their little discussion. "Privacy needed."

Derek opened his mouth to decline the offer, when he noticed a gray spiral of mist floating up toward Becca's face. "Um, Becca?"

"What?"

"Your stomach is smoking." He blinked. "Are you on fire?"

Justine stepped up next to him. "Holy crap."

Becca glanced down at the orange and blue flames roaring on her abdomen. "Bastard. Like I need to deal with this right now. He thinks it's so hilarious to send me notes this way." She scowled at them. "Do I look like I'm laughing?"

"You never laugh," Derek said. "Jesus, Becca! Do something! You're on fire!" He looked around for a fire extinguisher or help, but strangely enough, there wasn't another human in sight anymore. A chill ran up his spine and he eased his feet into a ready position.

"Isn't that painful?" Justine asked curiously.

"Of course it is. But I'm not giving him the satisfaction of letting him know." She eyed Derek. "I was going to tell you anyway, but I guess this is the best way. At least you'll probably believe me."

"Tell me what?" He gaped as the flame faded on her stomach, leaving behind a series of red scars. "What the hell's going on?"

She looked down at her belly. "Watch."

The scars twitched, convulsed and then began crawling over her stomach, rearranging themselves. "Jesus!" He jumped back, yanked up Justine's dress, and grabbed her dagger free before she could stop him. He gripped it in his fist, held it ready, ignoring the amused look Justine shot him.

"Quit freaking out and pay attention," Becca snapped.

"I'm not freaking out," he shot back. "I'm arming myself."

Justine touched his arm as she moved closer to him. "Look at her stomach, Derek. It's fascinating."

"Said by the woman who lives with a dragon and probably sees this stuff every day." But he dropped his gaze to Becca's midriff as Justine leaned forward for a better view. As he watched, the scars moved into letters . . . into words . . . He looked up at Becca as he read the words etched into her skin. " 'Kill them both'?"

She nodded grimly. "I work for Satan. And he just ordered me to kill you." She lifted her hand and a fireball formed in it. "Unfortunately, I have no choice but to do exactly as he commands."

How does immortality stack up against Satan's personal servant?

Justine decided it was probably best *not* to find out.

She threw herself to the ground as a fireball hurtled toward her. It exploded next to her hair and set it on fire, as well as two potted plants that had been decorating the front step of the restaurant.

"Dammit, Justine! You moved!" Becca shrieked as Derek stomped out the flames that used to be a very cute, very pricey highlighting job by *the* Joacque LaFlaire. She'd been on the waitlist for six months before she'd gotten in, and now it was burned up?

A total waste of money.

Derek pulled Justine upright, using his jacket to smother

the rest of the flames. She yelped as the cloth pressed against her head. Nothing like third-degree scalp burns to make a Guardian wish someone would behead her.

"You all right?" Derek squatted in front of her, his forehead furrowed in concern as he peered at her burned hair. "Looks bad."

Oh, how totally sweet. She actually had to blink hard to keep her eyes from filling up. She slapped his hand away. "Guardians don't need comfort. We heal quickly and are trained to be independent."

"But your head is burned. Doesn't it hurt?"

"Like hell." Hmm . . . speaking of hell . . . she shot a quick look at Becca, who was giving her a very unfriendly look. But at least there were no more fireballs in her hands. That was a start. "Derek? Satan's assassin is still here." She pushed him aside and hiked up her dress to grab her gun. Not that she was particularly optimistic about a gun's usefulness against Satan's servant, but it was worth a try.

"Back off, Becca." Derek moved between Becca and Justine, and Justine felt another flicker of warmth. Mr. Mortal Guy was protecting her, an immortal badass? How adorable. She paused to bask in the moment, then shoved him aside so she had a clear shot at Becca.

The doorman came outside again with another couple, and all three of them froze, their gazes fixed on her gun. Justine glanced at Derek. "A little help, please?"

"We have this under control," Derek said firmly. "Please go back inside and keep everyone in until we leave."

"No problem." The trio bolted back inside, and Justine figured they had about five minutes until the police showed up.

Becca didn't look happy. "I wouldn't have hit her at all if she hadn't moved." She scowled at Justine. "What were you thinking? Do you have any idea how much trouble I would have been in if I'd killed you?" She paled suddenly and sat down hard on the smoking flowerpot. Her breath started coming in wheezes, and she put her head between her knees. "She's okay," she muttered. "Didn't die. No harm done. Deep breath. One . . . Two . . ."

Justine glanced at Derek while Satan's helper counted to ten, then started over. He shrugged, then cleared his throat. "Becca? You okay?"

She snapped her head up. "Of course I'm not all right. I almost killed the Guardian! Do you have any idea what it's like to have Satan pissed at you?" She started to wobble, and returned her head to between her knees. "Goblet Girl, if you *ever* do something that stupid again, I'll follow you to the Afterlife and torture you for all eternity." She looked up, and her eyes were glowing red. "And trust me, I'm more than capable of doing it."

Derek cursed and took a step back, grabbing Justine's wrist and yanking her with him. "Good lord, Becca. What are you?"

"I'm a Rivka. Created by Satan, kept alive by his life force, destined to obey his every command, yada, yada, yada. I'm sure you've heard it all before."

"Um, no. I haven't. You were created by Satan? And he exists?" Derek looked shocked, his jaw muscles twitching as if he was trying desperately to process everything before he ended up dead.

Justine nudged his arm with her gun, and he glanced at her. "Derek. I don't want to be rude and interrupt this little educational session, but she hasn't killed us yet. If you'll step out of the way, I'll take care of this situation."

Becca stood up and brushed the flower remains off her butt. "Hello? Obviously, I'm not planning to kill either of you. If I was, you'd be dead by now."

Justine narrowed her eyes and trained her gun on the Rivka. "A little cocky, are you? I'm very difficult to kill."

The Rivka's eyes grew redder. Sort of looked like glowing embers. *Interesting.* Somehow, Justine couldn't drum up any regret that she'd managed to avoid Rivkas until now.

"I'm his best Rivka. Trust me, you'd be dead." Becca's fingers turned red and a fireball began to form in her palm.

"I'm the best Guardian in a thousand years. Trust *me,* you're no match for me." She released the safety and took aim on Becca's forehead.

Derek stepped between them and Justine quickly averted her gun. "Okay, hang on, ladies—"

"You're calling me a lady?" Becca asked suddenly. "Even after all this?"

Derek hesitated. "Sorry?"

"No! That's so nice!" The red faded from Becca's eyes. "No one ever calls me a lady once they know what I do. A freak, the damned, a murderous bitch who deserves to be dismembered, yes. But a lady?" She beamed at Derek, and a surge of something rushed through Justine. Jealousy, maybe? He was *her* man to kill, after all.

"Hey, Rivka," Justine said.

Becca glared at her. "My name is Becca."

Justine lifted a brow. "Is it?"

A faint red flushed her cheeks. "Well, it has been for five years. I kind of like it. Better than the one Satan gave me."

Something in the Rivka's expression touched Justine, something that said that Becca might understand what it was like to hate her job. Becca was someone who understood centuries of isolation. So she shrugged. "Fine. *Becca,* you said Satan had ordered you to kill us immediately, and you said you had to obey him. But you didn't kill us, and you aren't trying to. What gives?"

Derek raised the dagger again, his fingers relaxed around the hilt in an expert grip.

Becca sighed and spoke to Derek. "First of all, the 'them' referred to you and your brother, not you and her. Once you found Goblet Girl—"

"Justine. Call me Justine."

Becca glanced at her, and something in the air between them changed. It wasn't friendship, but it was an understanding. "Once you located *Justine,* you became a danger to her. You know, the whole kill-her-steal-the-Goblet thing? My assignment was to monitor your search for her. If you found her, I had to report in to Satan. Apparently, he has decided you need to be destroyed before you can follow through on your plan to do her in."

Derek blinked. "You mean the whole five years you've been working for me, you've actually been spying on me . . . for Satan?"

At Becca's nod, the dagger wavered in his hand and he let his arm drop to his side. He muttered something about Satan and hell and insanity, then sat heavily on the top step leading into the restaurant. "Didn't you think that was something I might have wanted to know?"

Becca shrugged. "For what it's worth, you're the best assignment I've ever had. I love working for Vic's."

Suck up. Justine patted Derek's arm and gave him a

warm smile. Deception was the worst. *She'd* never lie to him, especially not for five years. Kill him? Quite possibly. Lie to him? Never. Obviously, she was the better woman for him.

Becca eyed Justine. "Why would Satan care if you lived? Everyone knows he lusts after the Goblet, and having you alive doesn't help his odds."

"I don't know . . ." She frowned suddenly, her gut dropping. "Oh, God. I *do* know. He's courting my mom. He's probably trying to win her over by keeping me alive." She slumped onto the step next to Derek.

Derek shifted away from her. "Satan's courting your mom? Are you kidding?"

Becca stared at her. "Really?"

"Long story." Justine sighed and tried not to notice Derek's wary gaze. "I'm sure it's not that big of a deal. Really." When he didn't return to his spot by her side, she sat up straighter and tried to shake it off. "So, Becca, why is Derek still alive if you're supposed to kill him?"

Becca grinned. "Loophole."

Like the one that was going to let her worship Derek's body tonight, despite her Oath. Not that getting naked with him was high on her list of priorities at the moment. And he definitely didn't look like a guy with sweaty sex on the brain.

"What loophole?" Derek asked.

"Well, I have to do exactly what Satan says, but sometimes he's not specific enough." Becca nodded at the smoking remains of the petunias. "He said I had to kill *them both*." She blinked innocently. "I thought he meant the plants."

Justine grinned. "That's brilliant." If they'd met in other

circumstances, maybe she and Becca *could* have been friends. "I'm impressed by anyone with the gumption to go against Satan."

Becca returned the smile. "Thank you. I do my best to thwart him whenever possible. I might have to obey him, but it doesn't mean I have to make things easy for him."

"What about when he orders you to 'kill Derek LaValle now'?" Derek asked.

Becca wrinkled her nose and gave a nod of acknowledgment. "That will be tougher to evade. That's why we need to get this sorted out before he smartens up. Sometimes he gets the order right on the second try. Other times, it takes longer."

"Sort what out?" Derek asked.

"The way I see it, we have two options," Becca said. "My first choice, and the easiest one, is to have you kill Justine before I can stop you. Then you can steal the goblet and end the Curse."

"Um, hello? I'm right here." Maybe she and Becca wouldn't be so close after all.

Becca stood up and brushed the embers off her butt, ignoring Justine. "Quite frankly, Derek, you're a much better boss than Satan is, and I don't want you to die. I'm willing to trade Justine's life for yours, but if Satan gets pissed and kills you anyway, it sort of defeats the whole purpose of breaking the Curse."

Justine picked her gun up off her lap and wrapped her hand around it, letting it angle slightly toward Derek. "So much for being friends, Rivka."

"I have no friends," Becca snorted. "But if I let Derek kill you, then Satan will be pissed at me . . ." Becca's voice faded and she chewed her lower lip.

"We wouldn't want that, would we?" Justine tapped the gun against her knee, her grip loose but ready.

Derek looked thoughtful. "Vic's would be in trouble if Satan killed you. We really need you in charge of things. And I'm not *all* that high on killing Justine," he added. "So what's the other option?"

"Find another way to end the Curse besides killing Justine," Becca said.

Justine let the gun point toward the floor, and saw both Becca and Derek notice her action. He set the dagger down and gave her a nod. She grinned. "You were ready for me, huh?"

He grinned back. "Always." He was still smiling when he turned back to the Rivka. "So, how would we find out how to end the Curse, Becks?"

"I have no idea how to break curses," Becca said. "That's why it's my least favorite choice." She brightened all of a sudden and slapped her thigh. "I just had an idea! I'll go create a diversion somewhere else, and Satan will send me off to deal with it. While I'm gone, you can do whatever you need to do to Goblet Girl, and it won't be my fault, so he won't torture me for it. And if I can snare him some really good souls, he'll be in such a good mood he probably won't kill you." She nodded at Justine. "No offense, it's just that my options are pretty limited, you know? The Rivka rules only allow so much room for manipulation."

"No offense taken." Well, maybe a little. But only because Becca had actually come up with a way to avoid killing Derek. How bad could Becca's job be if she could outmaneuver her orders to assassinate someone? It wasn't as if Justine *wanted* to kill Derek, or anyone else, for that matter. But she did what she had to do, because the Oath wasn't nearly as poorly written as Satan's Rivka rules apparently were.

Derek frowned. "I'm not sure that's the best option, Becca . . ."

"No worries. I can make this happen." Becca winked at him, then lifted her chin and shot him a very restrained, professional look. "Boss, I'm taking a couple personal days from work. Everything is in order at Vic's and should run by itself for a few days, because I know you'll be busy 'taking care' of Goblet Girl. I'll be back when things . . . quiet down." She shook Justine's hand. "It was great to meet you. Sorry it couldn't have worked out differently." And with that, she turned into a black vapor and dissolved into the cement.

Derek cursed, grabbed for the dagger, and jumped to his feet as the black vapor vanished. "Do all Rivkas do that?"

"So I've heard." Justine held the gun tightly, watching his fingers around the dagger. His grip was still relaxed, so she didn't move. Yet.

Derek eased over to the spot Becca had been standing, lightly probing the ground with his toe. "I think she liked you."

"Liked me?" She snorted. "You're deluded."

Derek gave a small laugh as he finished his inspection of the ground that had sucked up Becca. "For the first time in my life, I almost wish I was." He flipped the dagger around, so he was holding the blade between two fingers. "My vice president is Satan's disciple. Sort of takes some adjusting."

She eased to her feet, watching the blade reflect the nearby street lamp. "You going to follow Becca's suggestion? Destroy me while she distracts Satan?"

He thumbed the tip of the blade. "I need to think on it."

The tension dropped from her shoulders and she smiled. "Good plan." Not that it changed anything; she still had to take him out. He knew too much. One encounter with a mind-reading Manasa and everything he knew would be on the Otherworld black market. Even now, a Manasa could be hunting him down.

She knew she needed to end this threat immediately.

But she didn't move.

Do it now, Justine.

He eyed her. "What about you?"

"Still deciding." *Fire the gun at him.* But her hands remained on her hips, the gun hanging loosely from her fingertips. The faint sound of sirens echoed in the distance, and she knew it was time to vacate.

He nodded. "I can respect that." He cleared his throat. "Listen, I think we should forgo the . . . interrogation session tonight. Things are complicated."

She pressed her lips together to keep herself from protesting. "I agree."

He glanced at her, and she was pleased to see the regret in his eyes. "So, I'll give you a call?"

"Sure." Annoyed at how fast she dug into her handbag for her business card, she managed to slow herself down to a respectable pace as she walked over to hand it to him. "You're the first guy I've given my number to since I took the Oath. Seems a bit anticlimatic, you know, with the whole 'I have to kill you' undercurrent going on."

He gave her a rueful smile. "Well, you're the first woman I've promised to call since I found out I was cursed, so we're about equally antisocial."

"Aren't we the perfect match?"

Something flickered in his eyes. "Maybe."

Ooh. She didn't like the way her belly jumped in response.

Grab the dagger and end it. She managed to get her fingers to curl, but that was it. She simply couldn't do it.

"Want a ride home?"

She gave a quick shake of her head. "Not a good idea. I need some air." Close proximity with Derek and his delicious scent and unbelievable kisses was not what she needed. She needed a slap upside the head and an ice pack between her legs.

He frowned. "Are you sure you'll be safe?"

"I'm immortal and I've been training in combat for over two hundred years." The sirens were loud now, and it was time to leave.

He didn't look convinced. "The city can be dangerous at night."

See? How was she supposed to shoot a man who worried about her, even knowing who she was and that he might have to kill her tomorrow?

Unless . . .

Nine

So what's the loophole?" Justine asked before her mom had even fully appeared.

Iris frowned. "What are you talking about?" She was sporting a gorgeous ruby ring and a pair of Manolo Blahniks that had seemed innocuous last week, but now hinted at things Justine simply didn't want to know about.

She decided not to ask about the source of the expensive accessories. "The loophole in the Oath. What is it?"

Iris's eyes immediately darkened. "A loophole for what? You already learned how to disinherit a successor and get her back. What now?"

"Killing someone who knows about Mona, who knows everything. Where's the loophole so I don't have to kill him?" She held her breath. *Please let there be a loophole.* She'd decided that Derek must be the manufactured Qualifying Incident her mom had mentioned. He was tempting, but also a decent guy. She wasn't supposed to have sex with him, and he didn't deserve to die. Surely, she was supposed to do some innovative Guardian-ing and come up with another solution, right? That was the test?

She didn't want to consider the alternative. That he was a real threat and she had some really tough decisions to make. "So? Loophole?"

Iris collapsed onto the kitchen chair, whooshing right through it and disappearing through the floor.

"Um, Mom?" She leaned over to peer at the tile, but there was no sign of Iris. "Where'd you go?"

Iris suddenly popped up through the floor and Justine jerked back, her heart jumping. "Don't *do* that!"

"Sorry. Fainting in the mortal world is a pain. I need a drink. Do you have any tequila around here?"

Justine plunked herself back in her chair, trying to calm her heart. "Above the fridge, where you left it."

Iris floated over to the cabinet, pulled out a bottle and whipped off the top. She chugged it for five seconds before lowering it. "I needed that." She carried the bottle over to the table, ignoring the trail of tequila dripping from the bottoms of her feet as the liquid ran right through her. "Please tell me you aren't thinking of violating your Oath for a man."

"Well, no. I just want to know if there's a loophole."

"There's no loophole. Trust me."

As the resident expert on Guardianship, her mom would know. The Council had originally asked her to write the *Treatise on Guardianship,* a huge honor. Only the best were asked to write treatises. Of course, they'd changed their mind after she'd gotten herself killed, but that didn't change the fact that her mom was the expert. "Are you sure?"

Iris closed her eyes and muttered something about prayers and children who break their parents' hearts.

Justine cut her off before she could gain momentum. "Oh, come on, Mom. I don't need a guilt trip. It's a business question. I'm asking as a Guardian, not as your daughter."

Iris opened her eyes and gazed at Justine for a long

moment, before she sighed with resignation. "Here's the deal. The night I died? I violated my Oath."

"Really?" Justine inched forward. "How? For a man?"

Iris ignored her question. "I saved Mona, but I died, as you know." Iris took another swig. "When I got to purgatory, the Council showed me the penalty for Oath Violation."

Goose bumps popped up on Justine's arms as she leaned forward. "You mean the Chamber of Unspeakable Horrors? What is it?"

Iris shook her head. "It is literally a horror too unspeakable for words."

"Could you be more specific?" The *Treatise* didn't spell it out, and no Guardian had ever actually been sentenced to it and emerged with a sound enough mind to report on it.

Iris gave her a considering glance. "Well, imagine being skinned alive, then plunged into a vat of rubbing alcohol while getting your eyes stabbed repeatedly with burning hot needles. Imagine enduring that for all eternity without ever being allowed to sleep or take a break, while being surrounded by people you know and hate who are enjoying every single pleasure and joy you've ever yearned for in your entire life. Are you imagining?"

"Um, yeah." She blinked her eyes several times, forced herself not to cover them with her hands.

"Well, it's exponentially worse than that."

"Oh." Justine shook off the shudders and picked her gun up, stroking the cool metal.

"The Council spared me from the Chamber because I saved Mona." Iris pointed the bottle at Justine. "But that I'd *almost* violated my Oath? I would have gotten an eternity in the bowels of hell for that little maneuver, if it weren't for the fact I had you. So don't violate your Oath, or even think about it. They'll know."

Crud.

"If someone knows details about Mona, you have to kill that person. End of story. There are no other options. Each day you delay moves you closer toward an official Oath Violation."

Justine pressed her lips together and tried not to scowl. "So there's no way to save him? Even if he's not a danger?" Not that he wasn't a danger, but on the chance he abandoned his quest to kill her and steal Mona, well, she wanted to be prepared to let him live . . . for the sake of her mom, of course. Going above and beyond to spare a mortal's life might meet the standards for a Qualifying Incident. If the Council was even the slightest bit modern, they might even consider creative problem-solving a plus. But since she couldn't afford the Oath Violation, her only choice was something that was entirely supported by the *Treatise.*

Iris shot her a look of total disappointment. "You know, as a mother, I worked very hard to set a good example for you. I ensured you had a roof over your head, and this is what happens? You consider violating your Oath? Spurning everything I gave you?" She sighed heavily. "I don't know what to do with you. I really don't."

"Mom, I'm not going to violate my Oath. It was just a suggestion and . . ."

"What's going on?" Theresa shuffled into the kitchen, wearing a lace camisole and silk boxers, custom-made of course, complete with a hole for her tail. "Oh, hi, Iris. Drinking again?"

Iris glared at the dragon. "You're supposed to be taking care of my baby girl. Justine is considering violating her

Oath. Why haven't you been on top of this? What have you been doing?"

"Cybersex."

Iris blinked. "Again? Every time I visit, you seem to be having cybersex."

"Justine won't let me kill people or burn things up. I need *some* outlet to keep my dragon instincts sated or things will get ugly around here. Besides, it's fun." Theresa yawned, her long tongue curling over her teeth. "What time is it anyway?" She wandered over to the fridge and pulled it open.

"Too late for you to be indulging in self-gratification. Your best friend is on the verge of descending into an eternity of unspeakable horrors," Iris sniffed.

"Mom! Get off Theresa's case. She's my friend, not my keeper." Justine gave the dragon an apologetic grimace, and got a puff of smoke in acknowledgment.

"You two are a team and she's dropping the ball because of a sex addiction. Pathetic. She should be replaced as your successor."

"Hey!" Theresa slammed the fridge shut, a gallon of orange juice hanging from her left claw. "I've been putting in my time for two hundred years. I've earned my spot as the successor!"

"Not if you have a sex addiction," Iris said. "If you don't shape up, I'll have to report you to the Council and—"

"I'm not the one planning to have sex with a man who wants to steal Mona," Theresa snapped. She yanked the cap off the juice and threw it on the counter. "Talk to your daughter." She upended the gallon and started pouring the liquid down her throat.

"Theresa! The Council could be listening right now!"

Justine yanked the plastic container out of the dragon's claws, ignoring the snarl of protest. "Can't you go stick your head in the toilet or something?"

"No, I can't." Theresa grabbed the juice and turned her back on them as she finished chugging.

Iris gave a groan of dismay and swung around to face Justine. "Is that really what the loophole question is about? You want to have sex with Derek?"

"No. Of course not. Hah. *Hah.*"

Iris took another slug of the alcohol, then let the bottle thud to the counter. After a moment, she gave the girls a determined look. "Okay, I'm a modern woman. I understand the need for sex. Women have sexual urges, just like men."

Oh, God. This was so not the conversation to have with your mom. "Never mind. It was just a thought. Anyone want a pretzel?"

"Do you think I'm immune when Satan talks about licking every inch of my body? I'm not."

Ugh. "Mom—"

"Licking is good," Theresa sidled up to the table and leaned on it, her golden eyes glittering. "I wouldn't mind Zeke licking me. The backs of my knees are my favorite place . . . or are they? I can't actually remember anymore. Cyber-licking isn't quite the same, you know?"

"I have fantasies like any other woman," Iris said, with a quelling look at Theresa, "but I'm not going to act on them. Sometimes you have to think with your brain instead of the throbbing between your legs."

"Mom!" Someone behead her now. *Please.*

"Oh come on, Iris. You've been out from under the Guardian Oath for two hundred years. Do you really expect us to believe you haven't been out there getting down and

dirty with the good-looking residents of purgatory?"
Theresa wiggled her eyebrows and grinned.

"Theresa!" Justine snapped. "Will you please shut up?
I do not need to envision my mom's sex life!"

Iris tapped through Justine's arm. "Sweetie, believe
me, I understand your womanly needs. They can drive
you to do incredibly stupid things that ruin your life and
your career." She frowned. "So, if you're really feeling
desperate, maybe it would be best if you *did* have sex. If
you controlled the situation, then you wouldn't end up in
trouble, like I did." She grimaced. "But even if you think
you can justify intercourse as necessary to Mona's safety,
it would be very difficult to get away with it. The Council
isn't stupid, you know."

"Okay, fine. I won't have sex. New topic."

"Chill out." Theresa tossed the empty plastic jug at her.
"You're way too uptight when it comes to sex."

"Only when it involves my mom, so back off."

Iris wasn't finished. "If you *do* have sex, you better be
very certain it's meaningless with no emotional attachment. No loyalty to anyone but Mona. It makes you vulnerable, and that leads to bad decisions." Iris tipped her
head thoughtfully. "But if you really did have to have sex
to save Mona, then how would you keep it meaningless? I
wonder . . ." She faded off into a ruminating silence.

"Really?" Theresa's tail switched with excitement.
"You think there might be a way we can get Justine laid?
She really needs to lighten up. She's driving me crazy
with all her rules."

"What, are you guys my pimps or something?" Justine
folded her arms across her chest and leaned against the far
counter. "Thanks, but I'm all set."

Iris rubbed her chin. "Maybe if you had him blindfold you, that might work. Then it would be faceless sex."

"I've never tried blindfolds." Theresa picked up a dish towel and fingered it thoughtfully. "Impossible to have cybersex blindfolded, you know? Logistical difficulties."

Iris continued her musings. "Or if there was simply intercourse without foreplay. But do you like foreplay? I do. I especially like it when—"

"Satan's Rivka almost killed me tonight," Justine blurted out. *Please, someone, spare me from this discussion.*

Iris blinked. "What?"

"See my singed hair? Burned scalp?" Hopefully there were a few scars still left. "She threw a fireball at me and almost melted my head off."

A slow flush rose up Iris's neck to her cheeks. "That son of a bitch told me he was going to send her to keep you safe. And I believed him." She lunged to her feet. "I can't believe he lied to me again! I'm going to go find him and—"

"It was an accident," Justine said quickly. Somehow, sending her mom off in a rage after the most evil being that existed didn't seem like a good idea. "She didn't mean to."

Iris took a deep breath and eyed her. "What exactly happened tonight?"

"She was aiming for . . ." Maybe she shouldn't mention the burnt flowerpots. No need for Satan to know how Becca had dodged his orders. ". . . Derek, and I got in the way."

"So, she didn't try to kill you? You swear?"

"I swear. She was trying to keep me safe." She studied her mom, who had sagged into her chair with relief. "How did you get Satan to send his Rivka to protect me? Why isn't he after the Goblet?"

"The power of withholding sex, my dear." Iris nodded at Theresa. "You should try it. Even withholding cybersex should work. Woman have power over men. It's nature, and you must take advantage of it whenever possible."

Not the advice she wanted with the memory of Derek's kiss still sizzling on her skin. Surely, liberal handing out of sex could be a weapon as well, couldn't it?

Iris sighed. "Now that I've thought about it, I don't think there's a way around the prohibition. I think you must continue to abstain unless you can get the *Treatise* updated." A high-pitched ringing filled the apartment. "I have to go."

"What?" Theresa's tail smacked the floor. "You can't announce Justine has to stay celibate and then leave without helping us problem-solve."

"Sure she can," Justine interrupted. "It's okay. Really."

Iris gave Justine a quick hug. "Make me proud, my dear, so I can brag to all the other parents in my neighborhood. I understand the need for sex, but Derek is simply too dangerous. Kill him instead. It's the least you could do for your own mama, so I don't have to spend eternity feeling guilty because I wasn't a good enough mom to keep my daughter out of the Chamber of Unspeakable Horrors." She leveled a finger at Theresa. "And you get some therapy."

And then she shimmered out of sight.

Theresa whistled. "She's really good at the guilt thing."

"No kidding." Justine picked up the abandoned bottle of tequila. "I feel like I should go sit in the corner for twenty minutes and think about my behavior." She stared moodily at the alcohol and wished she could drown her sorrows in it. Too bad the Oath banned all substances that could impair reaction time (page seventy-three of the *Treatise*). "I'm completely traumatized by all that sex talk from my mom. I don't think I'll ever recover."

"I'll distract you. How'd your date go?"

"He admitted he was there to kill me and steal Mona, then we almost slept together, but there was this whole fireball incident." She sighed. "Sort of killed the mood."

"Yeah, I can see how that would be a buzz kill." Theresa clucked with empathy, and Justine felt a little better.

"Then I learned that someone else also knows about Mona, so we have more than one enemy. Plus the Rivka works for Derek and is all cozy with him. She wants him to go ahead and kill me because she can't *bear* for him to die."

Theresa pulled three frozen pizzas out of the freezer. "Why does he have to kill you? It's not just about his quest for immortality and world domination?"

"Some curse apparently requires my death in order to break it. What kind of jerk would write me into a curse like that?" Justine grabbed a fourth pizza for herself and turned on the oven.

"A jerk with a personal vendetta against you."

"Me? What did I ever do to anyone?"

"Well, you've killed a few people."

"All in the name of duty. How could anyone take that personally? Derek doesn't take it personally."

Theresa cocked her head. "You should have killed him. Bad decision, girlfriend."

"I know. I guess I'll do it tomorrow." Justine swung the bottle from her fingertips, watching it sway back and forth. "He owns Vic's Pretzels, by the way."

Theresa snapped to attention. "You're kidding."

"Nope."

"Well, good lord, girl! We have to find a way to save him!" Theresa ran out of the room and was back with her computer in less than five seconds. "Tell me everything that happened. You can't kill him. He's my reason for living!"

Justine felt a surge of hope. "Mom says there's no loophole."

"There's always a loophole. Talk to me, sister. We will not relinquish the pretzels!"

"You've finally lost your mind." Quincy shoved his keyboard away and leaned back in his chair, his brow furrowed.

"No, I've finally found it." Derek perched on the edge of the chair across from his brother's desk. "I know it sounds crazy, but I saw all this stuff actually happen. I swear it."

Quincy picked up a pen and drummed it on his desk. "You want me to believe that Becca is actually a disciple of Satan?"

"Rivka. She's bound to him by his life force."

"And she shoots fireballs?"

"Yep. And Justine is the Guardian. We've already been through this. I need your help, Quin. I'm hoping you'll be able to see some pattern that will help us identify who originally wrote the Curse." He leaned forward. "We need one of your brilliant equations. That's all. You don't have to kill anyone. Just do what you like best."

"Sorry, Derek, but my answer is still the same as the last time you asked me: No. You need psychological help, not encouragement." Quincy punched the intercom on his phone. "Wendy, I'll take that number now."

Damn his brother and his close-mindedness. "What number?"

The door opened and Wendy sashayed into the room. Or rather, someone who looked vaguely like Wendy. This Wendy was wearing a fitted black top (since when had her chest been that big?) and a short red skirt that hit her hips in the right places and made her legs look like they went on for eternity. She was sporting some stylish new hairdo and was wearing makeup.

She didn't just look hot.

She was sizzling.

What happened to Wendy-the-librarian?

Even Quincy seemed to notice, if the way he was gaping at her swaying hips was any indication. "Thanks, Wendy."

"Anything for you, Quin," she purred.

Quin? Since when did she call him Quin? He studied his brother as Quin's gaze tracked Wendy's every movement. All the more reason to break the Curse, if Quin had finally found a woman.

She handed Derek a piece of paper. "At your brother's request, I did a little investigating. This is the name of a psychiatrist who specializes in people who have trouble separating fantasy from reality."

He crunched the paper in his fist and scowled at Quin. "Are you serious?"

Quin nodded. "Wendy did the research. This doctor is best in the field."

"You didn't tell her *everything,* did you?" He clenched his fist tighter as he thought of Justine and her gun. "It's a *really* bad idea for Wendy to know too much."

"Don't worry. She's sworn to secrecy." He gave his assistant a wink, and she shot him a sultry look, then sauntered around the desk and leaned next to him. Quincy slipped his hand around her waist, then hauled her onto his lap.

And then they were going at it. Hands roaming, lips smacking, little moaning noises coming from Wendy.

Whoa. Derek looked away, momentarily shocked by the display. After years of being too buried in his work to notice there was actually another gender on the planet, Quin chose *now* to get involved with a woman? Four days before they both died?

A low moan from Wendy drew his attention back to them. "Hey." He slammed his palm down on the table. "Quincy, this is really important."

Quincy broke the kiss and peered over Wendy's shoulder, even as his hands caressed her lower back. "I know it's important. Call this doc before you lose your mind. The line between sanity and insanity can be so tenuous." He rubbed Wendy's butt and shot her a look that promised things Derek didn't realize Quincy even thought about.

Derek frowned. "You feeling all right, Quincy?"

His brother gave him a very masculine look. "What do you think?"

Wendy twisted around. "Call the doctor, Derek."

"No." Derek stood and tossed the wadded up card on the desk. "You're too buried in denial to realize the truth, Quincy. Forget I asked. I'll figure it out on my own. And remember, if you die, you'll leave Wendy behind."

"Can't think of a better way to go." Quincy returned to the make-out session, nearly laying Wendy out on the desk with the force of his kiss.

"Spoken like a true nonbeliever."

When Quincy's only response was to slide his hand up the back of Wendy's sweater, Derek turned and stalked out of the office. Maybe he ought to give Becca a call and have her blow up Quincy's desk with a fireball or two. Then again, Quin might not take his mouth off Wendy long enough to notice.

"Derek!"

He glanced over his shoulder to find Wendy running down the hall toward him. Her shirt was half off her shoulder and her hair was a mess. "I'm not taking the card, Wendy." He didn't even bother to slow down. "I have work to do."

"No, not that." She reached him and lowered her voice. "I just wanted you to know that I believe you."

"What?" He stopped walking and she almost ran into him.

"I believe you." She clutched his sleeve and gazed up at him, her face unlined in its honesty. "I want to help."

He narrowed his eyes and uncurled her fingers from his arm. "Why? Hasn't Quin told you that no one ever believes me?"

"Yes, he did." Her cheeks turned pink. "But I love your brother, and if there's any chance he's going to die from a Curse, I want it stopped. I want kids and picket fences and a cute little house with him, and I'll do whatever it takes to save him." She reached for Derek again, her eyes wide with emotion. "Don't resent him. He's so buried in math, in logic, that he can't comprehend things that can't be explained with equations. He loves you, and that's why he's worried about you. The fact he can't accept what you're saying is simply because of how he's hard-wired. But I believe it and I won't lose him." She pressed a paper in his hand. "Here's my cell phone. Call me at any time. I can help you. I know people."

He folded his fingers around the paper, even as he studied her. "What people?"

"You don't think you're the only one to run into problems with the supernatural, do you?" She jumped when Quincy stuck his head out of his office and called her. "I have to go. Call me. I'll help you however I can." She then rushed back to Quincy, who put his hand on her elbow in a possessively male way.

Derek shoved Wendy's number into his wallet—not that he planned to get her involved. If Justine found out Wendy knew about the Goblet, she'd kill her. Call him old-fashioned, but there was only one woman whose death he was willing to cause.

By ten o'clock the next morning, Justine and Theresa hadn't found a loophole that would keep Derek alive, and she hadn't heard from him. The clock was ticking on Oath Violation, and she was getting antsy. "If he doesn't call soon, I'm going to have to track him down and kill him." She slammed the *Treatise* shut and dropped it on the coffee table, then flopped back against the couch.

Theresa didn't even look away from her computer screen as she scooped up the book with her left claw and tossed it back in Justine's lap. "He's the pretzel king. He's like a saint. You'll be damned forever if you kill him. We'll come up with something . . ." She clicked her mouse, then sucked in her breath. "No way."

Justine jerked upright. "What? Did you think of a loophole?"

"Just got an e-mail from Zeke. The golden aura is a sign of being possessed."

"Hah! I knew there was something off about the

surfer." She scooted next to the dragon and tried to lean over the two tons of flesh and scales to read the screen. "So, who was our surfer possessed by?"

Theresa scooted to the left and angled the screen slightly toward Justine, pulling her tail to the other side. "Someone from the Afterlife. He's not sure who."

"Afterlife, huh?" She scanned Zeke's e-mail, but there was no additional information. "Well, gold would imply someone affiliated with heaven, right?" She pulled back, careful not to snag her sweater on Theresa's scales. "But why would someone from heaven want to kill me and steal Mona?"

Theresa cocked her head. "Maybe it's the manufactured Qualifying Incident. Maybe the surfer was a test, and you let him go, so now they think you're getting soft. They realized Satan's Rivka is sniffing around, and they're worried you won't be able to resist a full assault by Satan. Maybe they want to eliminate you and bring in someone more ruthless. Like a dragon, for example."

"So I'm supposed to allow heaven's next assassin to kill me? Since it's for the greater good?" Justine snorted. "I won't even let Derek kill me, let alone some wimpy surfer."

Theresa rolled her eyes and gave her the "poor stupid roommate" expression. "No, you were supposed to kill the surfer."

"So killing an innocent who happened to get possessed would show I'm tough enough to be a Guardian?" She kicked a pillow out of her way and stood up, pacing the length of the room. "That makes no sense. Nothing makes sense."

Theresa settled back on the couch and folded her claws across her belly, her lips curved in an amused grin. "Maybe you're supposed to be smart enough to figure it out." The intercom buzzed, and Theresa used the end of her tail to hit the button. "Yello."

"It's Xavier. Justine's needed in the lobby— Umph." There was a crash, then a thud, then a howl of pain, then silence.

Uh-oh.

"That didn't sound good." Theresa's tail twitched and a cascade of sparks shot out of her nose. "Maybe I should investigate. Pretty please?"

Adrenaline rushed through Justine. "I think it's my party, but you can incinerate anyone who comes after Mona while I'm gone." This was turning out to be the most interesting week she'd had since she lost her virginity when she was seventeen. "I'll go check it out." She darted over to the bookcase, grabbed her gun, and raced to the elevator. A little action was exactly what she needed. Shoot first, think later.

"It could be a trap." Theresa's eyes were gleaming and her lips were pulled back to show glistening teeth.

"I know. Totally exciting, huh?" Justine flung open the door, dove into the elevator and pressed the LOBBY button. She tightened her grip on the gun, pressed her back into the corner of the elevator, and aimed at the doors. Whatever had grabbed Xavier probably knew she was coming, and it/he/she/they would be ready.

Well, so was she.

Ten

The elevator doors whipped open in the lobby and Justine barely managed to avoid shooting the old lady from the third floor as she waddled into the elevator. She waggled a crooked finger at Justine. "Drug addicts. Despicable. Prostitution will be next."

"What?" Justine slid the gun behind her back and edged past the woman, trying to catch a glimpse of what was waiting for her.

The woman pointed her purse at the lobby. "Gang war. Go back upstairs and lock your doors before society destroys all of us. I'm going to go donate money to Reverend Munsey on the religion network. Get him to say a prayer for us."

"Um, okay. Good luck." Justine stepped out of the elevator and let the doors slide shut behind her. The lobby was silent. No one was in there, but the security desk had been reduced to a pile of rubble. "Hello? Xavier? Are you here?"

"May I suggest you return to your condo and don't answer the door for a short while?"

Her heart lifted, and she spun around, letting the gun drop to her side. "Derek?"

He shoved the heavy front door out of his way and

stepped into the lobby. "I really mean it," he said. "You need to go back upstairs."

Gone was the millionaire businessman appearance. His jacket and tie were missing, his shirt was torn, and there was a raw red mark on his right cheek. Cheeks flushed, hair messed up. He looked rugged, masculine, and oh-so-hot. A designer suit guy *and* a warrior? *Yum, yum.* Her belly tightened and she had to order herself not to look at the curve of his bicep peeking through his ripped sleeve. *Focus on splintered desks.* "What happened to you?"

He lurched to a stop, as if it took all his effort to keep from moving forward. "Exactly how well do you know Xavier?"

"I don't. He's the doorman. Why?"

Derek scowled and took a reluctant step toward the remains of the desk. "Have you noticed he can make people do things merely by suggesting it to them?" He took another step, then turned around and grabbed hold of the front door, as if something were pulling him across the lobby and he was trying to fight it.

"What are you talking about?" She watched Derek's erratic movements and the hair on her arms began to prickle.

"Remember when I fell asleep in the lobby the other day? He told me to take a nap." He jerked back from the door, and one hand slipped free. He cursed and tightened his grip on the door with his other hand, muttering some not-so-complimentary remarks about Xavier.

"You're certain he made you fall asleep?" She'd heard of people with the power of suggestion, but had never met one. Or maybe she had, apparently. The ones of lesser power could influence only humans, but the really good ones supposedly could manipulate Otherworld beings.

They were considered highly dangerous, because if they were really good, you didn't even realize you were being influenced until it was too late. Combine a strong power of suggestion with a twisted sense of humor or something darker, and, well, it could get ugly.

"Yes. He seems to use those powers to protect you. Convinces people they don't want to bother you." His voice was strained, his biceps bulging with the effort of hanging on to the door, even as he pulled against it.

Well, no wonder Xavier was so effective at his job. "Obviously, it's a good career choice for him." She watched Derek's fingers sliding off the door and felt her adrenaline kick in as his hand flew off the door and he spun toward her with a grunt of aggravation.

"He's not merely a doorman." His brow furrowed and his jaw flexing, he worked his way across the room toward the desk, his path uneven and crooked, as if he were being yanked and he was fighting it. "I think he's here because you're here. I thought he was supposed to keep you safe. After all, he tried to kill me last time I was here. But tonight, he was different."

"Different how?" She watched as Derek reached the splintered desk and began kicking the boards aside in a frenzy. He was uncoordinated and his face was wrenched as if he was in pain. "What's wrong with you?"

He cursed, then bent toward the pile of rubble. "Tonight, when I walked in, he told me to kill you. Immediately and without mercy."

She jerked the gun up and aimed it at his chest. "Why would he do that?" The barrel wavered slightly and she had to use a second hand to keep it aimed at his heart.

Derek shoved aside several pieces of wood to get to a long sword, which glittered as he picked it up. "That's really not our major concern at the moment."

She sucked in her breath and took a step back from the one thing that could actually kill her. "Where'd you get that?"

He took a practice swing, like a batter warming up in the on-deck circle. "After he suggested I kill you, he gave me this. Said the only way to get the job done was to behead you."

She tightened her fingers around her gun and willed her hands to be steady even as the nose kept wanting to dip away from Derek. Dammit. This was *not* the time for her to lose her nerve. "Derek." She kept her voice calm. "What are you doing?"

"Isn't it obvious? I'm going to kill you." He slapped the blade against his thigh in visible aggravation.

She moved toward the middle of the lobby, so she had room to maneuver. Her heart was racing, and she couldn't take her gaze off the lethal weapon as he sliced it through the air. "I thought you were going to *think* about it."

He took another cut. "I did. I came up with an excellent plan that I need your help with. I have no intention of killing you yet. Unfortunately, your doorman has other ideas."

She kept the nose of her gun aimed at his chest, keeping a safe distance between them as he advanced on her. "Where's Xavier?"

"Unconscious in the middle of the street. I tried to convince him to rescind his suggestion, but he's a stubborn bastard." Derek's dark eyes flicked to her neck and then to his blade.

She eased her feet apart and raised the gun, her blood thundering in her ears. "So, that's how the desk got broken?"

"Mmm-hmm." He swung the sword thoughtfully, studying it with interest. "Quincy would be so interested in this. I bet there's a math equation to describe the perfectly balanced sword. It flows quite nicely through the air." He held it in a ready position and fixed his gaze on her. "I have to kill you now, but I'll do my best to allow you to get in a blow that will temporarily disable me. I expect his suggestion will wear off, and then we can have a civilized discussion."

" 'Temporarily disable'? All I have is a gun."

Tension flickered across his face. "I'm trusting you on this. I'll fight the compulsion, and give you a chance to knock me out or something. Don't try to kill me. I know you may have to ultimately but there will be plenty of opportunity for it later." He lunged and swung, and she barely dodged it in time. She got a nick on her shoulder, but nothing serious. Yet.

"Where'd you learn how to use a sword?" She spun around, keeping out of his reach, the gun trained on his heart. Steady and unwavering.

"Again, irrelevant at the moment. Can't you focus?" He moved slowly, circling her, his eyes fixated on her neck. "I don't know how long I'll be able to fight this off. Knock me out, already, will you?"

"How? If I get close enough to hit you, you'll cut my head off." He lunged again, and she dodged out of the way as the blow veered off to the right at the last second. It was a precise swing, lethal and perfect for beheading. "Derek, I'm really sorry. You're too dangerous. I have to kill you."

He scowled at her. "You realize that if we don't find a way to end this Curse, LaValle men will come after you until one of them finally succeeds, don't you? It's not just me you need to worry about."

Her gun wavered again. "I hadn't thought of that."

"Think quickly, my dear." And with that, he lunged for her again, and she knew instantly it would be a death blow.

She cursed as the gun barrel dropped ever so slightly, but she didn't hesitate. She pulled the trigger and the bullet thudded into his gut.

The sword clattered to the floor. He dropped to his knees, clutched his belly, already oozing with the bright red of fresh blood. "You call that temporarily disabled?" And then he fell to the ground unconscious in a puddle of his own blood.

And to think she hated her job. Go figure.

"You can't give him a drink." Theresa was lying on the kitchen floor next to Derek's body, her head resting against his cheek. "You're supposed to kill him, not break rules to save him." She snuffled against his neck. "My poor pretzel king. I'll miss him so much."

Justine chewed her lower lip as Derek bled all over the tile, a pool of blood spreading out beneath his hips. "If I don't give him a drink, he'll die."

"Should have thought of that before you shot him. You think they'll have to close Vic's Pretzels down? I mean, he was the creative genius behind it, right?" Theresa muttered an epithet. "So unfair. How am I supposed to survive without those pretzels?"

Justine laid her hand on his chest, slipping it under his shirt. Still warm, but barely. "But what about the Curse?

One of the LaValle men will eventually succeed." She shook her head. "I can't risk it. I have to keep Mona safe." She met Theresa's weepy gaze. "I have to keep him alive so we can break the Curse."

The dragon sat up. "No way, girlfriend. Bad choice. Even for pretzels, it's not worth it!"

"It's the only option." Justine jumped to her feet, hustled over to Mona, and poured a cup of the always-prepared frothy liquid. "One drink won't make him immortal."

"It's still highly forbidden. And after that whole Carl thing, you're really not supposed to be making this kind of decision without getting prior authorization." Theresa's tail was flicking and her pupils narrowed in her golden eyes as she stood up.

"Prior authorization takes seventy-three years, and Derek's going to die in about one minute." She knelt next to him, closed her eyes for a moment while she tried to clear her mind of all emotion. Logic only. *Am I making the right decision?* "Theresa?"

Theresa dropped next to her with a thud. "Fine. The fact you haven't slept with him yet and are still planning to kill him when the whole Curse thing is over does lend credence to your claim that it's purely about Mona's safety, even if it is *highly forbidden*."

Derek's body jerked and seized, and Justine knew he was near the end.

Time's up, Guardian. Make the decision.

She grabbed his head, opened his mouth and poured the steaming espresso down his throat. Her hand was shaking so much she barely managed to hold on to the cup.

Theresa steadied Justine's hand with a claw. "Easy,

girlfriend! You're going to give his esophagus third-degree burns."

"He'll heal." If she'd done it in time. She poured the last bit of steaming coffee over the oozing wound in his gut, then grabbed a pair of needle nose pliers and poked them into the hole in his stomach. She wiggled them around until she found the bullet, then pulled it out. God, she hated blood.

She tossed the bullet onto the floor, where it hit with a clank and rolled to a stop. Then she leaned back on her heels and waited, her chest tight. "Is it just me, or is it really difficult to breathe in here?"

"It's just you." Theresa's nose was inches from Derek's face, her gaze unblinking. "Come on, Pretzel King. You can do it."

Justine touched Derek's skin. Cooler than it had been. He was too still, too pale, and his breath was so shallow she could barely see his chest move. Blood was oozing freely from his belly, stirred up by her fishing around in there. "I think I'm going to be sick."

"He's too far gone. He needs more," Theresa said.

"But that'll be two drinks." Two drinks would make him almost immortal. Not quite, but too damn close.

Theresa sat up and leveled a stare at Justine, her claw resting on Derek's shoulder. "You've already given him one. You might as well do it again, revive him, and prove that you did it for the right reasons. If he dies now, you have no proof that saving him was the right choice. You'd just look like you wimped out."

"He'll be so much harder to kill." He'd been so skilled with that sword. Giving him a dose of immortality could seriously affect her odds.

"Didn't stop you with Carl."

"Yeah, but I was mad at him, and he wasn't exactly a competent opponent." She laid the back of her hand against Derek's face. Too cold. She jumped to her feet and ran over to Mona to fill the cup again. "Why did this happen?"

"Because you put a bullet in his abdomen." Theresa leaned back on her haunches, her gold hoop earrings swaying with the movement. "Haven't you ever heard of a kneecap?"

Justine pulled his head onto her lap and poured more of the espresso down his throat, stroking his neck to get him to swallow. "I've been trained to kill, not maim." She hadn't even thought of a kneecap. *Idiot!*

She poured the rest of the boiling hot espresso over his belly, then set the cup on the floor.

They waited.

No response.

"He needs more." Theresa was standing now, fiddling with the hem of her camisole as she watched Derek.

"No way. Two drinks are highly forbidden. Three drinks? There's no justification for that." Why wouldn't he revive? It wasn't supposed to end like this.

"I know. I just thought I'd point out that it was an option." Theresa ran to the freezer and pulled out a Vic's pretzel, carried it back to Derek and set it on his chest. "A memorial to our pretzel king."

Justine batted the pretzel away. "He's not dead yet! Cut that out!" She laid her hands on his cheeks and leaned over him. "Come on, Derek," she whispered. "Don't die on me. Not yet."

A puff of black smoke shot out of Theresa's nose as she

stalked away from Justine. "You're so ungrateful. I don't know why I waste my time hanging around with you."

"Because you're a dragon with no other friends and you need me to do your errands for you." She tensed as she saw a blue spark jump off Derek's stomach. Hope exploded through her body, shattering the lump that had settled in her gut. "Did you see that?"

"See what?" Theresa paused in the doorway.

Another blue spark popped up. Followed by a green one. And then a series of gold and silver. "It's working!" She set his head on the floor and backed up as fireworks began exploding off his body. Relief rushed through her as a whistler erupted from his shoulder and spun off toward the ceiling, whipping around with a high-pitched squeak as white sparkles hit the floor. Whistlers were a really good sign.

Theresa pranced over to Derek, sighed with delight and leaned over him, letting the sparks hit her in the face. "I love this part. I wish I could produce fire of different colors." Her skin sizzled as the sparks landed on her scales. "It's so beautiful. It's like the Fourth of July."

Justine sat down by the door, out of the range of most of the sparks. "I forgot what this was like. I haven't seen the fireworks since Carl drank from Mona." It was a pyrotechnic display that would make any mad scientist batty with envy. "It's incredible." Now that she knew he was going to be all right, she could enjoy the moment. All they had to do was break the Curse and prove she'd made the right decision by giving him two drinks. Then she could kill him, and everything would be fine.

Because she would kill him. Because that was her job and she never shirked her duties. Right? Of course, right. It would be no problem to follow through. No problem at all. Everything was perfect. She pressed her fingers to her temples and tried to rub the sudden headache away.

Theresa beamed at her. "I think we should do this more often. Pick random people off the street, let them drink from Mona so we can see the light show, then kill them. Don't worry, as the only non-Guardian in the room, I'll do the dirty work."

Justine blinked at her friend, barely visible behind the cascade of vibrant fireworks. "Then why didn't you offer to give the drink to Derek instead of me?"

Theresa's mouth fell open. "Oh, wow. I didn't even think of it at the time. I was too traumatized by the thought of losing Vic's Pretzels. I'll do it next time, I promise."

"Oh, like I plan to be in this situation in the near future." Justine hauled herself to her feet as the fireworks subsided. "Thanks for nothing."

Theresa's tail switched, banging into the cabinet. "What does that mean?"

"It means that you're supposed to be my right hand, and you contribute absolutely nothing around here. You eat, you have cybersex, and that's about it."

Theresa stood up, her tail whacking a chair into the wall. "It's not my fault you were too freaked about your sex toy dying to think of it yourself."

"I wasn't freaking and he's not my sex toy!" Justine leaned into the dragon's personal space. "I was relying on you to ground me in a moment of crisis, and you let me down. In fact—"

"Hey! Don't be taking it out on me just because you almost killed lover boy by mistake! That was your fault and—"

"Um, hello?"

They both looked down. Derek was lying between them, and he was covered in ash. He gave them a weak wave. "I don't mean to interrupt, but Theresa is spitting on me."

"Derek!" Justine's first reaction was to drop to the tile and hug him, but instead, she took a step back. "How's the murderous inclination?"

He cocked his head to study her, and something inside her gut curled. "I seem to be back to my normal feelings about you."

"So you're not going to try to kill me?" God, he looked hot, stretched out on the floor, covered in soot and blood and his belly spouting sparks.

"Not at the moment." He touched his stomach, where a red scar was still generating small sparkles. "Can't say the same for you, apparently. I said temporarily disable me, not put a bullet in my stomach."

"Um, well . . ."

Theresa cleared her throat. "Well, I'll just leave you two to work out your lovers' spat. I'll be in the other room if you need me." She dropped a dish towel on Derek. "Fire-retardant fabric, so you can use it while you're still on fire. Sorry about the ash." She then spun around, narrowly missed Derek's head with the spike on the end of her tail, and stalked out of the kitchen.

Justine managed a weak smile for Derek, who had propped himself up on an elbow, his partially burned, blood-soaked shirt falling open to reveal a heavily muscled chest. What to say to a man after you've almost killed him? She couldn't exactly apologize, since she'd been shooting to kill. "Um . . . you have nice chest hair. Just the right amount. Not too much. Not too little." Oy. How pathetic was that? Did she have no brain at all?

He raised an eyebrow at her. "You could have just asked me about it. No need to go to such lengths just to get my shirt off."

She grinned and felt the tension ease from her body. "You're not mad?"

"Well, I'm a little offended." He levered himself to a sitting position, leaning heavily against a cabinet. "I thought we had an understanding."

"Instinct. Sorry." She cocked her head. "Don't you owe me an apology? I mean, you tried to kill me first and all."

"Hey, I did all I could to avoid killing you, a claim you can't make, I might add. It's Xavier who owes you the apology, not me. Where is he, anyway?" He let his head drop back against the wood and closed his eyes.

"I have no idea. I've been occupied with saving your wimpy mortal behind."

He frowned and fingered the red mark just above his cute little belly button. "How am I not dead?"

"Yeah, about that." She chewed her lower lip. "I sort of broke a rule, so I think I made up for shooting you."

He opened his eyes, and raised his eyebrows. "Dare I ask?"

Justine avoided his gaze and busied herself with brushing ash off her jeans. "Well, it's kind of complicated . . ."

"She gave you two drinks from the Goblet of Eternal Youth," Theresa shouted from the other room. "You're not immortal yet, but you're close. Be sure and thank her with appropriate body massages—with hot oils. I have some in my bathroom if you want to borrow them."

Her cheeks swelled with heat as Derek grinned. "Theresa! I'll handle this!"

"No, you won't. You're sitting there being all girly." Theresa threw the kitchen door open and stuck her blue head into the room. "Here's the deal, Derek. You guys have to break the Curse now, or Justine's in deep shit. So quit sitting around and get on it. Don't you die in like three days or something? And clean up the mess you made on the kitchen floor. You're such a bleeder." She let the door slam shut, muttering about inaction and useless mortals.

Eleven

Derek couldn't believe what he'd just heard. "You immortalized me?"

"Not all the way, but pretty much." Justine cleared her throat. "It was the only way to revive you. I couldn't let you die yet. For Mona's sake."

He cocked an eyebrow at her addendum. "Mona, huh?" She looked cute, sitting there with a guilty flush on her cheeks, her clothes still covered in his blood. He grinned at the thought she'd broken the rules for him. Yeah, maybe it was about saving Mona, but she'd still done it. She hadn't saved his ancestor, had she? Point for him.

"Of course. For Mona."

"Well, thanks, I guess." He flexed his arms. He didn't feel any different, he still felt weak actually. Although, he did feel surprisingly well, if one considered the fact he'd almost died about three minutes ago. "So, what does two drinks do to me?"

"Well, it'll take you a few centuries to get old and die. And you'll heal from most things, but a serious deathblow would still do you in." Justine chewed her lower lip, her brow wrinkled. "A third drink would make you immortal, for all practical purposes."

A glimmer of hope rushed through him. "You think two drinks will be enough to stop the Curse?"

"Even three drinks wouldn't be enough." Her gaze flicked to his chest, then back up to his face. "You could still be beheaded. Even now, beheading would be my best bet to kill you. I don't think the gun will work on you anymore, unless I shoot you in the head repeatedly or something."

"Well, as long as you have a strategy to ensure my demise, I feel *so* much better." He stretched his arms over his head, as strength began to return to his body. "But I guess that means Mona won't break the Curse then. So much for that plan." He was two-thirds immortal and still on track to die in three days. Ironic.

Justine stood, her face suddenly tense. "Was that your plan? To drink from Mona?" She set her hand on her hips. "Did you set up that whole scene in the lobby hoping I'd shoot you and then revive you?"

"I own a multimillion dollar pretzel company. Do you really think I'm stupid enough to actually think that would be a good plan?"

She tilted her head. "I don't know. Maybe you inherited the business and Becca keeps it going. Maybe you're only a figurehead and in reality your brain is capable only of changing engine oil and watching baseball games."

He snorted. "For your information, I invented the No-Carb Pretzel as a tribute to my dad, Victor LaValle, whose life goal had been a no-carb waffle, and then I took the company public, all before I hired Becca. Becca has merely managed things while I've been dealing with the Curse issue."

"A little testy, are we?" She looked amused.

Great. So glad he could provide entertainment. "No. Just

because my entire family thinks I'm insane and a liability doesn't mean it bothers me when someone questions my basic intelligence." He pulled himself to his feet, leaning against the counter as his legs adjusted to his weight. "I don't care at all." There'd been a time, yes, but not anymore. He had more important things to worry about than what other people thought of him. Funny how the threat of a Curse will put things in perspective.

"Would it make you feel better if I told you I thought you were brilliant, incredibly sexy, and a man worthy of me?"

He grinned. "Do you?"

"No. I just wanted to know if it would make you feel better if I did."

But he caught her glance at his bare chest, and a sense of satisfaction breezed across him. "Liar."

She lifted her chin and met his gaze. "I never lie. So, what's your grand plan? It better be worthy of two drinks of Mona, or I'll have to kill you immediately."

Right. They had more important things to deal with than whether the heat from the dance floor was still buzzing between them. "Basically, we need to find out who cursed my family, then make them undo it."

She folded her arms. "For this, I saved you?"

"You saved me because you couldn't bear to have me die."

Something flickered across her face. "Don't even say that, Derek. You know I can't afford to have you live."

"Why not? If I don't have to kill you, why would you have to kill me?"

She paced to the other side of the kitchen and leaned against the counter, her hands braced next to her hips. "You know too much about Mona. I agree that we need to break the Curse to keep other LaValle men from coming after me, but after that . . ." She grimaced. "I can't let you live."

Okay, so he didn't really like that answer. His end goal, after all, had been to continue living. And now apparently, he had several centuries worth of living to lose out on, not just another fifty years. All the more reason to try to stay alive. "You're really going to kill me? Regardless?"

"Yes." She cleared her throat and shifted her weight. "And I can't sleep with you either. It would violate my Oath! The only sex I can have is meaningless, empty sex designed to save Mona."

He leaned against the counter. The strength was slowly returning to his body. "I can live with that."

Her cheeks flamed red, and the tension in the room skyrocketed. She wasn't immune to him. Not one bit. And awareness of that hit him low in the gut. He levered himself off the counter and began to walk across the kitchen toward her.

She held up her hands as if to block him. "I'd still have to kill you."

He reached her and came to a halt, his body mere inches from her, but not touching. "You'll try, you mean."

She planted her palms on his chest to block him. Her hands were warm, her fingertips soft. "Why are you doing this to me? There have to be plenty of women in this world who'd sleep with you willingly."

He could feel his heart thudding against her touch. "You're the first one who hasn't thought I was insane. Plus, the fact you plan to kill me takes away a lot of my guilt that I'll have to kill you if we don't solve the Curse. You balance me."

The corner of her mouth curved up. "You have such low standards."

"I'm a man. We don't have any standards." He reached up, twisted his finger in a strand of her hair.

She didn't push his hand away. "I have to kill you, not sleep with you."

He lifted his other one and cupped the back of her head. "What if I promise never to tell anyone what I know?" Er . . . anyone *else*, and he'd make sure Becca, Quin, and Wendy didn't talk either. "I'm very trustworthy. Ask anyone I do business with—I'm the epitome of ethical. Let me interrogate you. It would benefit both of us to have this Curse eradicated, but if you can't drop your natural defenses and let me in, we might not succeed."

She leaned forward slightly, until her mouth was barely an inch from his. The scent of mint and freshness curved into him. "It doesn't matter who you tell," she said, her breath warm against his lips. "A Manasa could get all the information out of your mind before you knew what had happened. And then it would be on the black market and I'd be in so much trouble."

Manasa. Another word he didn't know. "Okay, I give. What's a Manasa?"

"A Manasa looks human and they live in the mortal world like any human, but they can extract even the deepest secrets out of anyone's brain. They then usually sell the information. Nowadays, they use eBay. Fastest and easiest way to set up an auction. It's very lucrative, actually. Newspaper reporters love them, because they can get the scoop on stories. They usually buy the exclusive rights so the Manasa can't resell it. Manasas are pretty common, though they vary in their skill level. There are probably at least twenty or thirty in New York at any given time." She licked her lips and fixed her gaze on his mouth. Then she trailed her finger over his jaw.

He closed his eyes for a second, then dropped his hands and stepped back. He took a deep breath. *Focus on the priorities.* His life. The Curse. The mind-reading Manasa. "These Manasas, what if they're not reputable? What keeps them from reselling?"

Her hands dropped from his chest and she cleared her throat. "Basically, once they extract the info, it morphs into a printed document that pops up wherever they store all their files. Usually a locked safe or something. If someone buys the exclusive rights to it, the Manasa gives them the original file. Once the Manasa turns over the original, they can't remember or access the information. If it's a nonexclusive sale, then the Manasa gives them a copy. As long as the Manasa has the original in their possession, she'll always know exactly what's in it." Justine fiddled with her sweater, smoothing nonexistent wrinkles, then moved away from him.

He rolled that last bit of information around in his thoughts. "So, could a Manasa read my mind and figure out who cursed me?"

Justine stopped fidgeting and looked at him. "Maybe, but what about everything else they would learn? Too much risk." She shook her head. "I can't let you do it."

"I'll buy the exclusive rights."

She rolled her eyes. "Impossible. Do you have any idea how much a Manasa would charge for a preempt on information about Mona? It'd be astronomical."

He shrugged. "I have tons of money. Ending the Curse

seems a decent thing to spend it on. Do you know any Manasas?"

"Well, not personally—"

The door burst open and Theresa walked into the kitchen with a phone book. She was already leafing through the pages. "There are some listed in here. Why don't I start calling?"

"Don't you have anything to do other than eavesdrop?" Justine asked.

Theresa looked up, surprised. "You know I don't. I have no life. I live vicariously through you." She turned to Derek. "By the way, I'll sleep with you. You're quite protected by Mona, so I probably wouldn't burn you to death. I've loved you for years, ever since I bit into my first Vic's Pretzel. It would be my honor to take away your sexual frustration." She puckered her lips in a dragon kiss.

Derek shot a glance at Justine, who was looking amused and annoyed at the same time. He looked back at the dragon, in her sports bra and jogging shorts. He wasn't sure rejecting a dragon was a good idea, and sleeping with one was probably a worse choice. "Tell you what. Let's solve this Curse thing first and then see how things go."

Theresa shrugged and went back to reading the yellow pages. "Fair enough. I'll have you know though, that before I became a dragon, I was well known for being the best lay in the entire township."

He blinked. "Seriously?"

"When a girl has been celibate for as long as I have, sex is not something she jokes about." Theresa held up the phone book. "I found a Manasa that has a big ad and a top rating on eBay. She's practically around the corner. She even takes credit cards, so you're golden." She tore out a page and handed it to Derek, fluttering her eyelashes at him. "Here you go. I'll be waiting here if you *need* me."

He grabbed the page. "Thanks. I think."

Justine scowled at her roommate, then grabbed Derek's arm. "Come on, Derek. We have a Curse to eradicate." She didn't let go, her fingers tight around his arm.

He stole a glance at the dragon over his shoulder, and she winked at him.

Twelve

Justine paused outside the ramshackle storefront, complete with bars on the windows. She checked the paper she held in her hand one last time, and looked back up. "FAST CASH," she read from the battered sign above the door. "It looks like one of those cash-advance places that screws desperate people."

Derek peered over her shoulder, and she tried not to inhale his delicious scent. "It's the right address. You think she's closed down?"

"Maybe." She tucked the paper in her pocket. "Listen, this is a sign we're not supposed to visit a Manasa. I've heard lots of horror stories about them, and I think it's best if we don't . . ." He pulled open the door and stepped inside. "Derek! Just because you're almost immortal doesn't mean you can ignore me."

"I was perfectly capable of ignoring bad advice even when I was completely human." His voice faded as he disappeared from view.

She stalked into the ramshackle store. There was an old countertop with bars protecting the employee from customers. The carpet was smelly and tattered—it might have been green once. A few fluorescent lights dangled from the ceiling and one of them was flickering in a most annoying way. "For your information, Mr. Pretzel King, it wasn't bad advice, it was . . ." She stopped talking when a little old lady waddled out of the back room. The wrinkled woman looked familiar . . .

She took one look at Derek and snorted. "Drug addict. I don't deal in that nonsense. Get out."

Justine snapped her fingers in recognition. "You live in my building."

The crone eyed Justine, then her face brightened. "Of course, you're that gal from the top floor. What are you doing with the drug addict who brought gang warfare into my building? He threw our nice doorman out in the street. Is he pimping for you?"

Derek grinned. "Yes, she's my best gal. My clients love her."

"Shut up." Justine elbowed him aside. "He's not a drug addict, though if he was, he'd at least have an excuse for his behavior. We're looking for a tenant who used to be here."

The woman's forehead wrinkled even more, if that was possible. "I've been here for fifty-seven years, dearie. I'm afraid the previous tenant is long gone."

Justine frowned. "So, are you the Manasa?"

The woman suddenly stood taller and the wrinkles seemed to melt off her face as she whipped out a handheld PDA and typed into it. "Buying or selling?" Even her clothes seemed to take on fresh life.

"Buying my own information," Derek said.

She thrust her hand toward him. "Let me see the cash, please."

"I plan to pay for it with a credit card," Derek said.

"If it's a credit card, payment must be made before I give you the information."

"Fine."

She beamed at them, and opened a black door. "Come to the back. The cash-'n'-go business is a front to keep the undesirables from stalking me."

"But you advertise in the yellow pages," Justine pointed out.

"Of course. How else am I going to get business?"

"But if you're trying to hide, why advertise?"

The Manasa rolled her eyes at her. "You aren't a business expert, you?"

Justine made a face at the Manasa as she led them into a green room. Kelly green actually. Floor, walls, ceiling, carpet, furniture, framed paintings that blended into the wall, curtains. Nothing but green. "You're a green Manasa, I take it?"

"No, I just like the challenge of working in an antistim environment."

Green and sarcastic. This was going to be fun.

"What does 'antistim' mean?" Derek asked.

"It means working in an environment that isn't conducive to my powers, one that does the opposite of stimulate: antistim. It's really not that difficult to understand, even for a human." The Manasa went to a green closet and pulled out a green jumpsuit and a green wig. "Every Manasa has a color that opens their mind for reception. Mine's green." She began putting on her outfit. "As a youth, all I needed was to be wearing a green stone in my earrings, but now that I'm older, it takes a little more." She picked up a makeup jar and began spreading green face paint on her cheeks.

Derek frowned. "I don't mean to insult you, but the information we need is buried deeply. Even I don't know what it is. If your power is fading—"

"Silence!" She snapped her fingers sharply. "You obviously know nothing about Manasas. I'm very insulted. Are you sure you're not a drug addict?"

Justine touched his arm. "A Manasa grows in power with age, which is why they need more of their stimulant color. If she needs this much green, it means she draws on a tremendous amount of power." She smiled at the Manasa. "I've never been in the presence of such power. I'm very honored you will see us."

The Manasa harrumphed. "The man is annoying in his ignorance of Manasas. Can we leave him outside? I don't like to work in the presence of annoying people."

Justine grinned at the startled expression on Derek's face. "He's the one with information and money."

She grunted. "I'll have to charge a hardship fee, then." She held out her hand. "Credit card, please."

Derek kept it in his pocket. "Not until I see what you can do."

The Manasa narrowed her eyes. "Then I don't help."

"Fine." Derek turned to leave, grabbing Justine's wrist. "I heard blue Manasas are better anyway."

She had to stifle a grin as the Manasa leapt over the green couch and flattened herself across the door. "Fine. We'll negotiate fee after information is on the table. Come, come. Sit, sit."

"We negotiate the fee, now," Derek said. "This isn't a carte blanche."

The Manasa tilted her head, her arms still spread across the door. "So, what do you want?"

"I would like you to uncover some information buried inside my mind, and I want to buy the exclusive rights immediately," Derek said.

The Manasa was shaking her head before he could finish speaking. "I cannot set a price until I know the information. Then I assess what I could get on eBay and I let you preempt. A recipe for chocolate cookies would not go for the same price as instructions on how to break into the World Bank. You see?"

Justine touched Derek's arm. "It's how they do it. You have no choice. See why I didn't want to come?"

"That's why I'm very rich." She beamed at them. "You stay?"

Justine caught his arm and pulled him aside, lowering her voice. "Derek, you can't do this unless you're prepared to pay whatever price she asks. There's no way we can afford to have her put it on eBay."

"What price do you think she'll charge?"

She shrugged. "I don't know. A couple million dollars at least. Not for the Curse, but for the information on Mona that she'll inadvertently run across."

He rubbed his chin. "I'll block it, then."

"You can't block a Manasa! A pink one maybe, but a pink one would never be able to get to the Curse."

The Manasa clapped her hands. "Come, come. I have an enema in an hour. No time to waste."

"Fine." He turned to face the Manasa. "I'll offer you one hundred thousand dollars for any information you find. If it's valueless, you still get the money. If it's worth more than that, you can't raise the price."

The Manasas eyes widened. "Must be valuable."

"To me. I don't want you raising the price if you decide I really need the information. One hundred grand or we go to . . ." He slipped the phone book page out of Justine's back pocket and scanned it. ". . . to Manasas-R-Us."

"No! They are trying to put me out of business! I will not let you go to them. One hundred it is." She ran to a green desk, pulled out a green sheet of paper, filled in the blanks, then handed it to Derek. "That's the contract. You must allow me to access the information, and you must pay me one hundred thousand dollars for exclusive rights. My grandson is a Wall Street attorney and he wrote a most excellent contract. Ironclad, he says. Sign."

Derek signed, then handed over his credit card.

"That's some kind of pretzel business," Justine observed as his card went through for the agreed-upon amount.

Derek grinned. "Chicks love rich guys, right?"

"Not enough to let them live if they should be killed."

"A woman who can't be bribed." He brushed his hand down her arm and gave her hand an affectionate squeeze.

She frowned at the tingle in her arm and stepped away from him.

The Manasa tucked the credit card receipt in her pocket and patted it several times. "Sit. We begin."

Derek sat, and Justine stood off to the right. "Will this put me out of your range?"

"Yes, you'll be fine there," the Manasa said. "Why? Does the lady have secrets?"

"Everyone has secrets." She ignored the sympathetic look on Derek's face. "I've kept Manasas out of my mind so far and I'd like to keep it that way." She folded her arms over her chest and scooted a few more feet to the right.

"I'm a professional. I don't read uninvited. Usually." The Manasa sat across from Derek. "Ready?" At his nod, her eyes went really wide, and then the sound of bubbling water filled the room. Then her eyes turned kelly green and began flashing alternately, like Christmas lights.

Derek, to his credit, didn't even move. The man was adapting to his Otherworld experiences with impressive aplomb. Not bad for a mortal . . . er . . . *almost* mortal.

"You have a crooked penis."

Derek gagged. "What?"

"Chill, Derek. I won't tell anyone," Justine said, but she couldn't keep the laughter out of her voice. "Does it still work okay?"

"Of course it works! And it's not crooked. What kind of scam is this? We want to know about the Curse," he snarled at the Manasa.

"You lost your virginity to a prostitute," the Manasa continued.

Justine's nose wrinkled. "A prostitute? But that's . . . gross."

Derek spun to face Justine, his face so white he looked like he might pass out. "I didn't know she was a prostitute, I swear. My cousin Les paid her off and I swear I didn't know until later. I was fifteen! I didn't even know what a prostitute *was*."

The panic on his face convinced her. "I believe you." He relaxed slightly.

"But you should know, I'm free. So you might not be interested in me . . ." Justine added.

"This is over." He stood up and headed for the door.

She grabbed his arm as he tried to storm past her. "The Curse, Derek. You need this info."

"Then you need to leave." He wouldn't even look at her, and his cheeks were tinged pink.

She couldn't suppress a smile, and she gently patted his shoulder. "That's fine. I'll wait outside."

"I require a witness," the Manasa said. "Too many cheaters. Especially since he's a drug addict."

"I'm not a drug addict," he growled. "Surely you can see that."

The Manasa had followed him across the room, her green eyes still flashing. "You gave up the woman you loved because you are overly moral and protective. Afraid you would die on her, and you felt that was selfish. But you cried when she married someone else."

Derek's mouth dropped open and he pulled away from Justine. "I didn't cry. I don't cry. Hell, I didn't even cry when Justine shot me."

The Manasa leaned closer, until the light from her eyes cast a greenish glow on Derek's skin. "You cried for three weeks when your father died. His death is why you refuse to get serious with a woman. But you crave intimacy and want to fall in love. You are jealous of your brother that he is with a woman who loves him. Angry that he can rise above this Curse."

"I'm not jealous, and I never cry, and I don't want to fall in love. I'm too busy to fall in love. I just want to stay alive! Why can't you see *that*?"

Justine couldn't suppress a chuckle and she lightly slugged him in the upper arm as he pushed past her to go back to the couch. "You're such a softie. I thought real men didn't cry."

He slammed himself down on the sofa. "I'm *not* soft."

She sat next to him and tucked her arm through his, leaning her head on his shoulder. "You could be my big, strong man. Kicking ass and writing poetry for me later that day."

He tried to extricate his arm. "I don't write poetry."

"You wrote a poem to a girl in your ninth-grade class."

The Manasa returned to her kelly green chair across from him. "Then you cried when she said she didn't love you and was nice to you only because she had a crush on your brother."

Justine burst out laughing at the look of agony on Derek's face. "Don't look so worried, Softie. We all have our secrets." She tightened her grip on him and leaned against him.

His shoulder relaxed under her cheek and he touched her face briefly before he focused on the Manasa. "Can you please get to the point with the Curse?"

"As you wish." Silence. Then, "The Goblet of Eternal Youth. You have drunk from it." The Manasa sounded shocked. "It is real. You know where it is."

Justine's amusement vanished and she dug her fingers into Derek's arm.

"The Curse," he said. "That's what I want to know. Please focus."

The Manasa leaned forward, her eyes flashing even faster. "The Guardian. You know her. She is . . ." The Manasa let out a squawk and the light in her eyes stuttered. "The woman who sits with you! The Goblet is in my building!"

Justine's heart seized up and a cold chill swept over her. "Derek," she whispered in a strangled voice. "This was such a mistake."

He said nothing, but he flexed his biceps under her hand. A reassuring gesture the Manasa would never be able to see. "The Curse, please." His voice was calm, firm. In control.

Did he truly understand how bad this would be if it got out? They had to kill the Manasa. There was no other choice. Qualifying Incident failure, she was so sure. She was going into the Chamber, her mom to hell, and—

Derek set his hand on her inner thigh and slid it north until his little finger was almost touching one particular seam in her jeans. He began rubbing his thumb in leisurely circles on the denim, drawing heat to her nether regions in about a millisecond.

As distractions went, this was one of the better ones.

And it worked too. There was no sense in freaking out about unspeakable horrors and moms in hell. The info was already out and they'd deal with it in a few minutes.

"So, the Curse," he repeated.

The Manasa's lips curved back into a twisted smile, her eyes practically vibrating with flashes of green light. "Many years ago, but the magic is strong within your body. A complex pattern. Very complex. Encrypted? Yes, encrypted. No one but the creator would be able to undo it."

Justine watched Derek's face. As much as it sucked to be tied to a self-absorbed goblet, being cursed might be worse. The guy had even denied his true love because he didn't want to die on her. But it was probably for the best. Seriously, it clearly wasn't his true love or he wouldn't have been able to walk away.

The Manasa let out a high-pitched squeal and a green laser beam shot from her left eye and burned a hole through the wall. "You have been cursed by evil! The ultimate evil!"

Derek barely glanced at the smoking Sheetrock. "And what evil is that?"

"Satan!" Two more streaks of light shot from her eyes, and both Justine and Derek ducked as the glass picture frame behind them exploded.

"Satan *again*?" Derek sat back up and helped Justine do the same. "Are you sure about that?"

The Manasa's eyes swelled to grapefruit-sized orbs, then burst in an explosion of green light. All that was left behind were her regular, human eyes, regarding Derek with a calculating expression. "I am certain. All curses must be signed by the curser, in order to activate it. It was Satan's signature. Not a signature as you humans use to sign a check, exactly, more of a magic mark, until you get the printout of the file. At that point it's translated into human-speak as best it can." Her gaze flicked toward Justine. "So, you are the Guardian. Many people are very interested in the Goblet."

Derek's hand returned to her leg as Justine scooted to the edge of the couch. "You signed a contract," she said. "Ironclad. You must give us the original file."

"Oh, certainly." The Manasa walked over to the wall, flipped a painting aside to reveal a safe. She shielded the safe with her body, then punched in a code. The door opened and she pulled out a green file folder. "Here it is."

Derek took it and handed it to Justine. "Inspect it."

She opened it. All the information was there, right down to Derek's crooked penis and the fact Justine was the Guardian. Relief tugged at her, but she didn't relax. "It's here, but I don't know if it's the copy or the original."

His shoulder rested against hers as he scanned the document. "I thought you said they had to give the original. That it was biological or something."

"They do." She lowered her voice. "But I don't like the look on her face right now." The Manasa's eyes were whipping back and forth in rapid bursts.

Derek grimaced when he checked out the Manasa. "So, how do we find out for sure?"

"I don't know." The woman's head was now spinning around on her neck. "Good heavens. What's wrong with her?"

Derek cursed as green rocks burst out of the ceiling and pummeled the Manasa in the head and shoulders.

The Manasa threw her head back and opened her mouth as a scream tore out of her throat. "Aaaaeeeiiiii-ieeeeeee!"

Justine slammed her hands over her ears and Derek jumped to his feet. Then the Manasa leaped up, ran to the safe, yanked out a red folder and thrust it into Derek's hands. "Fine! The original! It is done!"

Her head stopped rotating, the rocks disappeared, and her eyes stopped dancing around in her head. She glared at them. "Now you have both the original and the copy, and I can't remember anything, other than that something very big just slipped away and that I will never sign a contract before acquiring information again. Go away."

"We're leaving." Derek removed his hand from her inner thigh and stood up.

Justine had liked his touch far too much. For heaven's sake, a part of her wasn't sure what was worse: Derek no longer touching her or the fact he was cursed by Satan.

No, Satan was worse. Discovering they were going to have to take on the lord of the Underworld took precedence over physical contact with a man every day of the week.

She slammed the door on the way out.

Thirteen

As soon as they got into the cab, Derek called his brother. He got voice mail three times before Wendy finally picked up. "Quincy LaValle's line. May I help you?"

"Wendy. It's Derek. I need to talk to Quincy." He drummed his fingers on his thigh, ran his hand through his hair, shifted on his seat. "Is he there?"

"He's working on a theory and ordered me not to let him be disturbed. Can he get back to you later?"

Derek ground his teeth. He wasn't used to being screened. Quincy always picked up by the fourth or fifth time he called. It took that long to penetrate his subconscious. "It's really important. I need to talk to him."

"Is it about the Curse?"

Her voice carried in the cab, and Derek saw Justine's eyebrows raise. "Who are you talking to?" she mouthed.

He watched her fingers idly stroke her gun and realized the bloodthirsty Guardian had just found another threat to her secret life. He schooled his features into a blank expression, as if he had no idea what she'd said, then looked past her. "Yes, it is," he replied to Wendy. "It's very important I speak with him."

Wendy clucked her disapproval. "I don't think that would be a good idea. He really worries about you and this whole Curse thing. You'll just upset him and then he'll be distracted the rest of the night."

"He's always distracted." He'd tried to get Quincy a cell phone once, but he'd never remembered to charge it. Ever. It had been a total bust. He realized he was crushing the file in his fist, and he forced his hand to relax. "Let me talk to him, Wendy. *Now.*"

"I'm the one who believes you, not him. Tell me. Maybe I can help. As I said before, I know people, and I'm highly motivated to save his disbelieving behind. I want to marry him and I'm not going to get the chance if he dies."

He realized Justine had moved in a little closer to him, her ear only a few inches from the phone. A flash of interest crossed her face at Wendy's claim. "What people?" she mouthed.

Derek shook his head and moved the phone to his other ear, away from her. She stuck her tongue out at him and climbed over him so she could listen to the phone on that side, her hands on his shoulders, her hips skimming over his thighs. He let his breath out slowly and tried to concentrate on the call. "I need his math skills, Wendy. Unless you're as good with numbers as he is, put him on."

"Fine," she sighed. "But I'm doing this under protest."

Somehow, the thought of annoying his brother's secretary didn't worry him. It simply didn't measure up to being shot by a Guardian, almost defrauded by a Manasa, fireballed by a Rivka, and cursed by Satan. "Understood. Thanks."

Quincy picked up a few minutes later. "This better be critical."

"How are you at breaking through an encryption?"

"I love encryption. I thought this was about the Curse.

Otherwise I would have picked up the third time you called. What do you need?"

Derek opened the folder and pulled out the Manasa's report. "I have a six-page document that's encrypted. I need it deciphered in twenty-four hours."

"Sounds fun. Can you drop it by the office? I'll start working on it now. Do you have a key to the building? I don't remember if the outside doors are locked or not."

A spurt of energy shot through Derek and he grinned at Justine. If anyone could decode Satan's curse, it was his brother. "We're five minutes away, and your building doesn't get locked until after hours."

"Oh, great. So, when will you be here?"

"Five minutes, Quin."

"Excellent. I can't wait. Encryption is a blast. When did you say you needed it?"

"I'll write it all down for you." Derek watched skepticism cloud Justine's features, and she pursed her lips.

"Perfect. Will you be staying for dinner?" Quin asked. "I could have Wendy order something."

"No, Quincy. You need to start working on it right away."

"Of course I will. What else would I do?"

He grinned. "I'll see you in a couple minutes."

He hung up and Justine shot him a doubtful look. "You actually trust him to stay focused long enough to decode it?"

"Once he gets started, nothing will be able to pull him away. He's absentminded only because he's so focused on his projects." Derek ran his fingers over the symbols that made no sense. "How ironic would it be if he was the one who finally ended the Curse, and he doesn't even believe in it?"

Her forehead was still furrowed. "And if he can't do it?"

"We convince your mom to use her body to barter with Satan to save me. You told Becca and me that Satan was courting her, right?"

"Derek!" She slammed him in the chest. "Not funny."

No, but it was a good distraction to keep her from remembering that Wendy had asked about the Curse. As annoying as Wendy was with her protectiveness over his brother, he'd prefer not to be saddled with causing her death. Now that he knew about Satan and the Afterlife, well, he sort of had a vested interest in keeping his mortal sins as low as possible.

Derek managed to keep the conversation with Justine focused around the Manasa, the Curse, and their plan for Iris to interrogate Satan, until after they'd dropped the information at Quincy's office. He lost control of the discussion when their cab was about ten blocks from Justine's condo and they passed a woman dressed as a hooker. The instant he saw Justine's gaze flick toward the woman, he knew he was in trouble.

"Derek—"

"Don't say it."

"Do you cry when you get a splinter?"

He glared at her. "I didn't cry when you shot me." So difficult to maintain his dignity after the Manasa had revealed all. He would never get over this. So much for any subconscious desire for a hot affair with the Guardian before they engaged in a battle to the death.

"True." She gave him a speculative look that made him cringe. "Is it really crooked?"

He ground his teeth. "It has a slight curve." He stared out the window. It was better than looking at Justine's face while she imagined him with a deformed penis.

"How slight?"

He gritted his teeth, then turned and leveled a dark look at her. "I've been told it is exactly the right amount of curvature to enhance the experience."

Her eyebrow went up. "Is that so? By who?"

"If you're that curious, perhaps you'd like to make your own judgment."

She blinked, and a thoughtful expression came over her face. "You know, I think that's a great idea."

She sounded completely serious, and heat rushed through him. "I thought sex was off limits. Eternity of unspeakable horrors and all that." That was why he'd backed off. He was no hero, but he couldn't justify getting a little action at the cost of her soul. Especially if he had to kill her. He'd feel like major shit if he killed her *and* damned her to an eternity of unspeakable horrors. If he knew she was heading up to heaven for unlimited rounds of golf, well, he'd be able to live with ending her life as a tradeoff for all the future generations of LaValle men. He'd at least be less guilt-stricken.

"Sex *is* banned, but this isn't sex. This is purely business. Just a quick look-see is all I'm talking about." She grabbed the file and opened it. "Look here." She pointed to the title of the file. "The Manasa identified you as 'the drug addict client.' Maybe she was kidding, or maybe she's not one hundred percent accurate. If she's wrong about who cursed you, I'd like to know before we rush off after Satan."

He blinked. "And this has what to do with my body?"

She slapped the file shut. "If I can confirm some of her other claims, like your crooked penis, then I'll feel more confident that she was right about the Curse."

If Justine went digging around in his pants, there was no chance he'd be happy with a nod and a handshake. He'd kissed Justine already. He'd had her body pressed up against his on the dance floor. He'd tasted her skin and her lips. If he wound up with his pants around his ankles and Justine's face at hip level, it wasn't going to be so she could take one look and walk away. He cleared his throat. "I can confirm it."

She made a face and shook her head. "See, that's not enough for me. First, you call it curved and she said crooked. If it's really only curved, then how do we know she was totally right about the Curse?"

"Fine. It's crooked. Move on."

"No. Still not enough."

"You think I'd admit it if wasn't true?"

She folded her arms across her chest and gave him a quelling look. "Maybe you're biased. Maybe you think it's crooked because the prostitute told you that, but it really isn't. So maybe the Manasa was picking up on your neurosis, but not the facts. Which would mean she picked up on Satan because of the Rivka and the Curse isn't really by him." She paused to take a breath, her gaze flicked to his lap. "I can't go after Satan unless I know for sure it's the right thing to do."

"No! I will not have my penis treated like it's a clue to be read and discarded." Only a woman would suggest such a thing. They had no concept of its fragile ego.

She cocked her head, and he could practically see her

analyzing the situation. "Is the curve evident in its flaccid state?"

"Justine, let it alone."

She scooted forward and rested her hand on his waistband. "Is it?"

"No. So there you go. A clinical exam will reveal nothing."

Something in her eyes flashed. She looked like a warrior now, not a sensual lover. "Derek, my eternal soul, and quite possibly my mother's, rests on my ability to vanquish the Curse and save Mona from generations of threats by LaValle men." She swung her leg over his and straddled his lap, her face tense with determination. "I wasn't made Guardian for nothing. I can kill as needed and I can most definitely generate a hard-on without getting emotionally involved." She dropped her hips and settled against him.

He was pressed as far away from her as the seat back would allow. He could not make the same claim. "Justine—"

She threw her arms around him and slammed her body against his, her mouth hot and wet against his. It took less than two seconds for him to lose the battle. He dove into her mouth, his tongue desperate for hers. Skin. He needed skin. He yanked her shirt out from her jeans and plastered his hand over her bare back. She was warm, soft, alive.

God, he needed her.

Want. Wanted her. Not need.

She was higher than him, holding herself up on her knees as she poured heat into his mouth. *Yes.* It was all it had been on the dance floor and more.

Much more.

This was the woman who had shot him in the gut. That

was a bond he'd never had with anyone, and it was dragging him into her spell.

She deepened the kiss, her hands frantic in his hair, her hips moving against his, grinding, taking control, demanding his response.

God, it felt good to let her drive. He felt like he was always the one managing everything and everyone in his life. But not now. Not with Justine. The sense of freedom was exhilarating. Let her take responsibility, not him.

He let his hands roam, taking in every curve of her back. He massaged her shoulder blades, ran his fingers down her spine, dug into the muscles of her lower back, cupped her bottom, relishing the softness under his touch. Soft, yet firm. Justine was a woman, a sexual being that was driving him to the brink, yet at the same time, she was a fighter who would never let herself fail.

His other half.

If such a thing existed.

And right now, he simply wouldn't think about the fact they might be battling to the death in the morning.

Right now, it was about the feel of her breasts pressed against his chest, about her hips driving into his, commanding his body to reply. He had no chance against her, and that was fine with him.

She moved her head to the side, her lips trailing heat down the side of his neck as she tugged his shirt out of his jeans.

No problem. Happy to oblige.

He helped her get his shirt free and she shoved it upward, feasting on his chest as if she would die without the taste of him in every cell of her body. Her lips were tight around his nipple, her hands kneading his stomach, sliding lower, her fingers on the button of his jeans.

With a growl he didn't even recognize, he grabbed her around the waist and pulled her upward, burying his face under her shirt to taste the skin over her ribs. She tasted like vanilla, and something else. Something hot. Something dangerous. Something that teased him to take a risk.

He felt like he was hovering at the top of a cliff, peering over the edge, with Justine down below, beckoning him to jump, to risk, to fly. What was down there? Something dark. Something dangerous. Something so unbelievably amazing that it was worth risking everything.

He knew in that moment he wouldn't turn away. Not from this. Not ever. No matter what the cost to himself. He grabbed her hand and guided it to the front of his jeans. It was the start, and he knew it wasn't going to end there. They were both in it until the end. He knew it, and he could feel the commitment in Justine's body, in the desperation of her kisses. No matter what the cost to either of them, they weren't turning back.

The seat lurched suddenly, and they were flung forward. Justine smashed the back of her head into the Plexiglas divider with a thunk and a yelp, and Derek flew into her, and then they both were on the floor, tangled up in a mess of limbs, heavy breathing, and too many clothes.

"Sorry," the cabbie said. "Didn't notice the red light. Not that I was watching you guys, because I wasn't. Go ahead with your business. I can drive around for hours."

Justine groaned, and Derek looked at her. Her hair was a disheveled mess, her shirt was up around her armpits, and she was still breathing heavily. Raw heat surged through him and suddenly all he wanted to do was bury himself in her essence, to lose himself forever.

"Don't stare at me like that," she muttered. "Get off me and let's get out of this cab."

"Right." He grabbed the edge of her shirt and tugged it down over her breasts.

It took them several minutes, a few inadvertent gropes that sent hormones raging again, and a significant bribe to convince the cabbie to stop the cab and actually let them out, but they were finally on concrete again. One block from her condo.

They stood there for a moment, looking at each other.

Was the moment lost? Had sanity returned, along with thoughts of unspeakable horrors and curses?

Justine's gaze flicked to the front of his jeans, then back up to his face. "I'll race you to my place. Winner gets naked first." She took off running before he could even agree.

He loved a woman who took control.

Fourteen

Just as Justine knew he would, Derek caught up with her as she was yanking open the door to her building. He grabbed her around the waist, spun her around, and hauled her against him, shoving them both through the open door as he shackled her with kisses. She sighed and slipped her hands under his shirt, relishing the feel of his body under her fingers. There was nothing like a man's body, with all the curves and hardness that were so different from hers.

She could feel desire in his breath, in the way he clutched her against him, and it reached inside her and tugged at an answering need deep inside. They'd both been isolated for so long, and it was impossible to fight it any longer. He made her feel alive, and she hadn't realized how dead she'd been inside until he'd woken her up.

"I know Theresa Nichols lives here and I'm not leaving until you buzz her." Derek's lips trailed down the side of her neck as an unfamiliar male voice penetrated her sexually deprived haze. Alarm burst through her at the man's reference to Theresa.

No one knew Theresa even existed, let alone that she lived here.

"Derek." The word fell into his mouth, but he stilled instantly and pulled his head back.

"What's wrong?"

Justine forced herself to let go of him and turned around. Derek released her and followed her gaze, his body tensing next to her.

A man in his late twenties was standing at a brand-new security desk, arguing with Xavier. He was wearing a pair of jeans and a collared shirt, with the sleeves rolled up and the tail untucked. His hair was a bit long, a bit ragged, but it looked like he'd styled it that way. It was intentional dishevelment of the highest fashion. She wouldn't be surprised if his casual look cost more than Derek's nicest business suit.

The man was leaning on the desk, his body language relaxed even as he repeated his request to see Theresa.

"You are hungry. You need to go to a restaurant and get some dinner," Xavier said. His arms were folded across his chest, his dark face cold. He shot a glance at them, then his face tightened when he saw Derek. He touched his fingers to the stitches on his forehead, then gave Derek a slight nod before turning back to the man. "You need to go eat."

Justine stilled at his "suggestion." Who *was* Xavier?

"That doesn't work on me," the man said to Xavier. "I'm immune."

Adrenaline flooded Justine's body. If Xavier really had the power of suggestion and this man was immune, then their visitor was of the Otherworld. Someone with powers was after Theresa. And possibly her. And Mona. She eased the dagger out from under her left arm and hid it behind her right thigh, her heart pounding. "May I help you?"

The man turned his head, giving her an easy glance. His face was angular, dignified. Handsome, in a way that wasn't nearly as masculine as Derek's but good-looking nevertheless. There was no sign of gold dust and he didn't have the LaValle chin. "Not unless you know Theresa Nichols," he said.

She noticed then that Xavier had taken off his uniform jacket and was rolling up his sleeves. "I'll take care of this visitor, Ms. Bennett. Would you like me to take care of your lawyer as well?"

Derek frowned, and she knew what he was thinking. Where was the Xavier who'd tried to get her killed? This Xavier was about to knock two men around to protect her. Then again, she'd never seen Xavier resort to violence before, so this wasn't the old Xavier either. Something was up with him, and she doubted it was good. "No, Derek is with me. He's fine. As for him . . ." She nodded at the man. "Who are you?"

Their visitor gave a deep bow that bespoke of an old-world grace. "Zeke Siccardi at your service."

For an instant, Justine's mind was a blank.

And then she realized who it was and her adrenaline sent her heart into a pounding frenzy. Theresa's cyber lover! The one who had been doing research on dragons and gold auras and, apparently, where Theresa lived. How had he found them? She glanced at Derek, but he was watching Xavier, who, in turn, was intently focused on Zeke.

Zeke smiled, showing dimples to die for. "I'm here to surprise Theresa. You know her?"

"How did you end up at this address?"

"It's not too difficult to find someone if you know what you're doing." He held up a manila envelope. "I got some information she might like and I thought I'd deliver it in person."

She watched him wave the envelope. It could be instructions on how to turn Theresa back into a human. Or information about gold auras, or even about the Curse. She walked toward him, her fingers practically twitching with eagerness. "Theresa doesn't live here anymore, but I'll be happy to get that to her."

He frowned, and she noticed a small diamond earring in his left ear. Theresa would love that.

"Really? She moved?" He tucked the envelope back under his arm as Justine got close enough to grab it.

"Yes." Justine almost managed to look him in the eye as she answered. Almost. She was a terrible liar and if he had any brain in his head at all, he would realize it. Her heart was thudding so loudly she was certain he could hear it. *Calm down. Count to ten.* "But I can get the envelope to her."

"I want to deliver it myself." Zeke levered himself off the desk and stood up, ignoring Xavier as the doorman circled Zeke. He was plenty tall enough for Theresa in her human form, not quite big enough to make an eleven-foot, two-ton dragon feel dainty, though. "Where is she?"

"She isn't seeing visitors, Zeke. I'll get it to her." She held out her hand for the file, but he made no move to hand it to her.

He cocked his head. "She said the same thing when I suggested we meet. Why isn't she seeing anyone?"

Justine reluctantly dropped her hand, but didn't give him any room. "She's sick . . . Yeah. Contagious. Yes. That's it. She has a contagious disease and has been quarantined."

She felt Derek's look, but she didn't dare meet his gaze. She would crack if she so much as looked at Derek. Xavier was listening intently, his hands flexing at his sides as if he was ready to toss Zeke out on his head as soon as Justine gave him the nod.

"What kind of disease?" Zeke asked

Justine shifted her weight and tried to find a place to put her hands. "A parasite she picked up in the Amazon. It's deadly, and airborne. It wiped out a whole village in two days." *Don't laugh. Don't laugh.*

He lifted a skeptical eyebrow. "So, is she going to die?"

"Hopefully not. They've found a drug that keeps the symptoms under control, but she's still contagious. Deadly to anyone." He looked ready to argue, so she quickly added, "She's in an FBI lab at an undisclosed location. No human contact. I'm her only living kin, so the FBI allows me to send her packages once a week."

Zeke swung the envelope from his fingertips and studied her. His eyes were too penetrating, too knowing. "Why didn't she tell me? We IM all the time."

Shit. She could throw a knife with deadly accuracy from fifteen yards, but was about to put herself and Mona and Theresa in jeopardy because she couldn't lie to save her life, though she had a feeling that no matter how well she lied, Zeke would know. He was too astute, too savvy. Too dangerous. She shot a panicked "we're in deep shit" look at Derek.

Xavier tossed his jacket on the expensive, handwoven carpet and moved behind Zeke while Derek stepped up beside Justine.

Zeke didn't even twitch, but suddenly there was an awareness prickling off his body, and she wondered whether Derek and Xavier together would be able to take him. What was Zeke?

Derek cleared his throat and broke the silent standoff.

"Listen, Zeke, no one knows why women do what they do," he said easily. "I hate to interrupt, but Justine and I were on our way upstairs to . . . chat." He gave Zeke a very male look and held out his hand for the package. "Have mercy on me, brother. Give us the package and let me get her upstairs before the moment passes."

At Derek's comment, Justine lunged for his arm and wrapped herself around it, rubbing her breasts against him even as her adrenaline raced and she longed to conk Zeke on the head with her gun and take the envelope. "Oh, Derek. I thought you'd forgotten."

He slid his hand down her back and grabbed her butt, giving her a steamy look that made her want to climb inside his suit with him. "Not a chance, sweetheart."

Zeke shook off the tension with a visible shake, then flipped the package to Derek, though the assessing sharpness hadn't left his eyes. He was capitulating for the moment, but it was on his own terms. He was enough man for Theresa, and that might be a big problem. "I'm jealous," he said. "My woman is under FBI lockup, apparently. No action anytime soon for me."

"I feel your pain." Derek caught the package, then wrapped his fingers around Justine's wrist and tugged her toward the elevator.

Justine followed him, turning her head to bid farewell to her mysterious doorman. "Xavier, we need to talk later."

"Of course." Zeke and Xavier's male laughter followed them across the lobby, and she could practically feel the heat emanating from Derek.

The instant the elevator doors closed, he pressed her against the wall with its expensive flowered wallpaper. "Thanks for going along with the cover to distract Zeke."

She softened against him as he leaned into her. "It was a good plan. Thanks for helping me out, and protecting Theresa." His heat was pressing into her, curving into her body like sensual caresses. "I have to admit, it's really nice to have a partner who isn't driven by bloodlust and food cravings."

"Partners? Is that what we are?" He grabbed her wrists and locked them by her sides, pressing them against the brass bar flanking the walls of the elevator. Then he dropped his head and laid a soft kiss on the curve of her neck.

She closed her eyes and dug her fingers into the waistband of his pants, sighing at the feel of his warmth. "I think we are," she whispered. "For the moment. Until death do us part."

The door to the elevator slid open at her apartment, but they didn't move. "We're here." Derek's breath tickled her neck. "Shall we continue this?"

Yes, do me!

No, save my soul!

Yes, take away my loneliness!

No, I'm terrified of unspeakable horrors and I can't bear to send my mom to hell!

"Derek—"

"Resist the temptation!" The interior door flew open and Theresa shoved her head between them. "The Council just left!"

"Oh my God!" Justine shoved Derek aside and nearly fell over him as she lunged for the door. He caught her just as she tripped over his feet. "What did they say?"

Theresa clutched an empty pretzel box to her chest. "They were *not* happy you were gone for so long. I'm supposed to be emergency backup only! They had heard about

Derek and his drinks, and they were coming to check up. And you weren't here! Do you have any idea how difficult it is to stall three men who are over six hundred years old and have interrogated some very bad people?" Theresa's face was pale gray and her golden eyes were bloodshot. "They were here for *two hours*! I'm a total wreck!"

Justine's gut thudded to her toes as she stepped into her apartment. "They know about Derek's drinks?" She was suddenly cold, so cold, and she jumped when Derek shut the door behind them.

"Yes!" Tears welled up in the dragon's eyes as she sat heavily on the floor, rattling the china in the nearby cabinet. "What am I going to do if they abduct you and throw you into the Chamber of Unspeakable Horrors? I'm going to be alone here for eternity! I'll go insane. I can't bear my scaled exile alone! And you . . . what will happen to you? It's too awful for words! What if they come back? They'll find you, you know. They told me they would. You can't escape them!" She broke down into heaving sobs, her scales vibrating, her tail a limp rag on the floor. "You can't leave me here again. I can't take the pressure! And Zeke e-mailed me and said the gold aura meant he was possessed by Satan. Satan! The lord of the Underworld is after us, and so is the Council! I can't deal with this!"

"Oh, sweetie, I'm so sorry." Justine reached out to hug the dragon, then dropped her arms when the dragon didn't respond. A hug was so inadequate when everything she said was completely true. The gold aura was from Satan . . . not really surprising. The Council? Unexpected and *so* not good. Justine sat beside Theresa, resting her head against her friend. "I'm really sorry you had to endure the Council."

She didn't even look up from her sobs, until Derek tapped her forehead with the envelope he'd gotten from Zeke. "Got something for you."

Theresa took a rasping breath of tears and anguish. "Pretzels?"

"Better than pretzels," Derek said.

She sighed heavily, and the envelope caught fire on the corner. Derek cursed and smothered the flames with his hand. Then he looked in surprise at his palm, no doubt in awe at its instantaneous healing. Such a minor burn was inconsequential to him now. He glanced at Justine, then handed the envelope to Theresa. "We met Zeke. He wanted you to have this."

Theresa's head snapped up and her pale face reverted instantly to her traditional blue-green complexion. "Zeke? *My* Zeke? You met him? Where? When? Was he gorgeous? Did he have a wedding ring on?"

Justine smiled as Derek escorted Theresa to the couch, enthralling her with details about Zeke. He even told her about Zeke's dimples, and the fact he'd called Theresa "his woman." The look on Theresa's face when he told her that was priceless, and Justine felt her heart melt just a little.

He was a softie.

How was she going to kill him?

But what choice did she have? The Council was onto them.

There were no loopholes that could save either of them now.

As Theresa opened Zeke's envelope and squealed how he'd given her his research on how to turn a dragon into a human, Justine met Derek's gaze over the dragon's head.

She knew he realized the significance of the Council visit as soon as she saw the regret in his eyes. At least one of them was going to end up dead, possibly both of them, and possibly something much worse.

He gave her a quick nod, and she gave him a half smile. It was agreed: They would go forward as long as they could. Hell, they were taking on Satan. How much worse could the Council be? (And no, she didn't want to know the answer to that question.)

How long until the Council returned? How many hours did they have until they ran out of time? No idea. Five minutes? A day?

Like the threat of the Curse hadn't been enough of a challenge.

Iris checked the connection between the faucet and the hose, making sure there were no leaks. Plastic was spread over the floor to catch the flood she planned to make, along with any melting body parts.

Today was about full-scale warfare.

A musical knock sounded on the front door, and she pumped the nozzle on the hose, double-checking it was on its most powerful setting.

"My sex kitten, it is your stud muffin, responding to your e-mail," Satan trilled from the front step.

"Come in." She lifted the nozzle, steadied it with a two-handed grip, and aimed at the kitchen door. "I'm in the kitchen, naked and ready for you."

"Oh, my darling! I knew you would come around!" Satan rushed around the corner, and Iris hit him square in the face with a powerful rush of water.

Unfortunately, he was wearing a Gore-Tex rain outfit,

complete with goggles and a face mask. He threw his hands on his hips and stood under the assault of water. "You lie! You get my manly regions eager with anticipation of a sexual marathon, and you ambush me! I do not understand. I am emotionally shattered by your actions."

She released the trigger. Bastard. Since when did he get that smart? Water dripped off his hood, hitting the plastic sheet on the floor with rhythmic drops. "How stupid do you think I am? Did you really think I wouldn't find out?"

He sighed heavily. "Find out what, my love? If you're referring to my harvesting of two hundred and thirty souls yesterday, I ask you, what do you expect? I am Satan. It is my calling. My best Rivka found a cult that was looking for sponsorship, so I offered my services."

"Not that." God, she wanted to turn him into a pile of jelly. "Take off the rain gear. I promise I won't shoot you."

Satan chuckled and waggled a gloved finger at her. "Oh, my large-breasted fantasy woman, you are turning into my perfect mate. You lie without even one facial twitch. So impressive."

Iris frowned. He was right. She had every intention of shooting him. "Did you turn on your brain today or something?"

"My best Rivka challenges me daily. I realized I cannot always rely on my manly brawn and my special Satanic talents to overpower everyone. I am courting the souls of some Harvard Law School professors. Soon I pass the Afterlife bar exam and will write unbreakable contracts and issue incontrovertible orders." He sighed suddenly and sat down heavily on a kitchen chair with a loud squish. "It is very disheartening to realize how much I do wrong. I have much to fix."

Iris hesitated, trying to read his body language. His shoulders seemed too droopy for this to be another scam.

Not that it mattered. He was in trouble. She whipped the hose back into firing position. "Justine told me about the surfer."

Satan looked at her, but the goggles kept her from seeing his expression. Good. No need to be tempted by his come-hither eyes. "Which surfer?" he asked. "I have taken the souls of many surfers. They are willing to trade much for the perfect wave."

"The one who showed up at my daughter's condo with a gun. He tried to kill her and steal the Goblet."

Satan sat up straighter. "I protect her. Why do you refuse to believe me? I will go to great lengths to win your favor." Satan shoved the goggles up on his forehead, his face a picture of innocent confusion. If he hadn't nabbed so many Hollywood souls, she might even be inclined to buy it. "Why do you blame me for this?"

"Because he had a gold aura."

Something twitched in his face, then it was gone, but she was certain he knew what she was talking about.

Disappointment rushed through her, and she realized she'd been hoping he didn't. "*And* you cursed Derek LaValle. You're the reason he's after Justine." Her fingers twitched on the nozzle, but she held off. Answers first, torture later. "Your signature was on the Curse." She moved closer. "You betrayed me."

"No." His voice was soft. Angry. His fists clenched. "It is I who have been betrayed."

"As if! How do you figure?" If he tried to blame all of this on her just because she refused to let him steal Mona, she was turning him into a puddle.

He held out his hand. "Hose, please. I will give it back after I explain."

She tightened her grip on her weapon, knowing she was unlikely to get it back. But she needed answers quickly, and she did have a few water balloons stashed under the sink. Justine had said Derek's time was running out, but Iris had sensed another threat that Justine had denied. Nice. Her daughter met an attractive man and instantly starts hiding secrets from her own mother. It hurt so deeply, after all she did for her.

Satan leapt to his feet and laid his hand on her cheek. "My love pancake? What is wrong?"

"Nothing." She shook him off and shut down her desire to lean on him. As if Satan could understand the emotions of being a mother. "Take the hose, Satan. You better make this good."

"Oh, very good. I have a dark secret I have told no one. Until now."

A secret that the lord of all things evil considered dark? This was going to be good.

Fifteen

Satan turned off the faucet, emptied the hose into the sink, detached it, and threw it out the kitchen window. Then he took off the rain suit, revealing a very nice-fitting tuxedo.

"Going somewhere?" The man certainly knew how to dress. He looked ravishing. She wanted to run her fingers over that fine fabric and well-muscled body.

Instead, she walked around to the other side of the table and sat down.

He settled himself across her from and pulled an envelope from his jacket pocket. "I was going to invite you to an opera at the Met tonight. I have reservations at a very nice restaurant in New York. Five star." He pulled out two tickets and slid them across the table to her.

Disbelief and yearning rushed through her as she picked up the tickets. They were crisp and real, and promised a night she hadn't had since she'd died. "How can we go to New York? The only place I can go in the mortal world is to visit Justine, wherever she is." She was lucky to have gotten that much. Being a disenfranchised Guardian didn't give you much leverage for negotiating Afterlife benefits. If she'd retired in good standing with full Guardian perks, she'd have access to anywhere in the mortal world she wanted, at any time. She'd have a lovely house in heaven and . . . *Stop torturing yourself, Iris.* She'd made a choice and that was it. No point in still getting upset about it. She set the tickets back on the table and pushed them away. "I'm sure you're not allowed to take me there."

"I am Satan. I break rules." But his claim didn't have the same energy it usually did. "I realized I need to woo you. Lawyer soul told me that. Very wise man. Made me realize the many ways I screw up."

She moved her hand so her pinkie finger was touching the tickets, stroking them. "Tell me who went after my daughter, Satan. You say it wasn't you. So who was it?" *Exonerate yourself so I can accept your offer for a night in New York.* Not that she was going to sleep with him or consent to be his Underworld concubine, but she'd tolerate his company for a chance to go out in the city.

He sighed heavily. "After you broke my soul—"

"You mean, after I ruined your quest to seduce me and steal Mona?"

"Yes, that. After you cruelly rejected me despite all I had to offer . . . well . . . I was very upset."

Iris pulled her hand back from the tickets and clenched them in her lap. "How upset?" This was the first time he'd admitted her actions had had any impact on him. She was most pleased to know he'd been upset.

He gave her puppy-dog eyes, but she didn't buy it. "You were the first woman to reject Satan, the best lover in the Afterlife. My ego was very damaged. And I had big plans for the Goblet."

"Yes, I know." That had been quite the night to remember. It wasn't every day a girl got to foil Satan's plans.

"So, I needed to restore my manliness. Prove to everyone that I was still a red-hot lover who could seduce women at will." He puffed out his chest and thudded his fist on the table. "I decided to share my virile lovemaking with as many women as possible."

Something dark settled in Iris's belly. "You went on a *sex rampage* while I was trying to save my eternal soul from the Chamber?"

"Exactly!" He clapped his hands with delight as she shoved her chair back from the table and headed for her stash of water balloons. "Unfortunately, I had the misfortune of impregnating one of my conquests."

Iris whirled around to face him. "What?"

He sighed heavily. "Or so she claims. She named him Satan Jr. and has been trying to use him to get access to my kingdom."

She clutched the edge of the counter, fought off dizziness. "You have a *son*?"

He started to rise to assist her, then sat back down when she glared at him. "I believe so. Only someone with my blood would be able to create a gold aura very similar to mine—"

"But you don't have a gold aura." That had been her one hope when Justine had told her. Despite what the Manasa claimed, if Satan didn't have a gold aura, how could he have possessed the surfer?

A red flash lit up his eyes for a millisecond. "Do you think I am so weak I cannot control my powers?" He gave her an impatient sniff, and then was suddenly encompassed with a brilliant golden hue. He shut it off just as abruptly. "You wish to contest me further, or shall I continue with my tale of woe and misery?"

"My apologies." She worked her way back to her seat and sat down with an ungraceful thump, rubbing her temples. Illegitimate sons and gold auras. It was too much. "Please continue."

"Thank you." He was sitting stiffly, his shoulders turned away from her. "So, as I was saying, someone with my blood could possibly create a golden aura similar, but inferior, to mine. In addition, he might be able to impersonate my signature." He sighed heavily and some of the rigidity left his upper body. "How weary for my soul that my ungrateful love child has inherited some of my special skills. Genetics is unpredictable. He could have ended up an emasculated, powerless loser with less power than the average human, but no. How awful for me." He thumped the table with his palms and his eyes glittered with red. "I gave them much money for good schools and excellent personal chefs, but they want more. He wants to become my heir. How can a half mortal be heir to hell? What happens if he dies? Anarchy would be very bad." He threw himself back in his chair, nearly upending himself onto the floor. Only a quick grab of the table kept him upright.

Iris nabbed the tickets as they started to slide off the now-tilted table. "So, what did you do?"

"I told him he could have a job in hell." Satan pounded his heart and spread his hands wide. "Generous, no?"

"Offering your illegitimate kid a job instead of love? Sure, great idea." She frowned at the tickets, then tossed them at Satan and clasped her hands on the table. "Did he take it?"

"No. The youth of today think they are deserving of much, even though they have done nothing to earn it." Satan stroked the fine material of his suit, then sniffed his gold and diamond watch, giving a nod of satisfaction. "Satan Jr. decided that if he managed to get the Goblet, I would be so desperate for it that I would trade for it. Announce him as my heir in return for the Goblet."

Her empathy for Satan Jr. vanished at that revelation. Let the scum be tortured by his longings for hell *and* the Goblet. "Idiot."

"Precisely." Satan picked up the tickets and waved them at Iris, wiggling his eyebrows at her. "He almost stole the Goblet one hundred and eighty years ago. But by then I realized you were my true love muffin. So I saved your daughter and banished Satan Jr. from the Afterlife. I haven't heard from him since, but apparently, he is still around." Satan rubbed his chin. "He is half mortal. He should be dead by now, no? And since I banned him from the Afterlife, dead for him would mean he is nowhere. Gone. But he remains. How is that possible?" He slipped the tickets into his jacket pocket.

Iris watched the tickets disappear from view, wondering whether he'd ever taken Satan Jr.'s mom to the Met. She sat up the instant she realized what she was thinking and glared at Satan. How could she be such an idiot to be jealous, especially when her daughter's future was at stake? *He's not worth it.* "Listen, I'm all for hearing your travails about your namesake, but the bigger issue is: Can you undo the Curse? It's your signature."

"Alas, I cannot. It isn't my signature. He has to do it."

"So, make him do it."

"I cannot."

Iris snorted. "You rule the Underworld and you can't get your own flesh and blood to unmake a simple curse?"

Satan donned his wounded expression. "I am very powerful. I am a deadly force that all fear. Happily, I do not know where Satan Jr. is, nor do I care to. And even if I did, we hate each other quite a lot." He sighed heavily and propped his chin up on his hands, his elbows resting on the table. "Tell me, Iris, how is it that our children can disappoint us like this? I give him lots of money, I give him a job, and he still tries to kill the daughter of the woman I love?"

Iris felt her heart soften ever so slightly. "I know how you feel. Justine refuses to kill Derek, and she keeps secrets from me. Her actions could send me to hell, or put her in the Chamber of Unspeakable Horrors for eternity. I have given her all the advice I can, and still she disregards me. What else can I do?"

Satan reached across the table and wrapped his long fingers around her hand, rubbing his thumb over her palm. "My son will not die. Your daughter will not kill. How they can they be so selfish after all we have done for them? It is so difficult to be a parent today."

"Don't I know it." She stared at their intertwined hands and didn't pull away.

Satan laid his other hand on Iris's forearm, stroking her skin ever so softly. "I have a brilliant idea to help us recover from the betrayals of our children."

"I'll bet you do. And Justine didn't betray me." *Yet.* She had a bad feeling about Derek. No man was good enough for her daughter, and certainly not one who was trying to kill her.

"Go to New York with me. Let me show you off to the mortal world and let them long for the Afterlife where women of your mystique live. We shall dance, sing, eat, and have sloppy sex for days." He beamed and gave her hand a tug of excitement. "Excellent plan, no?"

To get away from everything . . . it was so tempting. And when would she ever get the chance to go to New

York again? And she did have a cell phone, if Justine needed to reach her. She turned her hand over and wrapped her fingers around his. "Fine. I'll go to New York, but no sex."

Fresh energy surged into his eyes. "Nonsense. An evening in my presence and you will be unable to resist me."

"Now I *really* won't sleep with you." No woman wants to be considered a sure thing, especially by Satan. "You're not that good-looking."

"Of course I am." He sashayed around the table, then pulled her to her feet. "We will rent a five-star hotel room and have hot sex for hours without stopping. I am the best lover in the Afterlife."

She allowed him to sweep her into his arms and twirl her around the kitchen, unable to resist the feel of his hands around her, his smile so irresistible. "Is sex different in the Afterlife than in the mortal world?"

His dimples deepened. "Oh, yes. Very much yes. Very, very, much yes. You will be so glad to be in this world once I bring you to ecstasy repeatedly."

Iris felt a glimmer of anticipation rush through her, so she released him and moved out of his reach. "I'll join you in New York only if you promise not to mention sex once. If you do, then I'll never sleep with you." She grinned at the horrified expression on Satan's face. No way could he risk testing her threat, but how would he ever make it through an evening without bringing up his favorite topic?

Should make for a very entertaining night.

Derek paused in his Internet research to watch Justine. Her forehead was wrinkled, her lips pursed, her face intense as she concentrated. She was smart, as well as tough and incredibly sexy. It was really unfortunate they hadn't met under other circumstances.

She was searching the *Treatise on Guardianship* for details on exactly what she had done wrong and how to fix it. She was making a list of arguments to buy them time should the Council show up before she and Derek broke the Curse.

She looked up and smiled when she caught him watching her. "Will you tell them you set up a trust to fund the LaValle men's quest for the Goblet for the next five hundred years? That you've left detailed instructions with six different attorneys on how to find me and what Mona looks like? So if I kill you before we end the Curse, I'll be fending off LaValle men forever, and eventually one of them will fail to succumb to my feminine charm and actually kill me."

"Feminine charm?" Oh, she had no idea.

She gave him a flutter of her eyelashes. "No? Then how else do you describe your hopeless infatuation with me?"

"Your breasts."

She grinned. "Really? I thought it was my scintillating personality."

"I'm way too shallow to be attracted to your mind, or your courage, or your toughness." He flexed his biceps and gave her a shallow leer that had her laughing, then he dropped the pretense. "Truthfully, it's because you're the first woman I've met, including my own mother, who's seen inside my warped brain and hasn't tried to get me committed. That, and the fact that your kisses suck my brain dry and leave me unable to think coherently. That's a real turn-on for a guy."

Her smile widened, and he grinned at her. Justine was no softie and he liked that.

She was still smiling when she looked down at her notes again. "So, you agree then?" Her tone was serious again. "You'll support the trust story?"

"Sure. I can even set one up just to prove it. It's actually not a bad idea."

Her smile faltered as she looked up. "Well, that's not really necessary. I mean, you don't really want to have me stalked for all eternity, do you?"

"Of course not. But I have my duty to my progeny."

She stuck her tongue out at him. "Duty sucks."

"I agree." He returned to surfing the Internet for information on how to destroy Satan. Surprisingly, there were quite a few sites devoted to that very purpose, though he hadn't found many that seemed remotely legitimate. He clicked open a link and scanned the page. "You think if we barbecue a banana and shove it up his nose, his head would really explode?"

"You go right ahead and try it." She flipped a page in the *Treatise*. "I'll be sure and visit you in the Afterlife after Satan kills you for smashing a mushy banana in his face."

"Wiseass."

She grinned at him as a high-pitched ringing filled the apartment. Justine's smile vanished and she slammed the *Treatise* shut. "Mom?"

Mom? No fair springing the mother intro on him without notice! He checked his shirt for stains, ran his hand over his stubble, then stood up and faced the kitchen door.

"Water. That's Satan's weak point. He melts when hit by water." The unfamiliar female voice came from behind him, so he spun back toward the kitchen just in time to see an attractive young woman shimmer to life in the middle of the kitchen table next to his computer.

He set one hand on the back of his chair and schooled his features into an impassive expression, resisting the urge to take a step back.

Justine's mom was wearing an elegant black evening gown, and was heavily weighed down with diamonds. Her hair was swept up in a knot at the back of her head. She looked almost exactly like Justine, except that she was refined and looked much more fragile.

He liked Justine's rough-and-tumble attitude better.

Justine rested her hands on the *Treatise,* her eyes wide. "Wow, Mom. You look hot. Where are you going?"

"The Met." The woman studied Derek, then walked out of the table and glided around him. He stood more erectly, then almost sat down when she walked behind him to check him out. "So this is Derek LaValle. Still alive, I see." She clucked her disapproval, then glided to a stop in front of him. "I'm Iris Bennett, Justine's mother."

"Nice to meet you." He reached for her offered hand, but his fingers went right through hers. He felt a sort of tingling where her image was. "First time I've met a ghost."

Her lips thinned. "I'm not a ghost. I'm in purgatory."

He grimaced. "I'm very sorry. My knowledge of purgatory is somewhat limited." When her face didn't soften, he added, "I didn't mean to insult you. You look lovely in that dress."

Justine came to stand by his side, tucking her arm through his. "Don't bother sucking up to her. As long as you're still alive, she won't like anything you do or say. Right, Mom?"

"Right." Iris passed her hand across his chest, leaving a

tingling behind where she'd been. "But I do admit, you have good taste. He's almost as good-looking as Satan. Nice muscle tone."

He couldn't keep the look of surprise off his face. "Satan's good-looking? I thought he had red skin and horns."

Iris narrowed her eyes and leaned her face close to his. "So now you insult my date for the evening?"

"No! I didn't mean to, I swear." He tugged at his collar. "I think we got off on the wrong foot." Iris turned her back on him and he ground his teeth. Good thing he wasn't planning on marrying Justine. Having a mother-in-law who wanted him dead and felt he was inferior to hell's leader didn't exactly bode well for the relationship.

Justine poked her mom in the back, keeping her hold on his arm. "Stop harassing Derek. You might as well let him enjoy his last few days in the mortal world."

"I guess." Iris threw him another long stare over her shoulder, her eyes dark and threatening. "If you kill my daughter, I'll torture you for all eternity. I have connections, you know."

Her hand moved toward his computer, and he wondered briefly whether he was about to be pummeled over the head by a laptop. He edged toward the table and curved his hand over the computer, tugging it until it was under his arm. "I believe you."

She harrumphed, then turned toward Justine, which suited Derek just fine. There was a dark power rolling off her that was positively daunting. "Darling, I must run, but I wanted to let you know what Satan said."

Justine tensed against him. "You're going on a date with him?"

"Yes." Iris folded her arms over her chest and dared Justine to challenge her. Like mother, like daughter.

Justine didn't back down. "I'm sick and tired of you guilting me with this Qualifying Incident to save you if you're already planning to go down on him . . . I mean go down *with* him. To hell."

Derek set his hand on her back and she moved a little closer to him.

"Who I have sex with is none of your business," Iris snapped. "But if I do decide to have sex with Satan, that doesn't mean I'm going to go to hell and be his mistress. The only way I'll end up in hell is if you don't get yourself together." She shot Derek a hard look for emphasis.

He gave her an innocent smile.

Iris spun away from them and walked through the table to the *Treatise*. She ran her fingers over the embossed cover, and a wistful longing passed over her features. Then she gave the book a firm slap and faced them. "Satan's illegitimate son Satan Jr. impersonated him. He sent the surfer and cursed Derek."

Justine's mouth dropped open and Derek had to concentrate on not doing the same. The bastard son of Satan was causing trouble with the identity theft of his leader-of-hell dad? Of course. How silly of them not to think of that.

"We have no idea where to find him or what he looks like or anything," Iris continued. "But apparently, he believes he'll win his daddy's love if he can steal Mona." She slanted a look at Derek. "We don't know why he cursed the LaValle men, though."

Justine let out a low whistle. "So, Satan knocked up some woman and refused to acknowledge his own son, turning him into a bitter, deprived psycho we have to track down? But you can't give us a single shred of information to help us find Satan Jr.?"

"Exactly." Iris blew them both a kiss. "I must be off. If you need me, call my cell. We'll be staying at the Waldorf if you need us."

"You're going on a date instead of helping us?" Justine asked. "Can't you at least get Satan to help?"

"We've done all we can. It's up to you. Good luck, sweetie, and don't forget to kill Derek as soon as you can. Derek, lovely to meet you." Then Iris shimmered out of sight with a high-pitched ringing.

"Okay, so do you have any bright ideas on how to track down a half-breed Satan who can hide from his own dad?" Justine tugged the computer out of his grasp and sat down at the table with it. "I don't suppose he'd be listed in the white pages?"

Derek pulled up a chair and sat next to her, shoving aside the feeling of despair hovering at the edges of his soul. "This is a good thing. At least now we know where to focus. We can—" He paused as an inky black shape formed on the kitchen floor.

"We can what?" Justine looked up from the screen just as the shape began to take the form of a woman he knew quite well. A woman who happened to be Satan's right hand. A woman who was awaiting direct orders to kill him. Justine cursed. "Oh, like we need to have time to deal with *her* right now. If she starts telling you to kill me, I swear I'm going to shoot her."

"She could have received her orders to kill me." He slowly eased his chair back from the table as Justine jumped up and darted across the room to where she kept her guns.

"Derek. Here." He turned just in time to catch a gun

Justine tossed at him. She cocked her own weapon and gave him a cheerful smile. "We decide how and when the other dies, and no Rivka's going to interfere. If she orders either of us dead, we'll kill her."

He frowned at the gun in his hand. "Aren't you afraid I'll use this to shoot you? Render you helpless while I grab a sword to do you in?"

"You're a softie, remember? You won't kill me unless you have to." She pointed her gun past his shoulder. "She's almost here."

"I'm not a softie." He cocked his own gun, but kept it by his side as his vice president took solid form.

Becca was wearing an all-black outfit: jeans, sneakers, T-shirt, and a leather jacket. Her short, dark hair was spiky and her fingernails were painted black. Over her shoulder was a bulky black bag that looked perfect for carrying machine guns or other such friendly accoutrements.

Not the pin-striped professional he knew so well.

She was a shark as a businesswoman. As a Rivka? She was intimidating as hell. "Hello, Becca." He slid his finger over the trigger. "Did I miss a meeting with McDonald's?"

"Probably, but that's not why I'm here," she said. "We have a major problem and it will be here in about two minutes."

Sixteen

Becca slung the bag over her shoulder and let it land with a thud on the kitchen floor. "Goblet Girl, I don't know who you pissed off, but you have a serious army on the way to this condo right now. Since you have to stay alive long enough for Derek to kill you and break the Curse, I'm here to help."

"Are you kidding? Why would an army be after me . . . ? Oh! Is it Satan Jr.?"

"It's not Satan Jr. It's Penhas."

"Penhas?" Justine nearly dropped to her knees as true panic slammed into her. "Are you sure?"

"Yeah, I'm sure." Becca unzipped the bag and hauled out a couple of machine guns. "I rarely get to use these because I'm supposed to use fireballs—Satan thinks it makes me scarier—but I thought you could use them."

"Could the Penhas be working for Satan Jr.? Maybe we could track him through them?" Derek slung one gun over his shoulder and accepted another one. "What are Penhas anyway?"

"Penhas are just another Otherworld being," Justine interrupted before Becca could answer. "Guns work on them, so no worries." *For him.* "Why are they after me?" She grabbed several guns and would have poached a few hand grenades if Becca hadn't given her an odd look. God help her, what had she done to deserve Penhas? Her gun slipped out of her grasp, and she had to wipe the sweat off her palms before she picked it back up.

"They're here to steal the Goblet and kill you. And I seriously doubt they'd sign on with Satan Jr. They don't get into stuff like turf wars over hell."

Derek walked to the window, his gun resting on his shoulder. "There's a string of yellow cabs lined up in front of the building." He glanced briefly at Becca. "If they're not with Satan Jr., then how would they know where to find Mona?"

"No idea." Becca kicked the bag under the table. "There's a lot of them though, and they must mean business because most of them are half naked."

Justine's heart actually stuttered and she had to sit down. "They're *half naked*?" Oh, God. She had no chance, did she? "Derek, you have to take the lead on this one."

He didn't look away from his vigil by the window. "Why? What's wrong?"

"Nothing." She stood up. How was she supposed to tell him? "Never mind. Just keep Mona safe if something happens to me."

"They know she's an espresso machine too," Becca added as Derek turned to give Justine a long look.

She refused to meet his gaze. Instead, she used Mona as an excuse when the espresso machine morphed into a bottle of erotic massage oil.

Becca stared at it. "Impressive."

The bottle flashed a hot pink color, then returned to a translucent red state.

"Stop showing off," Justine snapped. "Can't you turn

into a bag of rice until they're gone? I don't think sensual oil is the right thing to be when a bunch of half-naked men are on their way here."

Her gut lurched when Mona promptly became a two-liter bottle of massage oil, instead of a six-ounce bottle. "That's not helping," she hissed.

Derek walked away from the window, grasped Justin's arm and tugged her away from Becca. "What's wrong with you? Why are you afraid of the Penhas?" He kept his voice low, so Becca couldn't hear. "What's their power?"

She felt her cheeks heat up. "Sex."

"'Sex'? What do you mean?"

"They're like one big walking pheromone. Unless you've had sex lately, you won't be able to resist them." Her heart was racing so hard her chest was beginning to ache. "I've heard of women killing their own children to have sex with a Penha. The longer you've been celibate, the more power they have."

The understanding on his face made her want to crawl under the couch and die of embarrassment.

A light knock sounded on the front door, and Becca held out her hands and churned up a few fireballs. "All right, Justine. Let 'em in."

"*Me?*" God no, she couldn't face Penhas. Not in her state. Damn that *Treatise* for making her vulnerable.

Derek headed for the door. "I'll do it."

Thank God. Before he could open it, a shriek from Theresa's room jerked her attention. "Theresa!" Justine bolted for the back of the loft, even as the knocking on the front door grew louder.

Gun up and ready, she burst into Theresa's room. The dragon was standing in the center of a circle of dried fruit and some other mangled stuff Justine couldn't identify. Theresa was staring at her hand, her mouth hanging open like she'd lost her mind. "Theresa? What's wrong?" There were no Penhas in the room. Safe, for the moment.

Theresa finally looked up, and held her hand out to Justine. "Look at my fingernail."

"What?" She took a distracted glance at her roomie's appendage, then froze in disbelief. On the middle toe of her right hand, the claw had been replaced by a human fingernail, complete with a French manicure. "It's human!"

"I know! Can you believe it? It was one of the spells Zeke gave me. It was supposed to do all of me, but this is a start, don't you think?" The dragon blinked back a tear, and Justine suddenly felt her own throat get a little tight.

Then a loud thud from the front room made Justine jump.

Theresa's head snapped toward the other room. "What's going on out there?"

Justine winced as Derek shouted at her to come back. "We're being attacked by Pehnas. Come on."

Theresa's golden eyes widened. "Penhas? You're so screwed."

"I know." She hoisted her gun up and sprinted back to the other room, vaguely comforted by the thud of Theresa's feet right behind her.

They made it to the main area of the loft just as the interior door to the condo splintered. In stepped a man wearing nothing but a pair of jeans and the perfect amount of five-o'clock shadow. He had muscles in all the right places, and his eyes were a brilliant shade of green that matched the emeralds in the butt of his sword. He turned toward Justine and Theresa, and flashed them a smile that revealed straight white teeth. "Good afternoon, ladies."

Sweet mercy. He was perfect. Heat flooded her lower body.

Becca yelped and threw a fireball at him. It hit him in the chest and he immediately exploded in a puff of blue smoke.

Justine whirled on Becca, unfulfilled need raging through her. "Why'd you do that? He'd done nothing wrong!"

Becca revved up another fireball as the elevator door slid shut to return to the first floor. "He nearly got you, Goblet Girl." She nodded at Theresa. "Dragon."

"My name's Theresa, Rivka."

"Mine's Becca. Can you shoot flames?"

"Better than you can hurl a fireball," Theresa snorted.

"Have you had sex lately?"

"Several times a day. I'm good."

Becca jerked her chin at Justine. "What about you? You seem a little vulnerable."

"I have to stay. It's my job." Tingling zinged through her belly when Derek touched her shoulder.

"You don't have to stay." His voice vibrated with a sexuality she'd never noticed before. "Your vulnerability proves you're a good Guardian."

She shrugged off his touch and shifted restlessly, trying to shake off the urges pulsing through her.

"She can't stay," Theresa announced. "She'll be down on her knees offering blow jobs in less than a second." She patted Justine's shoulder. "You're like a dried up old maid, sweetie, and you need to bail."

At that moment, the elevator door opened and six guys walked in. The man in front was blond, tan, and wearing nothing except boxers and a light splattering of chest hair.

He gave Justine a brilliant smile as he casually swung a nicely polished sword from his fingertips. "You look lovely tonight, Guardian."

"Oh, my . . ." Justine dropped to her knees, vaguely aware of the machine gun hitting the floor with a thunk, of Theresa snickering next to her.

Becca disintegrated him with a fireball that had Justine moaning with frustration and fury.

"How could you kill him?" Justine grabbed her gun and jumped to her feet. "You can't invite yourself into my house and then go around killing all the beautiful, naked men who show up on my doorstep!" She unloaded fire and was satisfied when Becca vanished into a slither of inky black soot that melted into the floor.

The second man headed straight for Justine, a sword in his hand. All it took was a smile, and she dropped the gun. "Take me. Now." She held up her arms and ran toward him, but Derek sprayed him and the others with bullets, and all she got was an armful of blue smoke. She whirled on him. "That was completely uncalled for. You'll pay for that."

Seventeen

Given the mutinous expression on her face, Derek was guessing that their imminent battle to the death was going to happen *now*. "Justine? Maybe we can talk about this?"

"No." She stomped over to the gun and picked it up as the elevator door slid closed, no doubt on its way downstairs to pick up more Penhas. "How dare you!" She released the safety on her gun and pointed it at him. "I can't let you kill these gorgeous men."

He tensed and lifted his gun, vaguely aware of Theresa howling with laughter off to the left. "Theresa? How about a little help here?"

"Shoot her in the stomach. She'll survive, but that should get her out of our way long enough to deal with them."

He considered the woman standing before him with the twitchy trigger finger, flushed cheeks, and slightly glazed eyes. "I can't shoot her." He put up his gun.

Theresa snorted. "And you call yourself a man? No worthy man would resist shooting his woman for her own good."

"She's not my woman."

"You're pathetic. I rescind my offer to have sex with you. As desperate as I am, I still need a manly man."

Theresa made a groan of self-sacrifice, then tapped Justine on the shoulder with her tail.

Derek ducked when Justine jerked, and her gun shot a bullet over his right shoulder. "He's the pretzel king," Theresa told Justine. "Think carefully about how traumatized I'll be if you shoot him."

"What?" Justine glanced at Theresa, but her gun was still aimed in Derek's direction. "I have to kill him. Didn't you see what he did to my new sex toy?"

"Don't do it." Derek tried to assume a soothing tone as he inched closer, his eye on her gun. A few more feet and he'd be able to grab it. "You don't really want to kill me, I promise."

Then he noticed a dark shape appearing around Justine's feet. Becca?

His vice president appeared behind Justine, grabbed her in a headlock and wrenched the gun out of her hands. Gave her a quick elbow to the head that dropped her.

"Hey!" He aimed the gun at Becca. "You touch her again and you're fired." The elevator rattled and he knew it was on its way back up again.

She tossed Justine's gun to him and gave Derek an appraising look. "Interesting she didn't shoot you as soon as you killed one of them. She must be powerful to hesitate for that long, especially when she's that susceptible. And she must have a very strong aversion to killing you, as well. Notice how she didn't hesitate to shoot me?"

Theresa snorted her disgust as a sense of satisfaction settled in Derek's chest. So the Guardian wasn't as bloodthirsty as she made herself out to be, at least when it came to him. Maybe he could leverage that into a longer life expectancy . . . or something.

"I'll be resistant to the Penhas' allure for a few moments, but then I'll have to go, and even Theresa will eventually succumb." The elevator dinged its arrival and they all turned to face it. "Unless they send women, you should be fine. So it'll be up to you." The door opened and Becca shot a fireball without even waiting for their visitor to speak.

"How long are they going to keep coming?" Theresa asked. "I mean, they're totally hot and everything, but we can't keep knocking Justine out and shooting them."

"This is just the start. There's a lot of them. They'll come until they get the Goblet." Two more came in this time, and Becca hesitated for a fraction of a second until she incinerated them. A thump at the back of the apartment made Becca jump. "They found the stairs. Can't you feel them?" She shivered. "I gotta get out of here. I suggest you do the same." And with that, she vanished into the floor in a slither of blackness.

Theresa burned up the last two, then high-fived Derek as the door slid shut. "Oh my God. How fun was that? It has been *so* long! Have sex with me right now so I can withstand their allure for hours. Think how many I could kill! An endless supply of victims!" She held her front claws over head and wiggled her hips in a dance that was far more frightening than sexy.

He picked up a pillow from the couch and tucked it under Justine's head. "Can you stop celebrating long enough to tell me what other powers they have?"

"Just what you've seen, Wimp Boy. It's not like they can fly up here or break down the door with a puff of breath, so chill. They're generally peaceful and they have no battle skills whatsoever, except the sex thing, which is pretty much all they need with Miss Sexually Deprived here."

He smoothed Justine's hair off her face, and was dismayed to see her eyelids flutter. She was waking up. Not good.

"Unless they brought axes it's going to take a while for them to get through the back door," Theresa continued. "It's specially reinforced to keep any Mona-stalkers at bay."

Justine groaned and sat up. "That bitch hit me, didn't she?"

Derek eyed her carefully. "You want to kill me?"

She rubbed her head. "Do I want to? No. Do I have to? Well, we both know the answer to that question."

Relief rushed through him. She was all right. "Good. You're back to normal," he said gruffly. But they needed to get out of there before the next batch showed up. He turned to Theresa as he cupped Justine around the waist and helped her to her feet. "Can you fly?"

She grinned. "Of course I can. Justine never lets me, though. She's afraid I'm going to get shot down by an anti-aircraft missile or something equally dire."

"Well, you get to now." He ignored Justine's grunt of protest. "Can you carry both of us and Mona?"

"If I was in shape I could, but I haven't flown since we lived in the Amazon. I could carry Mona, but that's it." Her eyes were sparkling and he could practically taste her eagerness to do what she'd been denied for so long.

"Take Mona and go to my apartment. Just go through a window. I'll get it fixed later." He jotted the address down and handed it to the dragon. "Now, go."

"You got it." She grinned. "I can't believe I get to fly."

"Just don't get shot down," Justine said.

"I'll do my best." She danced out of the room, singing

about leaving on a jet plane. He couldn't help but smile at her excitement. The small joys in life.

The elevator beeped, and he swung around, unloading his gun through the elevator door before it even opened. When it did open, there was nothing inside but a lot of blue smoke.

A *lot* of smoke. Meaning they'd packed the men in there. The Penhas didn't need axes to get through. If they kept coming long enough, he'd eventually shoot the door apart for them. He needed a new plan.

Justine frowned at him. "I don't think I like that you just did that. I'm feeling a little hostile toward you."

"Resist it, Justine. It's the Penhas. They're getting to you." He pulled the emergency stop on the elevator, but the pounding from the back of the apartment intensified. How long until one of them ran off to pick up a few axes? But at least no more would be coming up in the elevator, unless they knew how to shimmy up elevator cables.

"Penhas. Right. I got it." She closed her eyes and hugged her arms to her chest, her lips moving in a silent mantra that he really hoped would work.

Theresa came back carrying the extremely large bottle of massage oil. "I'm okay for the moment. Never thought all my cybersex would come in so handy, but it's helping me. I do feel sort of weird, though."

"Then go. We'll catch up with you later."

"Don't rush. I'm going to take the long route. I haven't flown in forever." She got a dreamy look on her face that said she might zip around the New York skyline for hours.

Like they needed to have a dragon sighting right now. "I have an entire freezer full of experimental flavors of Vic's Pretzels. Help yourself."

Theresa sighed. "That's so cruel. You know I can't resist that."

"Just get out of here."

"You got it." She ran toward the window and broke through it, wings sprouting out of her back as she hit the fresh air.

Incredible. She was graceful and delicate as she soared through the air, with her horned tail flicking and puffs of smoke coming out of her nose. He had no idea how he knew it, but he was pretty sure that was happy smoke. Maybe he was getting the hang of Otherworld language. Go figure.

"I can't do it, Derek." Justine abandoned her mantra and opened her eyes. "I have to go let them in." She whirled and bolted for the back of the apartment, but Derek managed to tackle her as she went by. "Get off me so I can let them in!" She flung her knee upward. He twisted, and she slammed his inner thigh instead of her target.

He grunted with the impact as pain ricocheted down his leg. "Justine! They're going to kill you."

"So what? Death by sex is the only way to go." She dug under her arm, and he blocked the dagger as she thrust it toward his throat. "Release me so I can rip off my clothes and fling my body at their mercy!"

"If you die from sex, it's not going to be with a Penha." He tossed the dagger out of her reach. It clattered to a stop in the corner. "If you let those men kill you and take Mona, you'll go in the Chamber of Unspeakable Horrors, remember?"

Something moved in Justine's eyes. A faint recognition. "Penhas," she whispered. "They're here for me."

"Yes." He cupped her face with his hands, keeping her pressed to the floor with his body. "Focus, Justine. Fight it off. We need to get out of here. Just keep it together for five minutes."

"Oh, sure. No problem." He saw a desperation in her eyes that belied the sarcasm in her tone. A plea for help that he never thought he'd see in the eyes of his independent, self-sufficient Guardian.

It reached in his gut and yanked free something he'd kept locked up since his dad had died. It surged over him and exploded in his chest, and he dug his fingers into Justine's shoulders. "I won't leave you. I won't let you die." He'd thought those words about Quincy many times, but he'd never actually promised them to anyone. Until now.

And it scared the daylights out of him.

Then he heard them shouting her name, and he felt Justine tense under him. "I can't help myself," she groaned. "I need to respond to them. I have to . . ." And then she grabbed his head and kissed him. "Have sex with me, Derek."

"Now?" The pounding from the back of the loft intensified, and he thought he heard the sound of wood splintering. Call him old-fashioned, but it didn't exactly seem to be the most romantic situation for a seduction.

"It's the only way for me to resist them." She twisted under him, shoving at his shoulders. "If you don't, I'll kill you to get free and then we'll both die and Mona will be gone." A Penha shouted her name, and she winced. "Derek!"

"You're sure it'll be okay?"

"Yes!"

He took a deep breath, and then kissed her. For real. With all intention of full follow-through. She flung herself into the kiss, pouring her heart and soul into his mouth.

The power from her kiss stunned him, and he nearly lifted his head to break from the electricity rushing through him. It was too much, it hit too deep, it curled his gut painfully where he didn't want to feel anything.

Then he heard the Penhas yelling her name again, and her hands dove for the button of his jeans. "Now, Derek," she whispered into his mouth. She yanked his pants open and bit the side of his neck.

"Most men don't respond well to this kind of pressure," he muttered even as he raked his hands across her belly and tugged her jeans from her hips.

She arched under him, gasping as he slid his hands over her thighs, and he slipped the denim off. Her skin was so soft, so hot, piercing his fingertips like daggers. "You feel like you're on fire."

"I'm burning up." She shoved her hands under his jeans, her hands digging into his butt as she frantically kissed his neck, his throat, his collarbone. "For you. For us."

There was no mistaking the sound of wood splintering, and a banging coming from the floor of the elevator, along with the constant sound of men calling for Justine.

"Now, Derek."

He shucked his jeans and moved between her legs. She wrapped her legs around his hips, and he thrust hard and deep. She screamed and he couldn't suppress his shout. Their reaction was instant, explosive and branded them both as their bodies convulsed together. One movement, one response, two souls melted into one with a heat so intense he was certain there was smoke rising from their bodies.

She writhed under him, her fingers digging into his shoulders as he crushed her against him. He felt like every muscle in his body had triggered at the same time, and he couldn't stop himself from driving into her as far and deep as he could, and it still wasn't enough, until he felt her soul latch on to his, draining his body of its essence, absorbing it into hers and thrusting it back, revived, refreshed, and alive.

Alive. He felt so alive.

God. What had just happened to him?

He looked down into the face of his Guardian, and saw the same look of shock on her face he knew was on his. He kissed her softly and rested his forehead against hers. Closed his eyes and absorbed her, soaked in the moment.

"Mom says Satan claims to be the best lover in the Afterlife," she whispered against his lips. "That's only because you aren't dead yet."

He opened his eyes and smiled. "If I had time, I'd show you what I can really do."

A crash from the kitchen indicated that the door had finally given way, and a man's deep voice drifted through the loft. "Guardian? We are here for you."

"Time to go," she said. "Off, off."

He rolled to his side and jerked his pants on as she did the same thing. "Did it work?"

She grinned at him. "The only man I want to get naked with is you."

"Excellent." He tossed her a gun. "To save Mona, it was a worthwhile sacrifice."

"Sacrifice?" She aimed the gun at the kitchen door, and took out the front row of men in a puff of blue smoke. "You'll be dreaming about that interlude for the rest of your existence."

He killed the next group that swelled forward. "As will you. Got a fire escape?"

"Yep. In Theresa's room." She sprinted to the back of the loft, and he was right behind her. She yanked up the window and sprayed a few more bullets behind her just before Derek shut the door and shoved the armoire in front of it. A puff of blue smoke floated through the crack under the wood. "You first," she said.

"A gentleman never has sex with a woman and then leaves her behind to face possessed Penhas alone. You first."

She rolled her eyes and stepped out onto the fire escape. "There's no room in my life for chivalry."

"Maybe there should be."

She paused, with one foot on the ladder. "What does that mean?"

He frowned. It had sort of slipped out. Must be residual he-man urges after their moment of intimacy; taking care of his woman and all that. Instinctive response to sex. Neither of them could afford anything more than that. "It means you shouldn't argue when I offer to fight off naked men for you."

"I thought it meant you weren't going to kill me if we couldn't solve the Curse." She started to climb down and he followed her. "It's not very chivalrous to have sex with a woman and then kill her."

"Agreed. But it's not very ladylike to sleep with a man and then kill him." They both dropped to the ground, and sprinted for the nearest cab.

"As I said, there's no room for chivalry in my life," she said as she dove into the backseat of the cab. "And didn't you promise back there that you wouldn't let me die?"

He busied himself shutting the door. "I was talking about the Penhas."

"Ah. Too bad for me."

Too bad for both of us. He fell onto the seat next to her and gave the cabbie directions as scantily clad men began dropping from her fire escape. "Well, on the plus side, we managed to have sex without endangering your eternal soul."

She leaned back against the seat and closed her eyes, breathing heavily. "Maybe the Penhas will follow us."

"You think?" He slung his arm around her shoulder and pulled her against him, so she was resting against his chest. He needed her to be there, and she didn't seem to mind.

"I can only hope."

He kissed the top of her head. "Shall I leave a trail of breadcrumbs so they can find us?"

"Definitely."

Eighteen

Justine was still feeling a little dizzy by the time they arrived at the Waldorf-Astoria, after a thirty-minute ride around the city to make sure they'd lost the Penhas. *Sex.* She'd had sex. It had been over a half hour since he'd rocked her world, and her legs were still trembling, her brain was still consumed by some soft fuzzy emotion, and she didn't want to move out of Derek's arms. Ever.

She didn't even have the energy to tell Derek to quit being a gentleman when he helped her out of the cab and kept his hand on her back as they walked up to the front desk. She wanted him to keep touching her, to put his head next to hers and whisper sweet nothings.

And then she wanted him to rip her clothes off and take her right in the lobby of the hotel, in front of all these people and gorgeous pieces of furniture. Orgasm after orgasm. Lots of exposed flesh. Licking, kissing, caressing . . .

Oh, she was in such trouble.

"You all right?" His brow wrinkled as he peered at her, his eyes warm and soft.

"Just because we had sex doesn't mean I'm going to shirk my duty or put your life above Mona's eternal safety." *Yeah, yeah. What she said.*

One eyebrow arched in amusement. "Methinks the Guardian doth protest too much."

"Shut up."

Derek gave her an easy smile, then leaned on the reception desk, his hand still caressing Justine's back. In a moment, she would reclaim her independence but, for just one minute, she wanted to enjoy the sensation of a man doting on her.

How was she ever going to go back to her life?

"Can you ring the room for Iris Bennett please?" Derek asked the young man behind the desk.

Right. Forgot they were there to deal with Satan. Nothing like thoughts of evil Otherworld beings to help bring a Guardian down from the high of her first orgasm in two centuries.

The clerk gave him a practiced smile. "One minute." He studied the computer, then dialed the phone. After a moment, he said, "I'm afraid she isn't in. Would you care to leave a message?"

"No, thanks. We'll try again later."

Justine leaned around Derek. "Do you have a listing for Satan?"

The clerk barely managed to retain his bland expression. "I beg your pardon?"

"He doesn't use his own name. He's a celebrity." Well, he was, in a way. "Please check."

He did as instructed, and shook his head. "No Satan."

She glanced at Derek, then leaned closer to the desk clerk. "I don't suppose Iris has two rooms reserved?"

"No."

One room for her mom and Satan. Dismay curdled in her belly and she turned away from the desk.

Derek slipped his hand around her elbow. "It's not even eleven yet. They're probably still out on the town. Let's get a drink at the bar and wait for a bit. Decompress."

Right. She could use some decompression.

She followed Derek to the bar, and sank down into a plush couch next to a low table, while he went off to get drinks. She couldn't help but watch him as he walked away from her, his stride easy and long, his jeans fitting perfectly over his gorgeous behind. The one she'd been wrapped around only a short time ago.

He glanced over his shoulder, caught her looking and grinned.

She smiled back. Why pretend? After that sex, he had to know she had the hots for him.

She groaned and let her head flop back against the cushions. How could she kill the only man who'd given her an orgasm since she'd become a Guardian? And not just any orgasm, one that was so incredible she was still feeling sparks pricking her fingers and toes.

"Guardian?"

Her eyes snapped open. Three men stood in front of her. One was a pirate, right down to the gold earring and scabbard. Another was wearing a white robe and had a long white beard. A third man was wearing a navy suit and an understated tie.

The Council.

Uh-oh.

She gave them a calm smile—as if! "So good to see you again."

"We need to meet with you," the businessman said.

Yeah, I figured. "Have a seat." Derek walked up behind

them, and she tried to tell him to leave with her expression. He frowned and glanced at the men.

They sat in unison, one in each of the armchairs surrounding the coffee table in front of her. "Where is the Goblet?" the pirate asked.

Derek raised his brows when he heard the question, and he took a closer look at the men.

"She is with my designated successor," Justine said.

"Again?" The old man pulled out a notepad and jotted something down.

Somehow, she doubted it was a compliment about her excellent fashion sense. She cleared her throat. "According to article seven, section three, subparagraph A of the *Treatise,* entrusting physical custody of the Goblet to the designated successor is permitted in emergency situations." All that *Treatise*-reading had come in handy. "We were attacked by Penhas and had to separate. Deadly force was involved, which triggers the Emergency Response clause, which permits me to break all rules that, in my sole discretion, I deem necessary to ensure the Goblet's safety." *Hah. Take that, ye conservative old men in dated attire.* "As is my right, I have deemed that the emergency state will continue to be in existence until we end the Curse on this man." She pointed at Derek. "*And* until we find out who sent the Penhas after us."

The three members of the Council stared at her in surprised silence.

Guess they'd never before dealt with a Guardian who'd actually read the *Treatise.*

Derek moved past the men and sat down next to her, giving her a private wink. She grinned at his appreciation of her brilliance.

The pirate eyed him. "So, you're the Cursed one."

"I'm Derek LaValle, of the LaValle clan." Derek stood up and shook everyone's hands. "I'm working with the Guardian to break the Curse so later generations of LaValle men don't continue to come after the Goblet until they eventually succeed. Justine is a stellar Guardian and has tried to kill me on more than one occasion. I am fully aware she lets me live only for now, and when the time comes, she will kill me as she is supposed to."

"Sit," commanded the old man.

"At your service." Derek did as directed, and Justine could see the tension in his neck.

It made her feel better to know he had her back. Yes, she was accustomed to working independently, but he was a good addition. The Penhas would have been a wee bit difficult to manage by herself. She shifted her leg so her left thigh rested against his. It was a slight touch, but the contact made her feel settled. Grounded. Especially when he leaned back and pressed his shoulder against hers.

For now they were a team, and it was okay with her.

The businessman sat across from them, his gold watch flashing in the candlelight. "We are here to set a date for your Judgment."

A Judgment? That sounded like a really unpleasant thing. She'd skipped the section in the *Treatise* on Judgments, an oversight that might have been a bad idea. "Thanks for the offer, but I decline."

He raised his eyebrows. "You can't decline."

"Oh." Terribly unfortunate. It had been worth a try.

"Two days hence. We will come for you."

"Two days?" She dug her fingers into the arm of the

couch, but tried to keep her voice calm. "That's not enough time for me to prepare."

"The head of the Council has vacation planned next week. She needs to get this done before she leaves."

"Vacation? You're depriving me of enough time to gather evidence to save my eternal soul because she has *vacation plans*? Isn't that a due process violation? I'll—" She clapped her mouth shut when Derek increased the pressure of his shoulder against hers. *Don't make things worse, Justine.*

"It's plenty of time." The businessman stood up. "You'll still be allowed to present your side."

"Not that it will help you save your soul. The decision is basically made." The old man tucked his notepad into the folds of his robe and teetered his way to his feet.

Well, if that was the case, she might as well have wild sex with Derek until her brains melted. The memory could sustain her through an eternity of unspeakable horrors.

Then the pirate winked at her. "They're blowing smoke, my love. I like your approach. Shows innovation. Evolution of the position to adjust to modern society. Save the Goblet and you'll be fine."

"She's doomed either way." The old man latched on to the pirate's arm and gave him a quelling glare that had the pirate glowering at him. "Don't give her false hope."

"It's not false." The pirate whipped out his sword and pointed it at the old man's neck. "How many times do I have to tell you not to grab me?"

The old man flicked the tip away from him with one finger. "You're too volatile for this position. No wonder you died by a mutiny from your own crew."

"It wasn't a mutiny, you old bas—"

"Enough." The businessman stepped between them and confiscated the sword. "The decision hasn't been made," he announced. "Until all information is in, it's still *undecided*." He looked at Justine. "Unless you lose the Goblet. No trial if that happens."

"I'll save Mona."

Derek leaned forward. "*We* will save Mona. She needs me, and that's the only reason I'm still alive." She gave him a gentle bump of appreciation with her shoulder and he squeezed her thigh.

His support gave her the courage to smile at the Council as they loomed around the table.

"That's all. We'll be back for you in two days," the businessman said.

"Doomed," the old man said before the businessman grabbed his sleeve and prodded him to the door.

The pirate's golden earrings sparkled in the candle-light. "You'll be fine."

She touched his arm. "Do you mean that? Because if I really am doomed to an eternity of unspeakable horrors, I want to know now."

He patted her hand. "It's all up to you." Then he gave Derek a thumbs-up and wink. "Excellent job with the Penhas, Cursed One."

"Jerome!" the businessman shouted. "Now!"

The pirate's face darkened and he stalked toward the door, muttering epithets and extolling the virtues of piracy and the high seas.

She gaped after him, heat rising in her cheeks. "Penhas? How did they know what you did? Do you think they were actually . . . watching?"

Derek leaned over and kissed her hard. Deep. He sent

all her emotions rushing through her until her fingers were burning as she leaned into him, clutching his shirt. When she was oozing around the floor in a puddle of sexual bliss, he broke the kiss and grinned. "I don't want you thinking of anything but me when you think about what we did in your loft."

She sagged into his chest. "You're such an arrogant male. I hate arrogant males."

"Yeah, I can tell." He nibbled on her earlobe, his chuckle vibrating deep in his chest. "What do you say we go track down your mom and Satan and get this deal taken care of?"

She hoisted herself off him. "Let's do it. I have a Council to thwart."

Satan shut the door, leaned against it, and gave Iris a leering grin. "It is time to rock your world, no?"

Iris put her hands on her hips and tried to give him a stern look. "I told you, just because I let you take me to the opera and buy me dinner doesn't mean I'm going to have sex with you."

He wiggled his eyebrows and levered himself off the door, gliding across the plush carpet. "No, but the fact you didn't object to one room and one bed says much."

"It says I was looking forward to forcing you to sleep on the floor." She turned on the ornate brass lamp next to the embroidered sofa that framed the seating area.

He shrugged off his tuxedo jacket and tossed it on the king-sized bed. "We will sleep on the floor together. And on the bed. And on the coffee table. And in the shower." He came to a stop directly in front of her, his body only inches from hers. "I am the best lover in the Afterlife. We will have sex on every piece of furniture in this room. Twice. And then we start over."

She scooted around the sofa and flicked on the floor lamp. "No."

He gave her a wounded look and leapt over the sofa to land in front of her as she tried to skulk around the back of it. "But why? How do you find the cruelness in your soul to reject me? I have been waiting for you for two hundred and twenty-four years. Do you realize how long that is for a man of my virility?"

"It hasn't been two hundred and twenty-four years. You went on a sex rampage, remember?" She turned to go the other way, then froze when he caught her wrist. "Let go of me."

"I already forgot about all the other women. I have no mind for anyone but my love muffin." He traced his fingers lightly over the necklace he'd given her earlier in the evening. With its perfect diamonds and the way Satan had begged her to accept it, she'd been unable to turn it down.

"But you're a lying, manipulative bastard, remember?" *Yes, Iris, remember? You know he'll break your heart, use you and cast you aside. Just say no! It's all lies!*

But what if it wasn't lies anymore? What if he really wanted her for who she was?

"Of course I lie and manipulate. I am Satan. I can be no other way." He trailed his index finger over her collarbone, and a delighted smile broke over his face. "Goose bumps! I turn you on!"

"I'm cold." But it was getting more difficult to keep the hostile tone in her voice. How could she help it? He was Satan and he'd always had a place in her soul. What woman could resist those dimples? He wore his tuxedo like he was born for greatness, and it framed his narrow waist and wide shoulders perfectly.

"I shall heat you up, then." He moved closer and kissed her throat, his lips drifting over her skin like a butterfly. "I am Satan. I am heat. I am fire. I burn in you."

"What do you want from me this time?" Her voice was soft, her fingers curving into his fine shirt instead of blocking him. "No lies."

"I want you to be my queen. My eternal bedmate and adviser." He ran his tongue down the side of her neck. "If you want to rule hell, that's fine too. Whatever it takes to get you by my side."

"What about Mona?" Her voice was breathy, and she knew he noticed because of the smile that curved his magnificent lips.

"I want Mona very badly, but I have already proven I want you more, no?"

Damn. He was right about that. "I won't relocate to hell." She sighed and tipped her head back as he showered kisses over her chest, down to the neckline of her black silk gown.

"If you come to hell, you will learn how to torture innocent souls and ruin lives. We will use the misery of others as foreplay for our lovemaking. You will have unlimited access to victims on which to release all your violent and amoral instincts, and I will adorn you with obscene amounts of the finest jewelry. Plus I have a most excellent assortment of automobiles and wines. People have traded much to get their most important dreams." He purred softly and nuzzled her neck. "Hell is very nice. Nicer than heaven."

"I thought you were only supposed to take souls." She clutched his shoulders as he slid his hands over her lower back, holding her up as he nuzzled the neckline of her dress aside, his lips whispering over the tops of her breasts.

"I am Satan. I break rules. My flat-screen televisions and surround sound make me very popular for parties. Best in the Afterlife." His tongue flicked her nipple, and Iris couldn't suppress her quick inhale. "Come for a visit. If you want to leave, I let you go. If not, I worship you for eternity and value your mind and your intelligence. You will grow an enormous ego and be impossible to tolerate. It sounds wonderful, no?"

"But you betrayed me," she whispered. How could she forget that?

He lifted his head and met her gaze. "I am sorry."

She pulled back, and her heart thudded. "What did you say?"

"I apologize. I express my remorse. I admit I was a . . . scum-sucking bastard? Is that good? Or, how about . . . royal pinprick unworthy of dog doo? Or . . ." He wrinkled his brow. "I know! I deserve to have my manly regions slathered in athletic cream that makes them burn until I scream like a girl."

She smiled. "You've been rehearsing your apology."

"Oh, yes. Does it show? I am very remorseful. Will you allow me now to bring you to ecstasy that only those who have been at my sexual mercy can even begin to understand?"

She tilted her head and felt the ache in her chest. The one that had been with her since the day she'd met him. "Satan?"

His eyes were glistening, his hands tight against her lower back, his thumbs rubbing circles against the thin material of her dress. "Yes, my burning hot pile of lusciousness?"

"I—"

A loud knock on the door interrupted her before she could finish. "Mom! Are you in there?"

Oh, *no.* "Justine? What's wrong?" She shoved Satan off her and lunged for the door, but Satan grabbed her and hauled her up against him, his body hard against hers.

"Satan, that's my daughter. I have to go." She couldn't let Satan and Justine meet. She had to find a way to stop it. "Release me, now."

"Not yet." And with that, he kissed her. A soul-searing, burning kiss that stole her mind, wrenched open her heart, and infused her with heat, passion, and something else that made her knees tremble and her hands shake.

He broke the kiss and stared down at her, a startled look on his face. "I hereby declare myself your servant for all eternity, Iris Bennett."

That was all he said, but the stark honesty and vulnerability in his voice reached her in a way nothing he'd ever said had before.

Nineteen

Justine was just about ready to kick down the hotel door when it opened and her mom slipped out.

She was still dressed, thank heavens. "Justine, sweetie, what are you doing here?" She shut the door firmly behind her and leaned against it, keeping a tight grip on the knob.

"I am your servant," a man's voice said through the door. "I lick the ground you walk on. I cry when you leave my sight."

Her mom's cheeks flushed. "Ignore him."

"If you make him sign that in triplicate, it might be worth it to have the ruler of the Underworld be your servant," Derek observed.

He stopped observing when Justine elbowed him in the gut. "If Satan can stop begging for a few minutes, we need to talk to him," she said.

The jerk on the other side of the door tapped firmly. "Satan doesn't beg! I throw my offended nature back at you! I worship the woman with the legs most lovely. That is not begging!"

Iris shook her head sharply. "You can't speak to him."

Justine wrinkled her nose. "He's naked, isn't he?"

"I am not naked, but I can be very quickly. Would you

like to inspect my manhood before I take your mother to the highest mountains of pleasure?"

"No!" He sounded like a love-stricken teenager, not a badass lord of the Underworld. "Keep your clothes on!" She caught a glimpse of Derek grinning broadly, and she glared at him. He immediately wiped the smile off his face and sucked his cheeks in.

"Satan! Go lather yourself up in the bathtub," Iris snapped.

"I cannot drag myself that far away from you, my luscious love monkey." There was a thud as if he'd fallen against the door. "I must press myself against this wood until I can feel your flesh against my body."

Iris's cheeks turned pink. "Can't we deal with this tomorrow?"

"Trust me, Mom, I really don't want to be here, but we can't leave until we talk to him about Satan Jr."

"Sniveling bastard," Satan announced. "I spit on my velvet soft sperm factory that created him."

Derek turned away and erupted into a coughing fit.

Justine smacked Derek on the shoulder. "It's not funny."

"I know. I'm sorry." He coughed again and his eyes were tearing. "I'll stop."

"It's really important that we ask you a few questions," she told the door. "Let us in."

"Certainly. Anything for the daughter of the woman I will caress for all eternity." The knob started to turn, but Iris squawked and lunged for it.

"Don't come out." She gave Justine a worried look. "I'm afraid if he sees you, it will stir up longings for Mona that are too strong for him to resist."

"I am Satan. I am strong. I can resist." Pause. "Do you have the Goblet with you, daughter of my fantasy woman?"

"No, I don't." As if she'd be dumb enough to wander around New York with Mona in her back pocket. There was a reason she was the best Guardian in a thousand years.

"Then I am Satan. I am strong. I can resist." He knocked on the mahogany. "Release me, beautiful one. Let me assist your daughter."

"You could save her life and it won't get me to move to hell with you," Iris said. "Don't even think you can manipulate me."

She glanced at Derek, who was still grinning broadly.

"I'm sorry, Justine, but this is hilarious," he said. "I can't believe I'm listening to Satan try to seduce your mom."

"Man-to-man, if you assist me, I will grant your greatest wish," Satan called out.

"I'd like the Curse ended," Derek replied.

"Oh. Except that. Would you like a larger manhood? I could arrange that."

"I'm all set, thanks." He shot Justine a look that had her cheeks heating up.

And her mom noticed, if the raised brow and stern, albeit disappointed, look on her face was any indication. "Justine? A private word?"

"The Council visited tonight," she blurted. "They're having a Judgment in two days. If I can't break the Curse by then and prove I did the right thing by giving Derek the drinks from Mona, it's the Chamber of Unspeakable Horrors for me."

Iris paled and clasped a hand to her chest. "Sweet mother Mary. I was afraid of this."

"My love pumpkin! I sense your distress! I come to your rescue!" With a loud tear, Satan ripped the door off the hinges and flung it behind him. He threw himself through the doorway and hauled Iris against him, nearly suffocating her by pressing her face into his chest and cooing disgustingly sweet things into her ear.

Satan was drop-dead gorgeous, no pun intended. At least six four, broad shoulders, dark hair, penetrating eyes, and a jawline to die for. No wonder her mom had sex fantasies about him. How could she have resisted Satan's full-court press for so long? Impressive.

Derek cleared his throat and sauntered up behind Justine, breathing softly against her neck. "Don't even think about it," he said.

An unfamiliar flutter danced in her belly. "Are you jealous of Satan?"

"No." He snorted. "I'm just looking out for you. Don't read anything into it."

"Mother of all evil souls and destroyer of lives!" Satan yelled suddenly. "I cannot believe what I see!"

She whirled around to find Satan had shoved Iris off him and was staring at Justine as if she was a . . . well . . . she wasn't sure what Satan would find terrifyingly odd, but whatever it was, she seemed to have cornered the market on it.

Iris cursed and tried to shove him back into the hotel room, but he sidestepped her so quickly she missed and tumbled past him onto the carpet. He leaned toward Justine, not speaking. Not trying to touch her. Just staring. And sniffing.

"Is it just me, or are his eyes glowing red?" Derek whispered in her ear.

"They are," she whispered back. "Do you think we should be concerned?"

"It's very possible," he said.

Satan leaned closer, his eyes pulsating with red and orange as he continued to suck in her scent. She pressed back against Derek's chest. "Too bad we tossed the machine guns in the Dumpster."

"Because I'm sure they would work on the leader of hell."

"Good point." A thin spiral of smoke popped from the top of Satan's head and began to curl toward the ceiling.

Derek's arm slipped around her waist and he moved them both backward, ever so subtly. "I think maybe we should leave."

"No. We need his help." She glanced at her mom, who was trying to untangle her stilettos from the floor-length dress. "Mom? Please do something. He's getting a little scary."

"I think it's the fact that I can actually see flames flickering in his eyes that's really intimidating," Derek said, his arm tightening around Justine as the carpet under Satan's feet burst into flames.

"On second thought, we could come back later," Justine said.

"Satan!" Iris finally freed herself and climbed to her feet. "You're scaring her."

He whirled around, clutched Iris's shoulders, and yanked her close. "What is this about?"

"Hey! Let go of her." Justine grabbed Satan's arm, and she was instantly repelled backward and slammed into Derek.

"You all right?" He peeled her off his chest and set her upright again.

"I've always wanted to be flung across the hall by an unseen force emanating from the leader of hell, so yes, I'm great." She took a moment to regain her balance. "We need to save my mom."

"He's too in love with her to hurt her." Derek nodded at the bickering couple.

Satan's hands were on her mother's shoulders, but Justine could tell his grip was gentle, even as he was arguing with Iris in low, frantic tones and the smoke coming out of his head continued to thicken. Iris was trying to get him to shut up by covering his mouth with her hands, but she didn't appear to be having any success.

"Does she know?" Satan shrieked. "You must tell me!"

"She has no idea," Iris said. "And stop yelling!"

Satan screamed suddenly, a horrible noise of anguish and pain and devastating loneliness that had Justine and Derek collapsing to the floor, crushing their hands to their ears to drown out the horrific noise. Pain blistered her eardrums and she screamed.

Then he vanished in a puff of gold bubbles and Justine nearly cried with relief as the pain vanished. Beside her, Derek groaned.

Iris stomped out the carpet fire. "Sometimes his temper tantrums are so annoying."

Her ears were ringing but she could still hear her mom. She glanced at Derek, and he nodded he was all right. "That was a temper tantrum?"

"Yes. Don't worry, you get used to them. Hardly bothers me at all anymore."

Justine tugged at her earlobes to shake off the residual ringing. "What does he do when he's really mad?"

"The Chamber of Unspeakable Horrors. Come on in. We need to talk."

Justine staggered to her feet as Derek rose next to her. "The Chamber? He did that?"

"Yes, and the Council bought it from him to use for their administration of justice." She flicked on the overhead light and moved Satan's tuxedo jacket off the bed. "Satan meant it as a joke, but they actually use it. Makes you wonder whether hell is the bad place, doesn't it?"

"Um, no, not really." Justine followed her mom into the room, and Derek lifted the door off the bed and leaned it into the frame. "What's Satan pissed about?"

"Sit."

Justine chose the bed, and Derek sat next to her. Iris stood in front of them, shifting her weight back and forth, fiddling with her rings, not meeting Justine's gaze. "I'm telling you this only because if I don't, he will."

"Telling me what?" Her mom's agitation was making her nervous. "What's wrong?"

The room shook suddenly and Satan exploded through the wall. He was carrying a five-foot-high teddy bear and a box of condoms. He thrust them at Justine. "For you."

"Thanks. I think?" She looked at Derek, who took the box of condoms.

"I'll carry these," he said.

"Sweetie?" Iris cleared her throat. "You know the man I had an affair with before you were born?"

"The one you won't talk about?" She tried to move the teddy bear to the side so she could see her mother, but Satan moved it back so it sat on her lap.

"For you," he repeated.

"Okay." At least there wasn't smoke coming out of his head anymore and his eyes had returned to ordinary black.

"Justine, meet your dad. Satan, this is your daughter." She sighed heavily. "Enjoy."

"What?" Justine jumped to her feet, leapt backward, tripped on the bed, and landed sprawled on her back.

"Fruit of my loins! Do not despair! I will rescue you!"

She rolled to the side just as Satan landed where she had been. "Derek?"

"Got ya." He pulled her to her feet and put himself between her and the ruler of the hell, who was puckering his lips and making kissy noises at her. "Back off, old man," Derek said evenly.

Justine set her hand on Derek's back as he shielded her, unable to suppress the surge of warmth toward him for stepping in. When was the last time anyone had protected her from anything? She didn't usually need it, but right now? Derek glanced over his shoulder at her, and she smiled at him.

He nodded, then turned back when Satan pointed a finger at Derek's chest. The finger was glowing red. "No man touches my daughter without my permission. Unhand her, you mortal oaf!"

"Satan! Down!" Iris grabbed his arm and shoved him onto the bed. "Stay!"

He bounced up and down on the gold-flecked comforter, his face beaming. "I cannot believe we share offspring. This is too wonderful. You cannot reject the father of your beloved daughter. We shall bond and be together for all eternity."

Justine's mind was spinning. And if her father really

was Satan, then maybe her head actually was spinning too. "Mom?"

Iris sighed again. "You know that dark side I mentioned the other day? Well, it's Satan's genes. It's a bit of a burden to overcome, I'm afraid."

"I'm half Satan? Is that what you're saying? I'm *half Satan*?" Oh, God. It had been hard enough to avoid the Chamber when her only baggage was letting Derek live when he shouldn't. Once she was known to be Satan's daughter, what chance did she have?

"Why did you keep this fertility accomplishment from me?" Satan demanded. "I was unable to provide birth control for my daughter's first sexual encounter. How will I ever recover? She is destined to be the best female lover in the Afterlife and I have not been present to give her advice on the matter! How do you forgive yourself?"

"That explains the sex at your place," Derek said under his breath. "I thought it was awfully good."

She elbowed him. "That was me, not my dark side."

"Well, then channel your dark side and kill me that way when you decide it's time for me to go. I'll die with a smile on my face."

"The reason I didn't tell you," Iris said to Satan, "was because you seduced me and then disappeared for twenty-four years. By the time you came back, Justine was a young woman and all you wanted was Mona. You didn't deserve Justine."

Satan held his hands to his heart and fell back on the bed. "You wound me with your words. If I had known my sexual potency had resulted in an offspring I did not have to spit upon, I would not have lied to you, convinced you to give me Mona at the expense of your eternal soul, and driven you to the point at which death was your only escape from my charms and the bonds of your Oath. See? It is your fault, but I will forgive you because I love your breasts and respect your intelligence."

"Excuse me?" Justine held up her hand. "Is that what happened that night you died? You were going to give him Mona?"

"Yes." Iris leaned against the ornately carved dresser with a sigh of resignation. "When he came back the second time, he confessed he was Satan and that he wanted the Goblet. I was so in love with him I didn't care. I was handing Mona over to him when I realized what I was doing. I was under his spell and I couldn't stop myself, so I chose death instead."

"Wow." Justine looked at Satan, who was still sprawled on the bed. "You really are an asshole."

He propped himself up on his elbows and beamed at her. "That I am. You are proud of your papa, are you not? Satan is the only one dastardly enough to trick a Guardian."

"One of two," Justine corrected.

Satan stood up so quickly, she didn't even see him move. One second he was on his back, the next, he was vertical. It made her fingers twitch for her gun, just in case he decided he wasn't entirely pleased to find out he had a daughter. "Who else has tricked a Guardian?" he demanded.

"Carl LaValle. I gave him three drinks of Mona and designated him my successor before I realized he only wanted Mona. He came to kill me and steal her." She eyed her mom. "I chose *his* death though, not mine."

"Well, you didn't love your betrayer," Iris said. "I did." Her gaze flicked toward Derek. "I fear the past may repeat itself."

Derek said nothing, but his eyes narrowed and he glanced at Justine.

What did that mean?

"You admit your love! I am helpless with bliss over your declaration!" Satan dropped to the carpet in front of Iris and laid his lips on the tips of her designer heels. "And your love still burns in you like the orgasm that would never end."

Iris tapped him in the chin with her toe. "Explain to Justine what happened to Carl, you thieving son of a bitch."

He jumped to his feet and kissed her hard. "See? You would not call me such pet names if you did not love me back." He smiled at Justine, who was still standing near the bed with Derek. "We will be a big happy family. I have large house with many amenities."

"Carl." Iris's voice was stern.

Satan nodded. "Of course. I shall reveal all."

"Good boy." Iris patted his head, and Derek coughed again.

"He's whipped," Derek whispered. "I think the balance of power has shifted over the last few centuries. You have nothing to worry about with your mom."

"Said by a man who doesn't have Satan sniffing at his mother's knees." But he did have a point. "Think we could figure out a way to use it to our advantage?"

"Probably."

Satan knelt in front of Justine and took her hand in his, then pressed his lips to the back of it. "My darling, Satan Jr. made deal with Carl. He was terrible artist, but Satan Jr. promised him wealth and fame if he steal the Goblet and kill you. Like all other mortals, his greed was strong and he took the bargain." He puffed out his chest and gazed up at her. "But even then, I must have sensed our familial bond because I interfered to save you."

Iris snorted, but Satan ignored her. "I offered Carl a better deal to confuse him, and it caused him to go after you in blatant way that gave you time to behead him. Then I banished Satan Jr. from Afterlife." He frowned. "But it appears he managed to issue the Curse. He was quite displeased with Carl's failure." He leapt to his feet and pummeled Derek on the back. "You are cursed by my bastard offspring who tries to steal my kingdom. It is bad. I feel your shame. 'Tis ugly to be marked by such a man." He held out his finger and it glowed red. A spark shot out the end of it. "If shame is too great, I kill you, yes?"

"No, thanks. Appreciate the offer, however." Derek shot an undecipherable look at Justine, but she was too stunned to worry about what it meant.

"Carl made a deal with Satan Jr.? But I thought he was my friend, a friend who got too greedy." She pressed her fingers to her temples. "How could I have been such an idiot as to trust him?" She felt Derek's hand on her shoulder. Derek had been honest with her. So what if he had to kill her? At least he admitted it and didn't deceive her. She patted his hand and smiled at him.

Satan waved his finger at her. "First lesson, offspring, no friends. You end up having to kill them all. I think we should name you Satanette. No Satan Jr. I spit upon the name. Satanette would never steal my kingdom from me. For that, you become my heir. Most pleasing situation, no?"

Ack. "No thanks. I don't think running hell is quite my style." Satan looked so devastated, she had to look away.

Derek cleared his throat. "Can we table the parental lectures? We need to find Satan Jr. within the next forty-eight hours, or Justine gets to go into the Chamber you created."

"Or you die," she added.

Satan brightened. "That Chamber is lots of fun. You'll enjoy it."

"Satan!" Derek snapped. "Where is Satan Jr.?"

"Happily, I do not know. But he has probably made a deal with someone you know, like he did with Carl. That person can lead you to him. I will be very pleased to have him die. Good luck." He stood up. "I must have sex with the mother of my child now. If you survive the Chamber, Satanette, you will have to come visit hell. It is very luxurious."

Iris grabbed her purse and tucked it under her arm. "Sorry, Satan. But all this reminiscing has reminded me of exactly what a self-serving jerk you are. You don't deserve me, and you certainly don't deserve my daughter." She clasped Justine's arm. "Come on, sweetie. We're leaving."

She let her mom lead her out as Satan fell to the floor begging for mercy and crying for Satanette and his true love. Derek shot him a sympathetic look, then reset the door behind them. Separating them from her . . . father?

Oy. She was going to need some therapy to deal with that one.

And then the even more brilliant news. Satan Jr. was using someone else to betray her? Great. Just great. When she found him, she was going to kick his ass . . .

Wait a sec. Lightbulb moment.

If Satan was her dad, that meant Satan Jr. was her half brother, which meant she was supposed to kill her disinherited half brother? And then kill her dad, to protect her mom and prove her loyalty wasn't to her dark side?

Choose between Mona's safety or the lives of her black-blooded relatives?

Smelled like a Qualifying Incident to her.

No problem. All she had to do was find out which of her friends had signed a pact with Satan Jr., use them to find Satan Jr., get him to undo the Curse and render him unable to ever be a threat to Mona again without actually killing him, emasculate Satan so he couldn't use sex to lure her mom to hell, and find a way to avoid the Chamber of Unspeakable Horrors. Oh, and kill Derek.

All this was supposed to be accomplished in two days before the Judgment? No problem.

She stole a sideways glance at the man who was trying to convince Satan he was trustworthy enough to be allowed to leave with Satan's daughter. The leader of the Underworld hadn't had any difficultly getting through the broken door and now had Derek in a headlock. Then Derek broke Satan's hold, flipped the leader of hell on his back and then ground his knee into Satan's chest. Satan crowed with delight, pumped Derek's hand, and invited him to move to hell and work for him.

As she watched Derek help Satan to his feet, she realized Derek would trade a great deal to save himself and his progeny.

Would he make a deal with Satan Jr.?

Maybe.

Twenty

After sending Iris off to purgatory, Derek and Justine grabbed a cab to head back to his place. As soon as they got in, an awkward silence settled around them. Derek watched Justine as she picked at a torn piece of vinyl on the backseat and stared out the window, her forehead furrowed in thought.

"So. Satan's your dad." The words sounded strange rolling off his tongue. Sort of put into perspective the few times he'd had to meet the parents of women he'd been involved with. Little had he known how bad it could be.

The piece of vinyl tore off in her hand and she clenched her fist around it. "Apparently. Though I haven't decided whether to acknowledge him or not."

"Can you do that?" He frowned at the tension in her face.

She shrugged and let head flop back against the seat. "I don't know. Hopefully."

He opened her fist and extracted the vinyl. "I don't think I'll ask you to marry me anymore. Talk about a father-in-law from hell."

She glanced at him. "It's not funny."

"No, but given the other things on our list, the fact that your dad is the ruler of hell isn't that big of a concern." The mere fact he could make that last statement indicated just how much trouble they were in. "So your dad has a rap sheet? Big deal. If we don't find your half brother and break the Curse, either you'll be in the Chamber for all eternity, or I'll be dead and all the men in my family will continue to die." He dropped the vinyl on her lap. "That, my dear, is a big deal."

"Good point." She sighed and absently traced her fingers over his leg. "So, any more ideas on how to find my half brother?"

"Maybe we can leverage your paternity into working for us?"

She pursed her lips as she considered his question. "Well, since Satan Jr. wants Mona so his dad will acknowledge him, maybe if we got Satan to declare him heir, he'd back off and drop the Curse."

"Satan already gave that honor to you."

"Yes, but in a moment of brilliant foresight, I didn't accept, did I?" She gave a rueful smile. "Did you see how bummed out he was? I actually felt bad for a minute."

He hooked his thumb under one of her fingers and caressed it while he considered her comment. "So, you'll make a deal with Satan? You'll accept your inheritance if he'll give half of it to Satan Jr.?"

She scowled. "I really don't want to be heir to hell. I'd probably have to start torturing people and stuff like that. Killing in the name of Mona is one thing, but I really don't think I have the stomach to survive an eternity of poking skewers into people's eyes."

"Yeah, I can see that. That might not be much of an improvement over the Chamber." He slid his arm around her waist and rested his chin on her head. There had to be something else he wasn't thinking of. He needed more information. "Okay, so explain this to me. How come Satan and Satan Jr. can't help themselves to the Goblet? They both seem to know where it is."

She played with the hair on his forearm. "Mona has a built-in protection against Satan, and apparently his off-spring. They can't touch her. The Guardian has to hand Mona over to them of her own free will, though being threatened with death counts as free will. The Guardian is expected to choose death, like my mom did."

He idly rubbed her back as he considered that. "So, after your mom killed herself to save Mona, Satan was standing there in the presence of an unguarded Goblet and he couldn't touch it?"

"Yep." She snuggled deeper against him, relaxed but ready to react to any threat.

Her hair smelled like strawberries. So innocent for such a badass. He smiled and nuzzled her hair. "That must have been a serious blow to his delusions of grandeur. Total impotence."

"Hence the sex rampage and Satan Jr., I guess."

"So how come you can touch Mona if Satan Jr. can't? You're half Satan."

She shrugged. "I would guess I didn't inherit Satan's true evilness. Mona is in no danger from me, and she knows it. Satan Jr. inherited the gold aura thing, I didn't. Hopefully, I managed to bypass most of those truly Satan-esque attributes."

He nodded. "Makes sense. If you were really evil, your mom would already be in hell, huh?"

"Probably." She hesitated, then pulled away so she could see his face. "Can I ask you something?"

"Sure. What's up?" He caught a whiff of cedar smoke

when he released her. Was that her Satan genes? He liked it: cedar smoke and strawberries. It fit.

She furrowed her brow. "When Satan said that Satan Jr. had probably made a deal with someone in my life, someone who would want something Satan Jr. could provide . . . You fit the bill." She sat back, scrutinizing his face.

He gave a small smile even as a tinge of regret tightened in his chest. He'd wondered when she'd make that connection. "You think I'm betraying you to Satan Jr.?"

Her eyes narrowed and she deepened her examination of his face. "Well, you'd be the perfect candidate."

"True." He twirled her hair around one finger. "It would probably work, don't you think? Not a bad idea."

She knocked his hand away. "Cut it out. I'm serious. Did you do it?"

"Do you think I did?"

She lifted a brow. "You didn't answer the question."

Disappointment made his shoulders sag. "Neither did you." No statement of trust from her. "But no, it's not me, and if you ask me to swear it, I'm walking away."

But she smiled and he felt her relax. "I knew it."

The constriction in his chest dissipated at the conviction in her tone. "They why'd you ask?"

"If you'd just found out you were half Satan, wouldn't you start to doubt your own instincts? Wonder if you really had a clear grasp on evil? I mean, for all I know, you could have been a mass murderer, and my half-Satan gut instinct would have thought that made you a perfect candidate for a husband."

The last of the tension vanished from his body, replaced with a heady energy that had him wanting to jump out of a cab and run the last few blocks to his condo to shake it off. "Excellent point. I only murder people on Sundays after church, so you can go ahead with your plans to marry me."

"Great. One less thing to worry about then." She lifted her brow. "So what next?"

"Aside from planning our wedding?"

"Uh-huh."

"My place. We'll check on Mona, get some food, regroup. Figure out who Satan Jr. has working for him, then somehow leverage that into a viable plan of action."

"It's a little vague, but I'll keep thinking." She snuggled against him and tucked her head under his chin. He rested his cheek on her head and spun the information through his mind, trying to work out who might be Satan's accomplice. They *had* to find out who it was and find Satan Jr., because if they failed, one of them was going to die, and he wasn't sure any longer who he wanted it to be.

They walked into Derek's apartment to find his brother and Wendy pinned in the corner of the kitchen by a fire-breathing dragon who had turned the muted beige tones of the room into fashionable charcoal.

Justine stopped, her hand going for her gun.

Derek nodded at Quincy, huddled behind the chairs. "Hey, Quin. How's it going?"

"There's a dragon in your kitchen!" Quincy was pale and wielding a wooden spoon like it was a sharp knife.

Derek tossed his house keys on the kitchen counter. "Dragons don't exist, Quin. Are you all right? You seem a bit tense. A beer maybe?" He hummed to himself as he grabbed a beer and tossed it at his brother.

It hit the wall next to Quin's head and landed with a thud on the floor, rolling to a stop by Theresa's clawed feet.

"You need to work on your reflexes, bro." He selected a beer for himself and bottled water for Justine, who was in the doorway pointing her gun at Quincy.

"Don't kill them just yet." He pushed the barrel toward the floor and handed her the water. "I think we both need a drink."

She accepted it. "I can't make any promises about their safety."

"You can always shoot them later." He moved in front of her to block her line to his brother, whistling cheerfully. Somehow, he suspected Quin wouldn't be able to continue with his threats to have Derek committed anymore.

Wendy waved at him. "Can you call off the dragon?"

"I think you should be more concerned about Justine." Her gun was against her thigh, but she was studying his guests intently, no doubt engaging in full recon before taking action. He turned to Theresa. "Are you going to kill them?"

"I'll burn them up if you'd like me to," Theresa said. "Justine gets cranky if I incinerate people without weighing all my options first. You know, police get all agitated if enough missing persons get tracked to our door."

"If you want to fry these two, go ahead." Justine waved her gun at Quin and Wendy. "I don't like them."

Derek couldn't help but glance at his brother after that remark. Quincy's mouth was hanging open and Wendy was hiding behind him.

"Really?" Theresa looked at Derek.

"Not yet." He slung his arm over Justine's shoulder. She fit perfectly under his arm, and he liked having her there. He could feel a dagger in the sheath beneath her arm, and he stroked his fingers over it.

Wendy began to rise. "I don't think Derek's going to let it hurt us."

"It?" Theresa shot a flame at Wendy that caught the ends of her hair on fire. "Since when do I look like an *it*? Just because you have breasts and shave your legs doesn't make you some sexy siren. I am way sexier and way more feminine than you and if you call me an *it* one more time, I'll—"

"Sorry." Wendy patted out the flames. "Truly sorry." She elbowed Quincy. "Get up and quit cowering." She stood up, and Derek was surprised to see that she was wearing a snug-fitting tank top and a short black miniskirt. She had the legs and body for it.

Quincy eased to his feet. "I decoded the encryption."

Derek glanced at Justine, and saw his own hope reflected on her face. "What did it say?"

Quin set his briefcase on the table, keeping an eye on Theresa. "It's a Curse by someone named Satan Jr. The encryption wasn't particularly impressive." He pulled a computer printout from his briefcase and started reading. "'I am a god. I will inherit the throne. No one shall best me, not even some worthless mortal who can't draw. I curse the worthless mortal, and all his male progeny. Death to you and yours at the same moment the Guardian kills you, until I have the Goblet in my hand and the throne beneath me. Until the Guardian's last breath is gone by your hand. Until I am acknowledged as the ultimate ruler. Yours truly, Satan Jr.'" He looked up. "Is this a joke? An attempt to make me believe there really is a Curse?"

"You're looking at a dragon, Quin. You can answer your

own question." He sat down at the table and reread Quincy's notes. "Looks like the journal was incomplete. We have to set Satan Jr. up on the throne in addition to killing Justine and stealing Mona." He thrust the notes into Justine's outstretched hand.

"You're right." She sighed with a weariness he felt in his bones. All he wanted was to collapse in a bed with Justine and fall asleep with her scent wrapped around him. "So, we find him and negotiate?"

"Any suggestions on tactics?"

She rubbed her forehead with the back of her hand and sank down onto the seat next to him. "Well, the three things he wants most are his daddy's acknowledgment, me dead for screwing up his plans, and the throne of hell. If we can get him those three things, he might lose interest in Mona. As long as we can save her, I've done my job."

"Or we could try to save you as well. Just a thought."

"I agree with Derek." Theresa slapped her tail against a cabinet, leaving a dent in the wood. "Listen to the man."

Derek rested his arm on the back of Justine's chair and kneaded her neck. "If we could hand him hell, he might be willing to forego your death."

She shot him a soft smile. "Wouldn't that be something, if we both ended up surviving?"

He met her gaze. "The odds are against it."

"I know." She touched his hand briefly. "I know."

He cleared his throat. "So, we need to find him. Any ideas?"

She sighed. "Fresh out, unfortunately."

"I can help with that." Wendy was leaning against the counter, her arms folded, her gaze shrewd.

Theresa growled. Quin patted Wendy's arm and looked

proud. Justine hooked one arm over the back of the chair and raised her eyebrow at Wendy. "And who, exactly, are you?"

"I'm going to be the next Martha Stewart—except for the prison thing." Wendy fluffed her sweater and strutted around the table. "I will be the most powerful, richest, and most influential woman in corporate America." She stroked her waist, ran her hands over her butt. "And the most beautiful and the best in the sack. Men will worship me. Women will want to be me. And Wall Street will bug my phone in hopes they can steal some nugget of my brilliance."

Ah. Derek and Justine exchanged looks, then she thinned her lips and nodded at Wendy. "So, you're the one who made the deal with Satan Jr.?"

"World domination in exchange for handing over the Goblet and the Guardian, courtesy of the LaValle brothers and their unfailing quest to locate you." Wendy sauntered around the kitchen and sneered at Theresa. "You are nothing in comparison to me. You see how Quincy fell for me? He's just an example of how the world will be my playground."

Quincy frowned. "I was . . . practice?"

Wendy chucked him under the chin and Quincy's eyes narrowed. "I had to get close to you in order to keep tabs on the LaValle men, so Satan Jr. enhanced my sex appeal to snare you." She stopped by the refrigerator, set her hands on her hips, spread her feet, and surveyed the room. "As soon as I deliver all of you to him, he will kill you, and I'll control corporate America. It's time for a woman to be at the top of all the lists, don't you think?"

A stream of flames shot past Wendy's head and set the paper towels on fire. "You're an idiot," Theresa snarled.

Justine jumped up and knocked the flaming paper towels into the sink. "Did you send the Penhas after us?"

"All I did was report my findings to Satan Jr. He did the rest, though he did call off the Penhas when you killed so many of them. Something about pissing off the wrong person. So, technically, I've committed no crime." Wendy gave the room a haughty look. "I know what I'm doing. If he gets caught, I'm clean."

"Yes, so clean," Theresa growled. "Like a public sewer."

"You used me?" Quincy asked.

Wendy ignored them both, thrusting her breasts in Derek's direction. "So? You ready to die?"

"No, but we'd like to talk to Satan Jr." Derek watched as Justine moved behind Wendy and pulled out her gun. She motioned for him to continue. "Can you set up a meeting? Tonight?"

"Of course." At Wendy's reply, Justine lowered her gun and nodded with satisfaction. "He'll enjoy having the chance to kill all of you personally." Wendy glanced over her shoulder, moving to the side when she realized Justine was behind her with a gun. "He's staying in town. Shall we head over now?"

"Works for me." Justine gave Wendy an innocent smile and holstered her gun. "Derek?"

"I'm in."

Theresa's tail switched. "Do you think we should torture her first to make sure we can trust her?"

Wendy paled and moved next to Quincy, who immediately walked to the other side of the kitchen. Derek nodded at his brother, and Quin scowled back.

"She's already admitted she's taking us over there so he can kill us," Justine said. "What else would she be hiding?"

"I don't know." Theresa's tail switched again and slammed into Wendy's legs, knocking her to the ground. "Oops. Sorry." Her gold eyes glittered as Wendy dusted herself off. "I'll stay here and guard Mona."

"The Goblet has to come with us, now." Wendy shot Theresa a hostile glare. Theresa flicked her tail and then laughed when Wendy jumped and ran to the other side of the room.

Derek nodded. "Wendy's right. We need to bring Mona so we have leverage for our negotiation."

"Derek? I don't think that's a good idea," Justine said.

"It's the only option. Satan Jr.'s not a fool, right?" He slid a glance toward Justine as he opened the door to his china cabinet. "I mean, he recruited Wendy, after all." He selected his most expensive wineglass, hiding his smile from the preening Wendy.

The goblet had been part of a set of four, but the other three had exploded and killed his uncle in a "freak accident," according to his family. He held it up and Wendy's eyes widened. Justine nodded and Theresa gave him a thumbs-up.

"It's beautiful," Wendy sighed. "I can't believe it's still intact after all these years."

"Immortality works on crystal the same as on humans," Derek said. "Let's go."

"Right." Wendy's face was flushed with excitement and there were beads of sweat on her forehead as she practically skipped toward the door. "Satan Jr. won't believe it when I show up with all of you and the Goblet. I'm so awesome."

Derek reached the door first and pulled it open. In the doorway stood a large black man with a shaved head. His jaw was jutting out, his arms were folded across his chest, and his brow was furrowed in anger.

"She's the betrayer." Xavier pointed a finger at Wendy. "She's the one who forced me to turn Derek into an assassin. She's the threat to the Guardian, and I will not fail at my job." Then he pulled a gun out of the back of his black jeans. Justine shouted and lunged for his arm, but Derek was closer and slammed into Xavier's shoulder a split second after a shot rang out.

Quincy hollered a warning and dove behind the couch as Wendy dropped to the floor, turned gold, and then shimmered out of sight. Derek and Xavier smashed into the wall and ricocheted onto the floor, and Theresa cheered and lit a set of curtains on fire.

"Did you see that gold thing? She is so going to hell," Theresa said. "Satan's going to kick her butt for helping out his son."

Justine stomped over to Derek and Xavier and glared down at them. "Nice work, Xavier."

The doorman nodded, oblivious to her sarcasm. "You're welcome, Justine. Always glad to help." He kicked Derek off him. "Derek, I think you need to go—"

"Shut up!" Derek and Justine shouted at the same time.

"He's on our side," Justine added. "Don't you dare send him off into a deep sleep right now."

"But he tried to stop me." The big man tucked his gun out of sight as Derek rolled to his feet.

"I don't suppose you know where we can find Satan Jr., do you?" Derek asked.

Xavier frowned. "Who?"

Yeah, as he thought. Their one link to Satan Jr.'s whereabouts was now dead.

"You guys are totally screwed," Theresa said. "And I don't mean that in the naked, sweaty way that leaves you writhing with pleasure and begging for more."

Justine flopped down on the couch and pulled a pillow over her head. "This sucks."

"Anyone want a pretzel?" Theresa asked. "With all this doom and gloom, I'm jonesin' for some comfort food."

All hands went up.

Twenty-one

Twenty minutes later, they had practically cleaned out the freezer of pretzels, Xavier had confessed to being appointed by Iris to protect the girls, and Quincy was in shock.

And Satan Jr. was still at large.

Derek and Justine each had their laptops out and were searching the Internet, but it wasn't that easy to find a listing of Satan Jr.'s favorite hangouts or residences.

All of their combined ass-kicking skills and they weren't even going to be able to use them. She slammed her computer shut and shoved back from the table, her fists bunching in aggravation. She turned to Xavier. "Are you *certain* you have no idea what Satan Jr. looks like?"

Xavier shook his head. "As I already explained, I was talking to Wendy when I felt a cool draft over my back. The next thing I knew, everything I saw had a gold tinge to it."

"Probably the effect of being under Satan Jr.'s influence," Derek said.

Xavier shrugged. "All I know is that I had a sword in my hand and I was on my way upstairs to kill Justine. But when Derek showed up, I told him to do it instead. I thought maybe I could force myself to stop him, or that he'd be too strong for me to compel, but he wasn't." He looked at Derek in disgust. "You let me down, and then nearly got me run over by a city bus."

Derek didn't seem ruffled. "She's still alive, isn't she? I'd say I did all right."

Xavier grunted.

Justine stood up and walked over to Xavier, who was sitting on the couch with his feet up, eating pretzels with Theresa. "Xavier, I appreciate your trusting Derek not to kill me, but we really need to find Satan Jr. Did you see Wendy arrive or leave?"

"She took a cab."

"Alone?"

Xavier shrugged. "Honestly, I was watching her legs, not who was with her."

"She must have loved that," Derek said.

"I can't believe I fell for a woman who was possessed by the devil's spawn." Quincy was lying on his back on the floor, staring at the ceiling. "I'm such an idiot."

"Hey!" Justine said. "Satan isn't the devil, 'spawn' is a little harsh, and she was in cahoots, not 'possessed.'" Derek raised a brow at her, and she shrugged. "They're my family."

"Back off, devil girl," Quincy said. "I am now seriously considering the viability of Derek's theory that I'm going to die in two days. My world has been shattered and I appreciate being allowed to piss and moan a bit, if you don't mind."

Derek thumped the table in victory. "Do you have any idea how good this feels to have you believe me after years of being told I was crazy?"

"Well, I feel like shit, so back off."

Derek grinned at Justine. "He's a math professor. They get moody when they learn the world isn't all about logic and mathematical theories. He'll be fine."

"If you say so." Justine yawned and glanced at her watch as she weaved back to the table. Almost two in the morning. Less than forty-eight hours until Derek would die from the Curse, and they were wasting time talking about his brother. "I need caffeine." Lots of it. Too bad Mona was still massage oil. She was the best espresso around.

Theresa marched over to the table and set her laptop in front of Justine. "And you think I've been wasting my time with cybersex. Read it."

She leaned forward. " 'T, I can't believe you're locked away in an FBI cell. I want to meet you, bask in your smile while I hold your hand . . .' "

"Skip to the end," Theresa interrupted.

"Fine." She did as directed. " 'And if you still want to find Satan Jr., I've attached the Yahoo! driving directions to his place in Connecticut.' " Elation whooshed through her. "Are you kidding? Zeke found his place?" She double-clicked on the attachment, her heart pounding with anticipation.

"He's a genius," Theresa said.

"Apparently." Justine leaned forward to read the attachment, and felt Derek lean over her shoulder, his chest brushing against her back. She caught his woodsy scent and smiled.

Derek set his hand on her shoulder, in the crook of her neck as he read. It was automatic, instinctive, and it made something in her belly tighten. "That's about an hour and forty minutes outside the city," he said. "We can make it there before four."

Normally, getting Derek alone for two hours in the middle of the night would make her mouth water. Now? It was a little overshadowed by the fact they'd be on their way to track down an insane bastard son of Satan in hopes of averting a very nasty fate.

"You look like you haven't slept in days," Xavier observed from the couch.

"We haven't," Derek said. "Not really."

"You'll be a liability behind the wheel. I'll drive," Xavier said.

Good call. It would be a shame to be only a few miles from Satan Jr.'s house only to preempt the Curse with a fatal car accident due to one of them taking a nap while they were supposed to be driving.

"You guys should take this opportunity to catch some sleep," Xavier said from the front seat. "I'll wake you up if anything interesting or unusually dangerous occurs."

Justine was so tired she barely managed a nod. Derek grunted something, then Xavier raised the privacy panel.

And they were alone.

Completely and utterly alone.

Too bad she was too exhausted and strung out for sex. All she wanted was to sleep. She was sitting sideways on the seat, her feet tucked up under her, an arsenal of weapons on her lap. The fake goblet was in a box between her feet, waiting. Not exactly prime snoozing position.

"Come here." Derek held out his arm. "We both need some rest."

The offer was too tempting to turn down. She shoveled all the weapons onto the floor, then scooted next to him. When he lifted her into his lap and curled her legs under her, she didn't argue. Too tired, and his warmth felt too good against her.

She sighed and rested her head against his chest. His

fingers were drifting through her hair, while his other arm held her against his body. A cozy, intimate moment that could be so romantic if they were different people, in different circumstances, on a different mission.

"This could be it," he said. "In a couple hours, the Curse could be lifted."

She closed her eyes and nestled her face against the curve of his neck, letting the soft touch of his fingers in her hair relax her body. "Or the house could be empty."

"Or he could kill us with fireballs the minute we step out of the car."

She shook her head. "He won't kill us until I hand him the Goblet."

"And if you don't? He'll kill you eventually. And then you go to the Chamber." His fingers trailed down the side of her neck, and she shivered. "Unless you kill me first."

She pressed her finger to his lips. "Can we not talk about that?"

He lifted an eyebrow. "Is the Guardian getting squeamish?"

"No." She wasn't, was she? Nothing had changed: She was going to prove she was a worthy Guardian, save Mona, and wind up having her own chapter in the next edition of the *Treatise*. And life was going to be grand. Rah. Rah. Rah.

This is what she'd wanted. A chance to prove herself. A little bit of interest in her life. So what was wrong with her? Why wasn't she fired up? She had plenty of people to kill, to save, and to hate. Life was good.

She felt his warm sigh against her neck, and she shivered. "What about you? Are you still going to kill me?"

"It's you or my brother."

She lifted her head and looked at him, but his face was in shadow. "That's not an answer."

"I know." He caught her face between his hands and fastened his gaze on her just as they went under a street-light. The utter regret and pain in his eyes nearly broke her resolve right there.

Oh, God. She could love this man. Under other circumstances. She'd never be foolish enough to fall for a man who stood between her and the Chamber of Unspeakable Horrors. Never.

He dropped his head slightly, until his lips were almost on hers.

"Don't," she whispered.

"I can't help it." The words had barely slipped out before his lips touched hers. It wasn't a wild, sexual kiss of someone looking for loophole sex. It was the kiss of someone whose soul might be her perfect match.

She pressed her hand against his chest to push him back, but instead, her fingers curved into the fabric and she let her lips part under his. *Yes.*

Then a loud beep made her jump back. "What was that?" Her chastity belt alarm going off? Lord knew she needed one, apparently.

"Xavier." He kissed her quickly. "Don't go anywhere."

Better plan: Run away as fast as I can.

He reached around her and pressed a button while she pressed her hand to her forehead and tried to regroup. "What's going on, Xavier?"

"There's a man standing in the middle of the road up ahead and he appears to be aiming a flamethrower at the car. Shall I mow him down?"

Justine frowned. "What does he look like?"

"He's wearing a gold Elvis jumpsuit."

She met Derek's gaze. "Satan Jr.?"

"Gold jumpsuit, mechanically assisted fire-throwing? Sounds like a Satan wannabe if I've ever heard of one."

"Let's go deal with him, then." She scrambled off his lap, saved from herself by the psychotic son of the leader of hell.

"I agree." He hit the intercom button again. "It's probably Satan Jr. Stop the car." He let go of the button and caught her arm as she leaned down to retrieve her weapons from the floor. "We're going to have to deal with this, Justine."

She bit her lower lip. "By 'this,' you mean how are we going to approach Satan Jr.?"

He shook his head. "I mean *us*. It's getting complicated and—"

"No. I can't allow that to happen." She pulled out of his grasp and started gathering her arsenal. "This is about business, Derek. We can't forget it. Ever."

"When it's over, we're going to talk."

"Fine. When this is all over. If you're still alive, we'll talk." She shoved the last dagger in her ankle sheath. "You ready?"

He picked up his gun and opened the door. "I've been waiting for this moment my whole life."

Twenty-two

Derek stepped out of the car first, Justine on his heels. The car was stopped next to an alley replete with trash, Dumpsters, and the odor of rotting food and public bathrooms.

Xavier had his window down. "You want help?"

"You play backup," Derek said. "If things are going badly, get Justine out of here."

She shook her head. "No way. I'm the Guardian. This is my battle."

"I'm the one who's Cursed. It's *my* battle. I'm not going to let you get killed—"

"Helloooo? I have a flamethrower. I suggest you throw yourself at my feet and beg for mercy before I incinerate you." A flame shot over their heads. "I'm *very* dangerous."

They spun around to face their assailant, who was standing in the middle of the road, just past the entrance to the alley.

He was over six feet tall, with wavy blond hair, blue eyes and . . . eyeliner? His skintight gold jumpsuit accentuated his dark tan. Thick muscles in his shoulders and chest suggested he spent his share of time in the gym, and his quads looked like they would split the seams of his leggings if he moved.

"So, you're Satan Jr.?" she asked.

Perfectly coiffed white-blond eyebrows went up. "You've heard of me? Have you been to my Web site and seen my list of accomplishments?"

"Actually, your dad told us about you."

"Liar!" He shot a bolt of flame at them, and they barely got out of the way. There was a loud whoosh behind them and she turned around in time to see the contents of a Dumpster erupt in a tower of conflagration. What was *with* all these flamethrowing people in her life these days? Derek was the only one who didn't need a fire extinguisher hanging around his neck.

"My father doesn't speak of me!" Satan Jr. bellowed. "You lie!"

"Excellent plan to bring up daddy," Derek whispered.

"You have a better one?"

"Maybe." Derek took a step forward and raised his voice. "I've met Satan and he isn't nearly the man you are."

"Damn right he isn't. Have you seen what he's done with hell? Total disgrace. He needs an infusion of modern thinking." He kept the gun aimed at them, but he didn't pull the trigger. "So, you're the Guardian. About time I got to see what you looked like." He gave her a thoroughly male appraisal that made her want to kick him in the shin.

Instead, she folded her arms over her chest. "You stopped us on purpose? You knew we were the ones in the car?"

He rolled his eyes. "You killed Wendy. I don't have time to make another deal, and to be honest, I'm tired of you screwing up my partnerships."

Derek frowned. "But how did you know where we were?"

"I have a tracking device on all LaValle men. I've spent two hundred years waiting for one of you to find the Goblet, since I haven't had any success finding the blasted thing. It's about time you found it." He aimed the tip of the flamethrower toward Justine. "I'm tired of playing games. Hand over the Goblet."

She pointed her gun at him. "You know I can't."

"Of course you can." His gaze dropped to her chest and then returned to her face. "Hand it over, and then when you end up in hell after I kill you, I'll make you my love slave. Put you up in a nice house and all that stuff. It'd be a great deal for you."

Justine's belly roiled in disgust. "I appreciate the offer, but I already have my own plans for ensuring an eternity that doesn't suck."

Satan Jr.'s gaze flicked toward Derek. "Him? That worthless mortal?"

Derek breath was hot on her ear. "I'm in your plans?"

"He's not really mortal anymore," she told Satan Jr. as she glared at Derek to be quiet.

"*What?* He drank from Desdemona's Temptation?" At Justine's nod, he screeched and sent a burst of flame over their heads. "Everyone gets to drink from that Goblet except me."

"Your dad didn't," Derek pointed out.

Satan Jr. looked thoughtful. "True." He aimed the gun at Justine's chest. "Hand it over."

"I can't," she said again. "You know that."

The gun pointed toward Derek. "You can. If you kill her and give it to me, and then help me take over the throne by tomorrow, I'll release the LaValles from the Curse."

Her gut tensed and she tightened her grip on her gun, unable to look at Derek. It was everything he wanted. How could he turn it down?

"I'm not really the bloodthirsty type," Derek said. "I was hoping for a deal."

Relief, heat, and something else flooded her body and her gun dropped to her side. Her gaze blurred for a second, and she blinked several times to clear her vision.

"I like deals. What kind of deal?" Satan Jr. asked.

"Undo the Curse, and I'll get your dad to make you heir to the throne of hell. Isn't that your end goal?"

Satan Jr. narrowed his eyes. "Why should I believe you? What leverage do you have with him?"

Justine thought of her mom. "We have access to something he wants more than the Goblet."

"You lie. There's nothing he wants more." But he looked interested, and the nose of the flamethrower dipped about an inch.

"You think Carl betrayed you on his own? Satan interfered because he craved something more than the Goblet," Derek said.

"What? He interfered? Son of a bitch!" Satan Jr. hurled the flamethrower to the asphalt. "He refuses to acknowledge me, then the minute I start to make a success of myself, he interferes!" He stomped around on the street, kicked a fire hydrant, then added a howl of agony to his litany of complaints. He grabbed his flamethrower and tried to set the hydrant on fire. "Argh!" He finally whirled around and shot a tree, which obligingly went up in a small conflagration. He pointed his weapon at Derek. "Do you know he won't even admit I'm his son?"

"He admitted it to us," Derek said. "That's how we knew about you."

"You lie."

"I swear."

Satan Jr. stared at him for a long moment then kicked at a stray newspaper that was on fire. "He's still a son of a bitch."

"Agreed," Derek said. "Do we have a deal? We get him to claim you're a great kid and you take back the Curse?"

Satan Jr. narrowed his eyes. "Deal." He fastened a hard gaze on them. "But if you publicly embarrass me by dumping a pitcher of water over my head and making me melt to the carpet in front of all the girls, I will personally kill you."

Derek lifted his eyebrows but he nodded. "No water."

"We promise." Justine raised her voice. "Mom? Can you please come here?"

Derek gave her a bland look that she suspected was masking his surprise at this latest Otherworld talent. "Your mom can hear you calling and she'll just pop on up?"

"Yep." All in all, he'd done quite an impressive job handling the events of the last few days. He would have a future in Otherworldness if he survived the Curse and her sword.

Which he wouldn't.

Sigh.

No. No sigh. She was fine with it. She had to be. It was her job. Her destiny. *Get over it.*

Derek eyed Satan Jr. "Can you do any weird stuff?"

"Lots of it. You need to read my bio." He unzipped his jumpsuit and pulled a business card from among his chest hair. "My url is on here. You can see my list of accomplishments. I've done some great work with some of the gangs in Los Angeles. Lots of death and dismemberment."

Derek took the card and flipped it over. "I see you have some of your highlights here?"

"Yep. That first one? Twenty-three dead and six injured. Three of them were even innocent bystanders, and I still got them to sell their souls to me before they died." He puffed his chest out and smacked it with his palm.

At that moment, a high-pitched ringing filled the air, and Satan Jr. whipped the flamethrower back up, turning in circles and shooting at the air, shouting that he would not be taken alive.

"Satan Jr.! Chill! It's just my mom!"

"Oh." He let the weapon drop. "I knew that."

Whatever. Iris shimmered into view. "Justine? Where are we?"

"An abandoned city street in New York at two forty-five in the morning having a negotiation with Satan Jr." She eyed her mom's negligee. "Dare I ask?"

"Trust me, I haven't seen him since I walked out." Iris sighed wistfully and stroked the black silk. "He has such nice taste, though."

"Hey, lady." Satan Jr. swaggered up to Iris. "I don't know who you're pining for, but I can make you forget him." He did an Elvis pelvis gyration, with an extra thrust at Iris. "What do you say?"

Iris took one look at him, then patted his cheek fondly. "You remind me so much of Satan."

Satan Jr. did another hip thrust that brought him closer to Iris. "You want me, don't you? I can smell your lust."

Iris immediately smacked him through the face. "Don't be obscene. You can't smell my lust."

He howled with rage, and showered her with a burst of flame. "You will not reject me! I am the heir to hell!"

The fire faded and Iris stood there, glaring at him. "You can't burn me up, you dolt. I'm only an image in this world. No wonder Satan won't acknowledge you. You'd be quite the embarrassment."

Justine waited until a fresh burst of flames faded and her mom's image emerged from the smoke again. "Mom, you're really not helping the situation."

"What situation, dear?" She eyed Satan Jr. "Shoot me again and I'll make it rain all over you."

Satan Jr. whimpered and shot a glance up at the starry sky.

"Can she do that?" Derek asked.

"Not that I know of, but given how little I apparently know about my own mom, I'm not going to claim anything for sure," Justine whispered. She raised her voice. "Mom, I need a deal. Agree to go on another date with Satan if he'll acknowledge his son."

"And make me heir," Satan Jr. said. "And tell everyone I'm great."

Iris raised her eyebrow. "You're going to barter off my body to save your own behind?"

"To save Mona."

"I'm retired," Iris said. "Mona's fate is no longer my concern. I've officially cut Satan off and I'm not allowing him back into my life."

"It still bothers you that you failed at Guardianship, doesn't it? A Guardian needs to be on duty for five hundred years to get benefits, and you didn't make it. You didn't even get to write the *Treatise*." Iris gave her a sharp look, and Justine pressed harder. "You and me, Mom. We can save Mona from Satan and Satan Jr. It's your chance for redemption."

"Hello? Anyone forget I'm here?" Satan Jr. waved the flamethrower. "Who is this woman and why is she talking about my dad like she knows him? There's only one woman Satan belongs with and that's my mom."

The three of them exchanged glances, then Derek said, "This woman is Satan's vice president of recruiting." It was better than admitting she was Satan's current crush.

Satan Jr. eyed Iris. "I'll have to fire you when I take over hell."

"Fine with me. I'll get Satan," Iris said and she dissolved.

She returned with Satan in less than a minute. Satan's hand was on its way down the front of Iris's lingerie when they appeared.

Satan Jr. howled and immediately lit his dad on fire.

Satan chuckled and zapped his son with a blaze that turned his gold jumpsuit into a ball of fire. The flames subsided after a moment, and both men were still standing. The only evidence of the flame war was Satan Jr.'s hair, which was a little charbroiled.

"Why aren't you burned to a wimpy pile of ash?" Satan demanded. "You obviously didn't inherit my supreme skill with fire, since you resort to using a flamethrower like an impotent mortal."

Satan Jr. narrowed his eyes. "Flame-retardant fabrics."

"Oh." Satan nodded. "Good thinking."

Satan Jr. blinked. Hard. "What?"

"Are you deaf?" He rolled his eyes at Iris. "The unacknowledged bastard of my loins is deaf as well as mortal. I am delighted to declare him beyond useless. Come, let us depart and invent new ways to engage in oral sex acts."

"Remember our deal," Iris said softly.

Satan Jr. gave a gleam at her mother's breasts that was too much for Justine to deal with. She tapped her dad on the shoulder. "I changed my mind. The deal you made with my mom is off. This one is with me."

He raised a brow. "What do you want?"

"Acknowledge Satan Jr. Tell him he's great and mean it. Have a birthday party for him. Set him up on some dates."

A sneer lifted one corner of his mouth. "Why should I?"

She turned to Satan Jr. "And if he does, you have to swear off Mona and drop the Curse."

He hoisted the gun up and rested it on his shoulder. "I already said I would. I want the throne though."

"Be happy with an acknowledgment and shut up. He's not abdicating." Justine walked back to Satan. "I'll acknowledge you as my father if you do this."

Satan blinked. "I don't need your acknowledgment."

"But—"

Derek stepped forward. "You can have my soul."

Satan grinned immediately. "That would be lovely. I hear you're a good warrior. I could make good use of you. Plus, Iris's daughter likes you. You could be quite the bargaining tool."

"Derek!" Justine grabbed his arm. "You can't give him your soul! That would make you his servant."

"*I* want his soul," Satan Jr. announced. "I want you to allow me to bring all the souls I've harvested into hell."

Satan swung around to face his son. "You've harvested souls?"

Satan Jr. flexed his arms and made his pectoral muscles wiggle. "Almost five hundred thousand."

"But you have no affiliation with hell."

Satan Jr. shrugged. "People don't realize that at the time."

"So you lie to them?" Satan asked.

"Of course."

He tilted his head. "And you offer them deals you can't fulfill because you do not actually represent hell?"

"Yep."

Satan inched closer to his son. "And then you trapped their souls in some empty space because you had nowhere to put them?"

"You got it."

"Huh." Satan rubbed his chin. "Do you torture them excessively and with great vigor and enthusiasm?"

Satan Jr. snorted. "Of course I do. What's the point in having them if I don't? Tortured souls are the only ones that are any good in hell."

Satan's eyes started gleaming. "And have you harvested any innocent souls that would have gone to heaven were it not for your deceitful and rude interference in their lives?"

Satan Jr. nodded. "Almost ten percent. I have to torture those the most, obviously. They'll be no good in hell if they're still clean."

Satan gave a full dimple grin and clapped Satan Jr. on the shoulder. "I had no idea you were so talented, my much-hated illegitimate cherub." He slung his arm around Satan Jr.'s shoulder and beamed at the group. "Did you hear what he did? Half a million souls with no training and nothing to barter with. I knew he was my son!"

At Satan's declaration of acknowledgment, relief rushed through Justine and she grinned at Derek. He gave her a quick nod of victory and even Iris looked pleased by the bonding.

"You tried to kill me every time we met, and then you

banished me from the Afterlife." Satan Jr. pulled away from Satan. "You've denied I'm your son since I was born."

"Of course I did!" Satan looked delighted. "It drove you to accomplish great things." He beamed at Iris. "I am the best father in the Afterlife. No wonder you had me sire your daughter." He slugged Satan Jr. on the shoulder. "You can have a job as my head harvester. How about that? It has been vacant since I killed the last one, but I bequeath this position of great honor and entitlement to you."

"But I hate you and want to destroy you and your kingdom," Satan Jr. said with a frown.

Justine's elation began to fade. "It's a great offer."

"Take it." Derek moved up behind Satan Jr. and eased the flamethrower off his shoulder.

Satan grinned. "What father would not be proud of your hostile attitude? Brilliant I am, for rejecting you for two hundred years and forcing you to become the man you are. We shall harvest souls and seduce women together!" Iris cleared her throat, and Satan blanched. "Well, you can seduce women. I will assist you."

Satan Jr. noticed Derek and yanked the flamethrower out of his reach with a scowl. "How badly do you want me?"

"You are my son! There is no degree. It is absolute."

"Then I spurn your offer and everything you stand for. I reject you as you rejected me. I will destroy your kingdom before your eyes."

Justine groaned and sat down on the bumper of Derek's car.

Satan blinked and wiped away a tear. "You are so perfect. I am bursting with pride for the fruit of my loins."

Satan Jr. turned to Justine. "You've given me the greatest gift of all, the opportunity to reject my father." He knelt before her and kissed her hand. "For that, I withdraw my quest for the Goblet."

"Really? That's awesome!" She leaned down and kissed him on the head. "Thank you so much!"

Satan Jr. bowed deeply. "At your service, Guardian."

"Saving Mona without bloodshed. Impressive." Iris sat next to her. "Not bad."

"See? Even he puts the woman over the Goblet." Tears were flowing freely now from Satan's eyes. "He is my son, and I worship him."

Satan Jr. stood and turned toward Satan. "I spit on your legacy and I reject your overtures." He set the weeping Satan on fire again, then snapped his fingers and a limo pulled out of a nearby alley.

He had just opened the door when Derek stepped forward and set his hand on the door. "What about the Curse?"

"The Curse continues. Watching LaValle men die is fun." He tried to open the door, but Derek shoved it closed with his hip.

Justine jumped to her feet. "What? You're not keeping your promise?"

"I'm Satan Jr. I never keep my promises."

Satan started sobbing, wailing about his love and pride for his son.

Derek's face darkened. "You'll keep this one," he said quietly.

"No, I won't." Satan Jr. blew a kiss at Justine. "When your lover dies, I will comfort you, and if he kills you instead, then I will have you in the Afterlife."

"She's your sister," Satan sobbed. "You cannot make love to her until her mind explodes."

Satan Jr. blanched and he looked at Justine. "You're my sister?"

"Yes. As your sister, I request you drop the Curse. I don't want to be stalked by LaValle men for all eternity."

Satan Jr. snorted. "If they do kill you, so what? I'll save you in the Afterlife and we can destroy Satan together. It'll be loads of fun." He grimaced. "But I don't want to see you naked. Gross."

Derek slammed his palm into Satan Jr.'s throat and shoved him against the car. "You will *not* walk away without undoing the Curse. End it now."

Satan Jr. made a raspy, choking noise. "No."

"Then you die."

"You do not kill my evil progeny!" Satan declared. "Unhand him now, you mortal beast!"

Derek's eyes were glazing now, his hand tight on Satan Jr.'s neck. "Undo the Curse, you son of a bitch. I won't let you force me to kill her."

A weak smile curved Satan Jr.'s lips. "You'll have to choose between saving the Guardian or your brother and all the other LaValle men. Either way, you will be tortured by your choice for all eternity. That's what makes it so fun. Kill me. I don't care. I can get Satan from the Afterlife just as easily."

"I love this boy," Satan sobbed. "He is so brilliant, is he not? I am so proud of him. I welcome him to my bosom."

Justine leaned around Derek's shoulder, pressing her face up against Satan Jr.'s nearly bloodless one. "Having trouble breathing, bro?"

Satan Jr.'s lips moved, but no sound came out.

"Withdraw the Curse," she said. "End it."

He shook his head and curved his lips into a small grin,

but she saw the flicker of fear in his eyes. Derek frowned and she knew he'd seen it. "Do it, Derek."

"My pleasure." Derek pretended to tighten his grip, and panic contorted Satan Jr.'s features. He started struggling, kicking Derek's shins, arms flailing, tears filling his eyes.

One more minute and they'd have him.

"No!" Satan shouted. "You will not kill my boy!" Then there was a flash and Derek was slammed into the limo. He fell to the ground, a six-inch hole through his gut from a fireball that had continued on through the side of the car.

"Derek!" Justine dropped to the ground next to him, her hands going immediately to his chest. When she felt his heart beating, she had to drop her head and close her eyes for a moment to gather herself.

"Serves you right," Satan Jr. said. He kicked some dirt on Derek, so Justine grabbed her dagger and plunged it into his thigh.

"Reverse the Curse, you bastard!"

He howled with pain, clutching his leg as he fell into the back of the limo. "Never!" He yanked the door shut and the limo sped away. She grabbed her gun and fired at the tires, but it was already out of range.

"Want me to go after him?" Xavier was suddenly by her side. "I can catch him."

She pressed her lips together and assessed Derek's injury. The wound was cauterized from the heat, and the Mona in his veins was keeping him from dying instantly, but even two-thirds immortal wouldn't recover from this. "No. We need to take care of Derek."

"But Satan Jr. will get away."

"If Derek dies now, then it won't matter if we catch Satan Jr. And we still have two days to find him. Help me get Derek in the car." Xavier hooked his hands under Derek's shoulders and she grabbed his feet. She scowled at Satan, who was looking immensely pleased with himself. "Go stick your head in a vat of purified water."

Satan beamed at her. "Aren't you proud to be my daughter?" He tucked an arm through Iris's arm. "Come, Iris, let us go celebrate. I owe you for bringing my son into my life again."

Justine staggered to her feet, hunched under Derek's weight. "You're going with him?"

Iris sighed and touched Justine's hair. "I'm so sorry, sweetie, but this was the way it had to be. Tell the Council you killed him. They'll be impressed and reward you. I know it hurts, but at least it's finally over and you didn't have to be the one to actually kill him." She took Satan's arm. "Come on, I think she needs to be alone."

They disappeared in a shimmer of gold bubbles, leaving Justine alone with Derek. Not dead yet, but on his way.

Twenty-three

On the plus side," Xavier said as they carried Derek toward his car. "With that hole in his gut, he'll die looking like the pretzel that made him rich. You should have an open casket. I'm sure he'd appreciate the irony."

"Shut up." She could see the asphalt road through his belly and it was freaking her out. They got him settled in the backseat, and Justine climbed in with him. "Take us back to his place."

"Certainly." He peeled out so fast she was flung into the door and Derek slid halfway across the seat.

She righted them both, then pulled his head onto her lap and patted his cheek. "Derek. Can you hear me?"

His eyes flickered open. "I was faking it. I'm fine."

"Liar." She bit her lip. "I can see the seat through the hole in your torso."

"Well, that explains the pain," he said. "What's up with you and your family all aiming for my stomach? Do I have a target painted on it or something?"

She managed a smile and wiped some charred bits off his forehead. "We're just a bloodthirsty bunch."

He nodded, then grimaced with pain. "Where are we going?"

"Your place."

A frown wrinkled his forehead. "To Mona?"

"Maybe." She avoided his gaze, picking some gravel off his shirt instead.

He reached up and tugged her hair so she bent over him. "We failed with Satan Jr., Justine. My life isn't worth you being in the Chamber for eternity. You have to let me die."

She blinked back the moisture in her eyes. "What about your brother?"

He closed his eyes and cursed under his breath.

She sighed and spread her hands on his chest, under his shirt. The skin was still warm, his heart was still beating. Mona was working hard to keep him alive, but she could sense his energy fading. "Drive faster, Xavier."

The only response she got was the rev of the engine and the squeal of tires.

"I don't suppose there are any loopholes for using Mona?" His voice was faint and gravelly.

"No." She smoothed his hair, even though it was so short it didn't need it. "Since the threat of Satan and Satan Jr. are gone, there's no reason to keep you alive. I have all the information I need to deal with it on my own. If I give you the third drink, I might as well start packing my bags for the Chamber."

"Then don't do it." His voice was so faint she had to lean close to hear him.

Her vision blurred, and she knew he was right. She had to let him die. "Derek, I'm so sorry."

He didn't say anything.

"Derek?"

He was unconscious.

* * *

Derek woke up to blackness, and he knew he was dead. He'd failed Quincy. Failed all the LaValle men. And he'd lost the girl. He groaned softly.

Then a warm hand touched his chest. "Derek?"

He turned his head, but it was too dark to see. "Justine? Where are we?"

"Your den. Theresa took over the guest room, Quincy's working in your room, and Xavier is making calls in the living room. You've been unconscious for almost two days."

"But I should be dead . . ." He reached down to his stomach. Intact. No pain. "You did it." Elation and warmth rushed through him, chased instantly away by an icy fear for Justine's future. He grabbed for her hand, crushed it against his chest. "You shouldn't have done it. You'll go to the Chamber for this."

"It's looking like that." He heard her take a deep breath, and then she laid her other hand on top of their intertwined fingers. "I took a chance. We had two days left. I thought maybe we could still find Satan Jr. and end the Curse."

"And did it work? Did you find Satan Jr.?" *Please tell me you found a way to save yourself.*

She sighed. "We spent the entire time looking for Satan Jr. but he has completely disappeared. Even Zeke couldn't find him." He laid his hands over her face, trying to read her expression with his hands. He could feel the furrow in her brow, the tense set to her mouth. "We tried. They're still trying. But Satan Jr. disappeared for almost two hundred years. He knows how to do it, and he won't be found unless he wants to. It's over, Derek."

He wrapped his fingers around her wrist and tugged gently. Smiled softly when she rolled on top of him. "I'm not worth it."

She hesitated, then her voice became brisk and businesslike. "It wasn't about you. I hoped that risking my future to save your life might be a Qualifying Incident. I did it to save my mom."

Was that really the only reason she'd done it? He traced her lips with his fingers, rubbing softly to release the tension from them. "You really think it would have saved her?"

Silence. "Maybe."

Ah, his sweet Guardian. "You've complicated my life, now, you realize?"

"How so?"

"How am I supposed to kill you, knowing that when I do, you'll go into the Chamber?"

She sighed heavily, her breath warm against his fingers. "Well, now you know how I felt when you were dying. It's a crappy position to be in, trading lives of people you lo— Um, care about."

He cupped her face with his hands. "Why did you give me the third drink? Tell me the truth." *If you tell me you love me, I'll walk away forever. I'll burn the journal so no LaValle man will ever be able to find you.* He frowned. Would he really trade his brother's life for hers? Yes. His brother would go to the Afterlife. Justine would go to the Chamber. It wasn't a choice. All she had to do was say the word. "Justine? Tell me."

Silence.

Finally, "The Council could be listening."

"So?"

"So, I can't give up yet," she whispered.

What did that mean? Did that mean she did love him, but that she wasn't willing to let the Council know? If she saved him because she loved him, there would be no escape clause. But if she proved she had saved him for Mona's sake, she still had a chance.

He wanted to hear the words before one of them died, just to know. But it wasn't worth her eternity to hear her say she loved him or to say those words himself. To anyone listening, it had to simply be about the Goblet. Not about love. Not about divided loyalties. He lifted his head, laying the tenderest kiss he could on her lips. A kiss he hoped told her how he felt.

For a long moment, neither of them moved or spoke. Then he felt her fingers brush against his cheek and he closed his eyes.

Then Justine took a deep breath. "I saved you because I decided you had a legitimate point about your progeny stalking me. I was hoping you might have a new plan, now that the Satan Jr. idea came up a dead end."

"Of course you did." He sighed and let his hands rest against her waist. Hmm . . . She was wearing something silky and thin. "It was a valid plan."

"Thanks. I'm still going to kill you, though. Just so you know."

"I believe you." Her body felt so good against him. Warm and soft, her skin so smooth. Why was she in bed with him? How would she explain that to the Council? How would *they* explain it, because he wasn't going to let her face them on her own. He let his hands slide up her body until he got to her hair, digging his fingers in the soft tresses as an idea formed in his mind. "I know why you saved me. I know why you're in bed with me now."

"Why?" Her voice was soft, tinged with desperation. "Tell me, please."

"Your mom and the Penhas are proof that celibacy weakens a Guardian. But sex enabled you to defeat the Penhas." He pressed his lips to her forehead and let his head fall back on the pillow. "If you let me make love to you all night, and then kill me, you'll prove to the Council that even non-Emergency sex doesn't weaken your ability to defend Mona. Sex makes a Guardian stronger, no matter what the context." He frowned and stopped playing with her hair. "So, basically, you're using me so you can have other lovers."

"Wow. That's brilliant." She thudded her palms against his chest. "That's exactly why I'm here with you. Because I'm a brilliant Guardian who is willing to risk her future for the sake of the Goblet and getting the *Treatise* and the Oath updated so I can protect Mona adequately." She shifted on him, her thigh nestling against his. "Will you have sex with me? For the sake of my future?"

No rushed sex on the floor of her condo with Penhas hanging from the rafters. Slow, passionate lovemaking with all the time in the world to bask in the other's body. He let his breath out slowly and let his fingers skim down her back, over her behind to the soft skin on the backs of her thighs. He traced the tip of her nose, her cheekbones, the curve of her chin. "How long do we have?"

"Seven hours until my Judgment. Eight until the Curse strikes you."

"Which means six hours and fifty-nine minutes to prove your case for saving your soul and getting your *Treatise* updated so your future is Chamber-free," he said. "The extra minute is for us to engage in a battle to the death before you go off to your Judgment."

She kissed him gently. "Just so you know, I'll feel really bad when I kill you. Really, really, bad."

"No worse than I'll feel when I kill you." He anchored her hips against his, his legs tangling around hers. Hmm . . . skin-to-skin on their legs, his chest was definitely bare, and he could feel the satin of her panties quite clearly as she pressed against him. "Am I naked?"

"Yes. Theresa insisted."

He grinned and slipped his hand under the silky camisole covering her lower back. Oh, God. The feel of her skin. So soft. So alive. So warm. "And you didn't argue? Try to protect my modesty?"

He felt a feather light kiss on his collarbone. "She's a fire-breathing dragon. I didn't dare interfere, but I thought I better sleep in here with you to make sure she didn't take advantage of you while you were passed out."

"Mmm . . ." He cupped her shoulder blades, pressing his palms against her, drawing her upper body down to him.

"Well . . ." He paused to lift his head and suck gently on her neck. Then he grabbed her tighter, wrapped his leg around hers, then flipped them over so he was above her. "We need to have really intense, mind-blowing sex so you can prove you're a worthy Guardian when you try to get the *Treatise* revamped."

"Exactly." Her hands pressed against his chest, her fingers tracing his nipples.

He kissed her breast through the silk and felt her arch against him. "Want to trade battle scars?"

"I have none. They all heal quickly." Her fingers dug into his shoulders, and she shifted under him. "You?"

"I have a hole in my gut."

"Yeah, that one might actually leave a mark." She slid

her hands down his chest to his belly, her fingers caressing. "It's a little smooth still."

He grunted and closed his eyes. It felt so good to have her against him, under him, touching him. Her skin hot against his, her flesh real and alive under his touch.

Justine felt like her insides were going to spill over with heat, passion, and other things she didn't want to put a name to. They had so little time. "Kiss me, Derek."

When his lips touched hers, it was as if someone had ripped her self-control from her body, replacing it with a burning heat that couldn't be restrained. She threw her arms around his neck and pulled him up against her, kissing him desperately, deeply, shoving all the heat and passion within her into his soul.

His tongue dove into her mouth, and she met him, danced with him, embraced him as he invaded her body. She needed him, needed his breath in her lungs, needed his touch on her skin.

He broke the kiss, and she felt a rush of loss, of loneliness, until she felt his hands span her waist, his lips caress her belly. God, she was totally quivering under his touch. Was she that desperate for the touch of a man?

No, she was that desperate for Derek's touch.

It was only him who could satisfy the need that had flickered to life inside her. It was as if she'd kept it doused for two hundred years, and his kiss had ignited it again. It would never go out. It would burn forever, yearning for him.

No, that wasn't good. She couldn't yearn for anyone, especially not him. "Derek . . ."

His mouth closed over her right breast and she couldn't remember what she'd been planning to say. She was vaguely aware of him sliding her camisole over her head, but the touch of his hands on her arms as he slipped it off, the feel of his teeth nibbling on her nipple, the heat of his breath on her skin . . . well . . . it was a little distracting.

A lot distracting. "Remember that love slave comment?" she whispered.

She felt the roughness of his whiskers against the soft skin of her inner thigh as he grinned. "I remember the love slave comment."

"If I kill you, then we might be able to arrange something," she whispered. She closed her eyes, relishing in the feel as his hands wrapped around her thighs, his lips caressing her. "Get you a portal to me or something."

He didn't answer.

She couldn't help her body from twisting under him, her legs from wrapping around him, skin-to-skin, the heat was building. God, she felt like she was on fire.

Derek traced his way back up her belly with his lips. "I feel like I'm burning up."

"Me too," she gasped. It was as if her blood were boiling, melting through her arteries, setting her heart aflame.

"Must be your dark side," he said, his knee moving between hers and his hands stroking every inch of her body. Here, there, again, his lips. Too much, so much, sensation overwhelming.

"Next to the bed," she managed, her voice too raspy to be hers.

Derek reached over and the sound of foil told him he'd found what she'd put there. "Aren't we both immune to diseases?"

"You want another Satan Jr. running around?"

"It would actually be Satan the third, and under certain

circumstances, it wouldn't be a bad thing." He tore the foil and shifted his weight.

His hands found her breasts again, his lips tugging at her nipples, and something exploded in her belly. Heat, fire, flames. Something hot. Something dark. "There aren't enough LaValle males in this world," he said as he rolled over, taking her with him. "Something needs to be done about it."

She straddled his hips, then eased herself slowly down. Sensation after sensation rippled through her, and she knew it was right. He was right. *They* were right. "You'd be willing to raise *Satan's* grandkids?"

"I won't have a son until the Curse is over." He grabbed her hips, moved with her, deeper, harder, until she was certain they were one. One body, one soul, one essence, one flame burning with deadly heat. He yanked her down on top of him, rolled again, until his weight was pressing her into the mattress, his strength against her, around her, inside her. "But if I ever get to that point, I choose you."

He loved her.

And then he drove into her again, so hard, so deep, and she felt his soul explode into her body. She screamed and clutched his shoulder, his arms, she didn't know what. All she had was his flesh, his skin under her hands, against her, holding her to this earth, keeping her grounded even as he shuddered against her, shouted her name, and held her so tight she thought they had melted into one.

Derek woke to the feeling of a cold blade pressing the side of his neck.

He didn't open his eyes, didn't move, didn't tense. He gave no indication that he was awake.

The mattress shifted under his hips, and he knew Justine was standing over him with a sword.

He'd stashed his own sword under his side of the bed, next to where his hand was draped over the edge. He moved his fingers ever so slightly and felt the handle. He wrapped his fingers around it, then waited for his opportunity.

She would need to take a backswing to generate enough momentum to slice his head off. He hoped he'd have time to take her out when she did it.

He could still feel her skin against his, hear her name on his breath as she fell asleep in his arms. This was not how it was supposed to end.

A light knock sounded at the door and he felt Justine jump and heard her suck in her breath. "What?"

"The Council is here," Theresa said. "They're waiting to escort you to the Judgment."

Justine cursed softly. "They're early."

"Can I fry the old one? He keeps making snide remarks about how the Chamber of Unspeakable Horrors is all warmed up for you. He's really pissing me off."

Give her permission. Don't let them rule your life, Justine.

"No," Justine said. "Leave them alone."

"Fine," Theresa said. There was a pause, then, "Derek's not worth your eternal soul, Justine. The Afterlife isn't such a bad place. He'll make new friends. He'll be okay . . . Hey!"

The doorknob rattled. "Justine, it's Quincy. Don't kill my brother."

Quin. Shit. He had to kill Justine now. If he didn't, Quin would die.

Justine cursed again, and he felt her weight shift and the blade disappeared from his neck. She was taking her backswing.

Instantly, he grabbed his sword, spun off the bed to his feet and raised his blade to her neck.

She stopped her blade so it was resting against his neck, mimicking his stance.

"Morning, love," he said. "Last night was great."

"Better than great. Blew my mind." Her gaze flicked toward his waist. "I see you're ready to go again."

"Don't cut it off."

A sad smile curved her mouth. "I wouldn't dream of it." She cocked her head. "You know, it's slightly curved, not crooked."

"What's going on in there?" Theresa asked. "Are you guys chatting? Just kill him, for heaven's sake."

"Why are you so bloodthirsty?" Quincy asked.

"I'm a dragon. It's my nature," she snapped. "Want me to prove it?"

"You try to fry me and I'll behead you. Derek's not the only one who's good with a sword. Besides, I have to talk to Derek. I found something out about the Curse." He pounded on the door. "Derek! Let me in! I have to show you something."

Derek and Justine exchanged looks. "What happens if you refuse to go with the Council?" he asked.

"They take me against my will."

"Can they do that?"

"Yep. Three against one and all that."

"What if it's four against three? I'm sure Theresa and Quincy would be willing to step up and provide assistance."

Justine felt a surge of hope swell in her chest, and she

immediately squashed it. "If I don't go, it will be another black mark against me. The fact I got Satan Jr. off Mona's case will go a long way toward sparing me, but if I refuse to go, I'm screwed." Dammit. She sounded like she was about to cry. Guardians didn't cry.

He cocked his head. "Do you want to kill me?"

"It doesn't matter." But her voice quavered ever so slightly.

"It matters." He raised his voice. "Key is above the door, Quin. Come in."

"Oh come on, Derek. You want me to kill him too?"

The door opened and Theresa and Quincy shoved their way through the door. Theresa stopped first. "Hot damn, Justine. He's a total hottie. He looks great naked!"

The corner of Derek's mouth curved up, and Justine poked him with the sword. "Show off."

"Gotta get her on my side somehow." He nodded at Quin, but didn't move the sword from Justine's neck. "What do you have?"

"I don't think Satan Jr. can actually curse people," Quincy said.

Derek groaned. "You're denying the Curse again? That's why you're in here? It's too late for that."

The old man, the pirate, and the businessman appeared in the doorway. Justine froze and felt her throat close up with fear. "Guardian, it's time to go."

"Back off, old man," Theresa growled. "She'll go when I say she goes." Then she set his hairpiece on fire and blew it down the hall with a gust of hot air. He shouted in protest and ran down the hall, covering his head and muttering about unspeakable horrors.

"One down," Derek said. "Two to go."

"All you've done is piss him off," Justine said, her gut sinking. She was in so much trouble. "It doesn't change anything important."

"Sure it does." Theresa slammed her tail into the other two and sent them crashing into the wall. "See? They won't bother us for a few minutes."

The pirate groaned and rolled onto his side, but the businessman was already fumbling for his BlackBerry.

Quincy stepped over the pirate. "Justine told us last night how Satan Jr. bragged that he harvests souls all the time, telling them he has the authority to make deals, even though he doesn't."

"He lies," Derek said. "So what?"

Quin paced the room, his hands flying with excitement. "So, what if he's lying about the Curse? What if he claims he can curse, but he can't?"

"Then why are we all dying?"

Justine's right arm was starting to tremble, so she added her other hand to the sword.

"This is ridiculous." The businessman shut his Black-Berry and stood up. "Guardian, it is time to leave."

"Let him talk," the pirate said. "I want to hear this theory."

Quin stopped in front of Derek. "Didn't you say that Satan Jr. enjoys watching us all die?"

"Yeah, so?"

"So what if he's showing up and doing it himself and there's no Curse. It's only Satan Jr. and the tracking device he already admitted he uses on us."

The pirate whistled softly. "He could be onto something."

"It's possible." Justine clenched her teeth and tried to

keep the sword at Derek's neck. Derek looked like he could go on for hours, and her arm was about to fall off. "He's slimy enough to do it."

Derek glanced at her, noticed her trembling arm, then sighed. "Why didn't you say you were getting tired?" He dropped his sword and then took hers. "We'll call a truce until we get this settled." He pulled her against him so he could rub her trembling biceps. "Why are you so stubborn?"

She leaned into him. "Because I refuse to be bested by a mortal."

"But I'm not mortal anymore, am I?"

The businessman perked up. "Not mortal?" He opened his BlackBerry again and began typing furiously. The pirate peered over his shoulder to inspect what he was entering.

Quin wasn't finished. "I ran some equations on the Curse, and it doesn't compute. It's not legit. I think the whole thing is a scam."

"Can you prove it?" Derek asked.

"My math is flawless." Quin sounded quite offended. "Though I haven't had time to recheck my work as thoroughly as I would prefer, given the repercussions of this particular situation."

Derek rubbed his chin on Justine's head. "So, we could set a trap for Satan Jr., then incapacitate him when he shows up. If I don't die, then we know there's no Curse. If I do, then your math was wrong."

"Then we both die." Quincy sighed. "Maybe it's not worth the risk. Killing her would be the safest option for us." He turned away and slammed his fist into the wall.

"If Derek dies, Quincy will still have ten minutes to try to kill Justine and steal Mona to break the Curse," Theresa said. "I vote against the plan. Behead them both now."

"Yes, kill them." Toupee guy was back with the charred ends of his hairpiece littering his head.

Derek picked up the sword and handed it back to her. "Or we can battle it out now."

She looked at the blade. "That's the low risk alternative. Highest likelihood of success for both of us."

"Yes, it is," he agreed. He raised his sword.

"Behead him," toupee guy said.

"Do it," Theresa sighed.

"I wish I had more time," Quincy muttered. "I really think this Curse is a sham."

The business suit guy took notes and said nothing.

"Interesting," said the pirate.

Justine raised her sword. "I have no choice."

"I know." He lifted his to meet hers. "Let's do it."

Twenty-four

The room was so quiet Derek could hear the crackling of the old man's still burning toupee.

Blades up.

Ready.

He met Justine's gaze, and he knew what he had to do. He'd lost the ability to choose long ago. "Justine?"

She nodded once, adjusted her grip on her sword.

He did the same, then blew her a kiss.

She tightened her lips, and then they both swung at the same time.

He slammed the butt of his sword into the back of toupee guy's head, Justine smashed hers into the businessman's gut, and Theresa screeched with delight and pounced on the pirate.

Quincy stood in the middle, looking startled.

"You'll regret this," the businessman gasped. "This won't look good in the report."

Pirate guy grinned up at them from under Theresa's tail. "Can I help?"

Forty-eight minutes later, they were ready.

A bunch of pillows were shoved under the covers on Derek's bed, a reasonable facsimile of Derek buried under the blankets. Derek himself was under the bed. They hoped that Satan Jr.'s locating device would track Derek to the bed, and Satan Jr. wouldn't take the time to assess whether the lump under the covers was really Derek or not. He'd see the lump, assume the obvious, and decapitate the pillows while the rest of the group took him out.

If Satan Jr. didn't fall for it, Derek was dead because he was trapped under the bed with nothing but a Super Soaker. Or if there really was a Curse, the pillow decoy wouldn't work either.

Everyone was in place, and now all there was left to do was to wait.

Justine was in the closet, only a few feet from Derek's bed, armed for her key role with her cigarette lighter and walkie-talkie.

She shifted position for the umpteenth time, then peered through the hole in the closet door, and wondered how Derek was doing under the bed.

Less than three minutes until he was supposed to die.

Derek dead.

She drummed her fingers on the wall, shifted again, then gave up and opened the door.

"Stay in the closet." His whisper was so low she could barely hear him

"No. Kill me." She kicked a sword at him across the floor. "Just do it."

He stuck his head out from under the bed. "No."

"You have to! I can't sit here and watch you die."

A small smile curved his lips and softened his eyes. "Then sit there and help me catch him."

"What happened to you wanting to kill me?"

"I can't kill a woman who loves my crooked penis. Where will I find another woman like you?"

"It's not crooked. It's slightly curved."

"And you love it."

"Maybe." Oh, who was she kidding. It wasn't his penis. It wasn't even the fact he was ready to kill her. She simply loved him and all he was. What other reason could possibly justify the fact she had two-thirds of the Council hogtied and gagged in the bathroom? Even if Derek lived, her soul was a lost cause. And her mom's, she was sure. "Derek, I can't let you die."

His grin got bigger. "Go back in the closet. We have just over a minute."

She scowled at him. "If you die, I will personally kick your ass."

"As long as you avoid the Chamber, you can kick anything of mine you want." Then his face tensed. "Did you hear that? The ceiling's creaking. He's here."

Her gut dropped and she grabbed the sword and held the handle toward him. "I can't let you die."

"Forget it, Justine. I'm not killing you. I believe in Quin. We're going to catch Satan Jr. and end this." He scooted out of sight. "We can argue later, but if this is going to work, you have to go back in the closet. That's how you can save me."

She took a deep breath. He was right. She was a Guardian. She could handle this.

"Go!"

"I'm going." She ducked back into the closet and hit her walkie-talkie. "Game on."

"Right-o," said Jerome, the pirate guy. Now that he was on their side, he got to be called by his real name.

She held her breath and watched her clock tick. Five seconds.

She stood up on the footstool and flicked the lighter on, holding it next to the smoke sensor.

Four.

Three.

Two.

One.

The ceiling collapsed and crushed the bed.

The sprinkler system went on.

The fire alarm sounded.

And someone screamed. And didn't stop. It was even worse than Satan's screaming when he had the temper tantrum. "I'm melting, you pigs! How could you do this to me? You will all die for this!"

"Let me burn him up," Theresa shouted. "Please, let me do it!"

"Get back," Jerome yelled. "I have water balloons! We have to make sure he can't revive!"

Justine dove out of the closet, straight for the bed. The mattress was buried under several feet of plaster, a coffee table, and a grand piano from the apartment above. The glass from a coffee table was sticking out of the mattress, having cleanly beheaded the pillow.

If Derek had been in the bed, he'd be dead now. But was he dead anyway? "Derek? Are you okay?" She shoved aside some picture books and an ottoman and stuck her head under the bed. "Derek?"

Silence.

Her heart seized up, like a vise in her chest. "Derek! If you're messing with me, I swear I'll behead you without a second thought!"

Then a hand crept out of the darkness and wrapped behind her head. She was met with a familiar set of lips, a tongue she loved very much, and the scent of a man that she could never live without. She grinned and let him pull her underneath the bed.

Justine fidgeted with her new suit, courtesy of Derek's favorite tailor and a special import of Italian fabrics.

Her mom, Theresa, Quincy, and Derek were sitting in the reserved seats at the front of the Judgement room. Satan had been given a special visitor's pass after providing proof of parentage, but he was still surrounded by six guards carrying bazookas filled with purified water. His arms were folded over his chest and he looked extremely cranky.

He hadn't spoken to any of them, including Iris, since they'd melted Satan Jr. into a puddle and stuck him in the freezer so he couldn't reform.

There was a door at the back of the room that was lettered in gold: CHAMBER OF UNSPEAKABLE HORRORS, CREATED BY SATAN.

Toupee guy had pointed to it several times in his speech. At least he hadn't had time to get a new hairpiece and looked ridiculous wearing his half-burned rug.

The head of the Council, Isabella Marcellini, looked at Jerome. "You have something to add?"

Jerome stood up, straightened his eye patch, and strode into the center of the room. "I think this incident shows that guarding Desdemona's Temptation is no longer a one-person job. Satan Jr. was a legitimate threat and it took a team to uncover it and take him down."

"A team," Satan said proudly. "My son is quite the badass, is he not? No training, and it still took a whole team to melt him. Imagine what he will do with more experience?"

Iris glared at him. "Ssh!"

Satan refused to look at Iris, but he shut his mouth.

Justine took a deep breath and tried to slow her heart rate. They'd done everything they could. Her speech had been great, she'd cited many clauses in the *Treatise*, and now Jerome was closing it out.

But even if she was spared, what would the Council do with Derek? He was immortal now, and he wasn't supposed to be.

"If Satan speaks again, shoot him." Isabella was well known for her conservative and ruthless views, and she was in a particularly bad mood because she'd had to delay her vacation for a day due to the temporary incapacitation of certain Council members who had been tied up in Derek's bathroom.

"Justine showed excellent instincts by recruiting a worthy staff to assist her and by breaking rules so she would be able to save Desdemona's Temptation," Jerome continued. "She succeeded in keeping the Goblet safe, and in my opinion, that is the most important factor to consider. I recommend that we create a job family. Promote Justine Bennett to Head Guardian, and assign Derek LaValle as Assistant Guardian. The dragon can continue to be Justine's successor, and Quincy LaValle can be Derek's successor."

Quincy stood up. "I respectfully decli—"

Theresa and Derek yanked him down. Theresa sat on him and gave Isabella a sweet smile. "He accepts. Please, go on."

"In addition," Jerome said. "I recommend you assign the retired Guardian, Iris Bennett, to update the *Treatise* to reflect a more useful and modern rule system. She will work with the current Guardian and the Council to redefine the rules. As a Guardian who failed partially due to the out-dated *Treatise,* I believe she should be given this honor to redeem herself. If she succeeds, I recommend we present her case again to consider reinstating Guardian benefits."

Iris let out a small gasp and clapped her hand over her mouth.

Justine grinned. They hadn't told Iris that part of the plan.

Then she realized Jerome had returned to his chair. The room was silent, and everyone was staring at Isabella as she read her notes and conferred with her assistant. It was now up to Isabella.

Even Satan was silent. Waiting.

As the silence dragged on, Justine's adrenaline faded. The Otherworld didn't evolve. It didn't become modern.

Isabella cleared her throat and surveyed the room. "I agree with Jerome."

What? Relief rushed through her and her knees started to buckle.

"Derek LaValle has proven his competence to protect the Goblet, and it is clear he and Justine Bennett work well together. I support forming a team and creating backup. Justine should have cleared it with the Council first, however, so I suspend her and Derek from Guardian duties for two months."

She fell to her chair, her chest constricted and her vision blurry. Derek was safe. It was over.

"In addition, the fact that Ms. Bennett orchestrated the melting of her own brother to save Mona shows that her light side trumps her dark-side loyalties. Therefore, I declare the Qualifying Incident met and both she and her mother will be spared hell unless they do something else to earn it."

Satan screeched and jumped to his feet in protest and Iris let out a whoop of triumph. Justine was too exhausted to do more than drop her head to the table and sag with relief.

"Subject, of course, to Satan's request for political relocation of Iris," Isabella added. "His petition will be remanded to committee for discussion. Decision due in three hundred years. The Council is in charge of updating the *Treatise,* subject to the expert advice of current and past Guardians. And Iris Bennett, though she still failed at the position, is nevertheless the best writer who has ever served as Guardian, so I regretfully give her the position of writing it. But she'll have to do an unbelievable job to have even a remote chance at benefits." She rapped her gavel on the podium. "Dismissed."

"Three hundred years?" Satan howled. "What about my son? You steal my woman *and* my son?"

"Oh, right." Isabella turned the microphone on again. "Satan Jr. will stay frozen until someone gives us a good enough reason to defrost him. Thank you again."

Justine lifted her head, staring at Isabella in stunned disbelief. They'd gotten everything they wanted? Even her mom getting to rewrite the *Treatise*. How was it possible?

Then she saw Isabella wink at Derek as she walked out of the room.

She spun to Derek as he reached to hug her. "What did you do?"

He grinned. "A lifetime supply of Vic's Pretzels. Even Afterlife judges like to watch their carb intake."

"You bribed her? I'm completely outraged by your absence of faith in Jerome's ability to sway her and your utter lack of morals." Then she threw her arms around him and jumped up, wrapping her legs around his waist. "You're too awesome."

He caught her against him, his hands wrapped around her bottom. "I told her I'd be too distraught to keep Vic's going if you were facing unspeakable horrors or if I was worrying about your mom." He kissed her nose. "I also said that if you were excused, then you and I would be visiting my mother-in-law in the Afterlife a lot, and that I would always bring pretzels when I visited. Lots and lots of pretzels." He grinned. "There are serious advantages to being a pretzel mogul."

"And what about the mother-in-law comment? Did you really tell her we were getting married? I mean, it's not like we've even talked about it." Or even had time to think about it. But she was thinking now. Oh, yes, she was definitely thinking about it.

"I had to tell her we were getting married to ensure it didn't sound like a bribe." He trailed his fingers along her collarbone. "You don't have to do it, though."

She clasped her hands behind his neck, unable to keep the grin off her face. "So you don't want to marry me?"

He lifted a brow. "I'm not cursed anymore. I'll take the first woman who says yes."

Her smile got wider. "What makes you think I would say yes?"

"Because no other man would be crazy enough to marry Satan's daughter."

"So, I'm desperate?"

"Yep. And so am I."

"You are? Why?"

"Because no other woman stirs my soul like you do."

He kissed her softly. "I'm a goner for a Guardian with a gun and an espresso machine. Especially a Guardian who loves me enough to save my life even at the risk of her eternal soul."

"I saved your life because I needed your help to end the Curse," she teased.

"But in the end, when it was all over, you didn't kill me." He pressed her palm to his lips. "That's when I knew you had it bad for me, Guardian."

"And you didn't kill me."

"Exactly. True love all around."

"Say it."

He caught her face between his hands. "I love you, and I'm going to use our two-month suspension to make love to you in so many different ways that only our immortality will keep us surviving all the orgasms. I figure we can get married today, and then take off on a honeymoon."

She hugged him fiercely, nearly overwhelmed by the love vibrating in her body.

He crushed her against him. "I hope you don't mind the vacation. She needed to punish you, so I made the suggestion and she liked it." He pulled back far enough to see her face. His eyes were bright, his smile brilliant. "I can't have my true love burning herself out. I insist on a vacation at least every two centuries. Let Theresa and Quincy earn their titles."

"I've never had a vacation. It's a great wedding gift." She grinned. "I love you too, and I will marry you." It was the most amazing feeling to embrace her love for Derek. There was nothing to hold them back anymore.

Oh, sure, Satan Jr. would eventually be unfrozen, Satan wasn't going to give up on seducing Iris, Theresa was still stuck in dragon form, Derek's vice president was Satan's servant, and she seriously doubted they were going to be able to convince Quincy to accept his new assignment and drink from Mona, but how dull would her life be without all of that?

True love, great sex, and lots of threats coming from all directions. Her life was *perfect*.

About the Author

Golden Heart winner Stephanie Rowe wrote her first novel when she was ten, and sold her first book twenty-three years later. After a brief stint as an attorney, Stephanie decided wearing suits wasn't her style and opted for a more fulfilling career. Stephanie now spends her days immersed in magical worlds creating quirky stories about smart, scrappy women who find true love while braving the insanity of the modern world and Otherworldly challenges. When she's not glued to the computer or avoiding housework, Stephanie spends her time reading, playing tennis, and hanging out with her own fantasy man and their two Labradors. You can reach Stephanie on the Web at www.stephanierowe.com.

About the Author

More
Stephanie Rowe!

Turn the page for a preview
of her new novel,

Must Love Dragons

Available in mass market Fall 2006

One

Theresa Nichols was going to starve to death and no one cared.

She didn't know which was ticking her off more, the fact that she hadn't had her No-Carb Pretzel fix in a week, or the fact that Quincy LaValle had apparently forgotten her yet again like everyone else in her life.

Her stomach growled and a sharp pain ground through her gut. Who needs to eat?

Certainly not an eleven-foot winged dragon under house arrest because no one in New York City could cope with the reality that dragons do exist. Heaven forbid she be spotted by anyone who could start the next world war with shrieks of invasions, Martians, and other such panic-inducing nonsense.

Because of the close-mindedness of humans, she'd been stuck behind closed doors for two hundred years, and quite frankly, it was getting old. Especially when she was withering away, alone and forgotten and starving to death.

She'd lost a hundred and sixty-one pounds in the last week since she'd been put under Quincy's neglectful care. Completely unacceptable! She was a dragon, dammit, and dragons had needs! Food, violence, destruction, incineration. None of which she was allowed to indulge in in Quincy's house.

Being deprived of food was making it that much harder to resist all her other dragon needs. She groaned and leaned her head against the fridge, crushing away her insatiable craving to blow up his kitchen.

She let out a deep breath that was a little too smoky for comfort, then marched over to the phone and punched the speed dial. Again. And again, his voice mail came on. "Quincy! It's Theresa. I haven't eaten in two days and I'm starving. I know you don't care about me or the Goblet, but your brother's now the Assistant Guardian, in case you forgot. He'll kick your butt if he comes home from his honeymoon to find that Mona has been stolen because you let the Interim Guardian die of starvation while you were obsessing about some stupid math equation that no one but you cares about. If you don't get home with food in thirty minutes, I'm burning down your house and moving in with Becca." She slammed down the phone and glared at the espresso machine. "Mona! This is all your fault."

The espresso machine said nothing.

Of course it wouldn't. In two hundred years, Mona had never so much as hinted at an apology for turning Theresa permanently into dragon form. Yeah, yeah, so Theresa was the one who'd actually drunk from the Goblet of Eternal Youth, which was currently masquerading as an espresso machine, but wasn't it the Goblet's duty to warn her that a sip while in dragon form would make her stay a dragon forever?

Apparently not.

Theresa yanked open the freezer and stared at the empty contents. She supposed she could eat some more ice cubes. She'd at least be hydrated when she died of starvation.

Or maybe she could eat some chairs. Nothing wrong with fiber, right?

Now that Justine, her best friend, roomie, and personal servant for the last two hundred years, was off on her honeymoon, it was all too apparent what kind of a life Theresa had: none.

No job.

No social life.

No friends.

And most importantly, no way to get food.

She slammed the door shut as her stomach rumbled again and a burning sensation clawed at her belly. She'd bet a box of Vic's Pretzels that her body was beginning to eat itself. Wouldn't that be a fun way to die?

No! A dragon should die a violent and fiery death!

Dammit! She slammed her tail against the fridge, too hungry to bother checking to see if she'd left a dent. She wasn't even allowed to order delivery because she was guarding Mona and it was a big no-no to have strangers parading up to the door when the Goblet of Eternal Youth was there. You never knew if the skinny little delivery boy might be packing a sword in his stay-hot pizza bag. Plus, how was she supposed to explain her appearance when she answered the door? *No, you're not really seeing an emaciated dragon with gold eyes. It's the scent from the pizza causing you to hallucinate.*

Yeah, right.

She stalked over to the window of Quincy's house and stared at the darkened suburb. If she was in her own condo, she could probably get Xavier the doorman to bring her some food, but no, their condo was still in shambles after Justine and Derek had gotten a little trigger happy with their machine guns.

She closed her eyes and dug her claws into the windowsill. *You are not hungry. You are not lonely. You are a goddess.* The shattering of the wooden frame jerked her back to the present, and she yanked her claws away from the window. Even the house wasn't built for helping a dragon through the throes of misery.

There was only one thing that would help her now. One man. If Zeke wasn't online, heaven help her and the neighborhood she was hiding out in.

Guess it was another night of cybersex to try to take her mind off her life and the fact that she was going to be the first size-zero dragon in the history of the world.

She grabbed her computer and IM'ed Zeke, the only man she'd had cybersex with in the last six months. Six months of monogamy for Theresa Nichols, former slut queen. Astounding, wasn't it? Just proved how good a cyber lover Zeke was. For him to satisfy a dragon that was completely deprived of all other outlets was quite the feat. Thank God for Zeke.

"Zeke? You there?"

His reply was instant. "Yep. You?"

Tension eased from her body at his immediate response and she smiled, imagining what his voice must sound like. Deep, manly. He probably had thick whiskers that would make women tremble with longing. He was definitely a badass. She could sense the undercurrent of violence in him. She loved bad boys. What dragon wouldn't? It wasn't as if she could date a pansy who couldn't deal with a girl who liked to burn things up and ate six pizzas for an afternoon snack. "I bought a new piece of lingerie off the Internet yesterday. Want me to describe it?"

Silence.

She frowned at his hesitation and an anxiety spark shot out of her nose and landed on the keyboard. "Zeke? Don't leave me hanging. Not tonight."

He finally typed an answer. "Listen, I think we should meet."

Panic rifled through her and she jerked upright in Quincy's microfiber recliner, slamming the footrest back to the floor with a thud. "I can't meet you." She scowled as a wave of longing washed over her, smashing her claws into the keyboard as she typed her response. "I'm still in isolation in the FBI containment center remember? They haven't figured out how to keep my contagious disease from infecting everyone who comes within ten feet of me." A little stab of guilt shot through her, but it wasn't as if she could tell him she was a dragon. Besides, being locked up by the FBI was sort of dramatic and cool, and way better than her real life.

"I think you're avoiding me."

She grinned at his perceptiveness, imagining his brow furrowed as he typed. "Tell that to the dude with the machine gun guarding my door."

"Give me his number and I'll call him up."

Some of her amusement trickled away at his continued pressure. "He won't get close enough to talk to me. Afraid I'll infect him."

"Isn't that convenient?"

Her tail switched at his thinly veiled sarcasm and she accidentally dropped a puff of ash on Quincy's hand-woven carpet from India. She'd been fending off Zeke's pressure to meet for months, but something felt different tonight. Or maybe her perception of reality was being distorted by the fact that her stomach was beginning to eat her brain. "No, it's not convenient. I'd love to meet you in person and engage in some real flesh-to-flesh activities." Understatement of the year. Cybersex was better than nothing, but it was no substitute for having a man wrapped around her. She'd even had Justine buy her some of the aftershave Zeke said he wore, and she sprayed it around whenever they had cybersex. The woodsy, masculine scent was nearly enough to give her an orgasm on its own, let alone when Zeke was working his magic with the keyboard.

And when she couldn't sleep, she sprayed it on her pillow and pretended he was there, not that she'd admit that to anyone. Dragons didn't need nighttime comfort, and she was no exception. She was just sexually deprived and she loved to bask in the scent of the man of her fantasies.

"Seriously, T, I don't care about your infectious disease. I can buy a biohazard suit anywhere on the Internet. We need to meet."

Theresa's heart started to pound and her hind claws curled into the floor. Zeke was her one contact with the outside world. The wild and daring cybersex they had was her only outlet that kept her sane, since violence, gorging on food, and incineration weren't options. She had to reel him in before he ruined everything, before he demanded what she couldn't give.

"What's the point in meeting if you're wearing a biohazard suit? We wouldn't be able to have sex."

His reply was quick, as if he'd anticipated her answer. "I want to know what you look like."

She scowled. She was an eleven-foot winged dragon

with bluish-green scales and golden eyes. Would that do it for him? She doubted it. "Sorry. No pictures, remember?" It had been so long since she'd been in human form. She wasn't sure she'd even recognize herself.

Silence.

At the hesitation, Theresa shoved the computer off her lap and jumped to her feet, pacing past the beautiful ash coffee table Quincy had warned her not to leave burn marks on. Heat roiled through her, struggling to escape. A spark slipped out of her nose and landed on the hardwood floors. She stomped it out, then spun back to the computer when she heard it beep.

After a moment, she lifted her chin, straightened her tail, and marched over to read what he'd written. "I think maybe it's time to change the rules."

She growled. There could be no rule-changing! Face-to-face meetings were not happening!

"T? You still there? I'm serious. Things need to change. I can't keep this up."

How dare he ruin the only decent thing in her life by demanding something she couldn't give, no matter how much she might want to? She wouldn't let him. Not tonight. "The scientists are here to run more tests on me. Gotta run. Love your body."

Then she disconnected before he could reply.

She slammed the lid closed on her laptop and stomped across the room, ignoring the pictures rattling on the walls. Well, wouldn't that be fine and dandy? Not only would she starve to death, but she would die alone and sexually frustrated.

Forget it. That was taking it too far. A girl had to have limits.

She smashed her hip into the kitchen door and shoved it open, ignoring the trickle of sparks that dropped on the tile. Quincy would just have to get over a few burn marks. He'd be lucky if she didn't burn down his house by accident. She narrowed her eyes at the espresso machine. "I have to eat, which means it's time for a highly illegal field trip. And you're coming with me, since I can't leave you behind unprotected." She picked up the espresso machine and tried to tuck it under her arm. Not comfortable, especially for a dragon who wasn't exactly in top flying shape. "I don't suppose you could turn into something smaller and easier to carry?"

The espresso machine didn't so much as flicker.

"What if I try to sneak you into a male strip club?"

Mona immediately changed into a pair of edible underwear.

Theresa grinned. "That's my girl. Maybe we can be friends after all." At least there was something in this world that was more hard up than she was.

Forty-five minutes later, Theresa was perched on the roof of the Vic's Pretzels that was down the street from the condo she used to live in. She was wearing her favorite come-hither outfit: a leather miniskirt (over the "edible underwear," of course), a black lace bra under a transparent white top, the topaz earrings she'd bought during their brief stay in the Amazon (so what if dragons don't have ears? The scales located on the sides of her head worked just fine), and she'd even put a new gold ring into the piercing at the end of her tail.

She might not have any breasts or even a waist to do the outfit justice, and her blue scales weren't exactly sexy, but one should never underestimate the effect that sexy clothes can have on a woman's mood. Or a dragon's.

She took a deep breath and inhaled the amazing scent of fresh-baked dough, letting it soak into her lungs. Vic's No-Carb Pretzels were her reason for living, definitely worth taking a forbidden trip out into the night air.

The sounds of the humans working the ovens drifted up to her, and she took a moment to sort out their scents. There were at least three of them, two male and one female. Too many to incinerate; someone would notice. Frustration tried to roll through her, and she shoved it aside. Food would have to suffice to appease her needs. All she needed was to get them outside for a few minutes . . .

She eyed the roof and found what she was looking for. Didn't anyone have the foresight to protect their vents from dragons anymore? She glided over to the vent (yes, she might weigh several tons but that didn't mean she had to stop practicing her double-jointed-hip walk that had brought men to their knees two hundred years ago) and pressed her face up to it. "Hope you all are wearing your gas masks."

Wasn't this going to be fun? She hadn't tortured humans in forever.

She grinned, rolled some smoke around in her chest, then expelled a huge cloud of black smoke into the vent.

Then for kicks, she did it again. The sound of coughing and the rush of human alarm drifted up to her, and Theresa flopped down on her belly and let the sensations wash over her. It wasn't actual destruction, but it soaked into her pores and eased the desperation of her needs.

It took less than three minutes for the humans to vacate the premises. While they were hacking away out front, she sat up, shook off the soothing effects of the assault, and coasted down to the back door. She tugged on it, found it locked, then grinned with delight and yanked it free, along with the doorframe. She tossed the entire unit into the alley and scooted inside the kitchen of Vic's Pretzels.

Three feet inside the door, she was hit with the intense aroma of baking dough and melted butter, and she fell flat on her face. *Holy mother of pearl.* She groaned and rolled onto her back, drinking in the heavenly odors. Cinnamon hot pretzels. Warm frosting. Her claws curved against her chest and she closed her eyes, inhaling deeply as euphoria slackened her muscles, slowed her heart rate. She would never move again. Just lie here forever.

A distant clang caught her attention, and she shook her head, trying to clear it. This wasn't a safe environment. She shouldn't be sprawled on the floor. She tried to uncurl her claws, but she was too relaxed, to overcome by lassitude.

Come on, Theresa. Block your olfactory receptors. Now she remembered.

That's what she was supposed to do. Basic dragon survival techniques. God, but how? She couldn't recall, and it felt so good. The freshly-cooked bread smelled so divine. She didn't want to block it out. She just wanted to lie here and suck it in.

No. She had to get up. *Get up.*

She held her breath, then rolled over, landing with a thud on her belly. Progress. Good.

Somehow, she managed to pull her feet under her and staggered to her feet. *Starting to suffocate. Need to inhale.* She closed her eyes and concentrated on shutting down her scent receptors, taking a careful breath through her mouth. She got a whiff of hot pretzel and almost went down again.

She slapped her claws to her face, pinching her nostrils shut. Two hundred years of being locked in a condo with no threats to worry about had obviously eroded all her dragon defenses. She'd gotten sloppy, and if there'd been real danger, she'd be dead now.

Not only wasn't she human, but she was also a sucky dragon. Life was looking better all the time. Her head began to clear, and she surveyed her surroundings. She was in the kitchen. The floors, shelves of pretzel ingredients, huge metal ovens, racks of cooling pretzels, pretzel-shaped potholders hanging on little hooks shaped like more pretzels.

Her stomach rumbled and her mouth began to water.

Surely having food in her belly would help her control her nose, wouldn't it?

She lurched toward the racks of cooling pretzels, took a deep inhale through her mouth, then released her nose to grab a tray of pretzels. She dumped the contents down her throat. Then another. And another. There was no time to savor them. She needed to eat and run before she collapsed again.

She was starting to feel dizzy again, so she grabbed a couple of potholders and wedged them in her nostrils. Better. She turned back to the pretzels and tossed six more down her throat, the intense ache in her belly barely beginning to ease.

This is what it must have been like when the dragon slayers would hit town, back when the Dragon Cleansing of 1788 wiped out the dragon population. In a normal attack, a slayer would disorient a dragon with his incredibly powerful scent, and then come charging in to gain the advantage before the dragon could recover. In the Dragon Cleansing, all the slayers had joined together in an unprecedented maneuver and they'd attacked at once. She shuddered at the thought of being hit with all that olfactory stimulation.

Any halfway decent dragon learned how to shut down their scent receptors before they were two years old. It was the first line of defense against the slayers.

Well, guess what? She wasn't a halfway decent dragon apparently. She'd almost been knocked out by pretzel dough. Imagine what a dragon slayer's scent would do to her? She was too pathetic.

"Holy Jesus! What the fuck is that?"

Theresa dropped the tray and spun around. A guy in a chef's hat was staring at her from the doorway, his mouth hanging open and his eyes wide with horror.

She immediately bowed low, kneeling before him. "You must be the pretzel chef. I adore your pretzels, and I am so honored to meet you."

He made a strangled sound and began backing around the corner. Theresa snapped her head up and narrowed her eyes at him. "Hey! Where are you going?" She couldn't allow him to report a dragon sighting.

He yelped and dove out of sight.

She sighed and stood back up. She was going to have to kill him to ensure his silence, wasn't she? Then she smiled, and her tail flicked. How fun! An added bonus for the evening. She always slept well for at least a week after she got to incinerate someone.

Then her tail sagged. But who would make the pretzels if she killed him?

Crud. What was she supposed to do? Protect herself or the pretzels?

Dammit. Exposing herself meant exposing Mona. She *had* to kill him. She stomped toward the door he'd vanished through. How unfair that she finally got to kill someone and it was a pretzel chef. The remorse was going to gnaw at her for weeks.

She stepped into what looked like a supply room, and saw the chef hiding behind a stack of boxes. She whacked the boxes aside with her tail, and he jumped to his feet. His face was stark white and terror was cascading off him.

"I'm really sorry I have to do this," she said. "But I promise to visit you in the Afterlife with pretzels, okay?" She closed her eyes so she didn't have to watch, but before she could incinerate him, she heard a loud explosion and a searing pain ripped through her left shoulder. "Hey!" She snapped her eyes open in time to see him aim his gun at her face.

She threw her arm across her face as he shot again, and the bullet ripped through her front claw, sending pain spiraling up her shoulder.

"Get out of here, you freak!" he screamed. "I'll kill you before I'll let an ugly monster take me alive!" He shot again, and the bullet tore through her tail, nearly taking out her new ring.

"*Ugly monster?* Are you serious?" How dare he insult her like that? She was already sensitive enough about her appearance without having some idiot scream insults at her.

"Your mother won't have to look at your disgusting face again after I get through with you!" *Her mother?*

Now that was going too far. She lunged for him, and he shot her in the neck as he dove over a box of yeast and crawled behind an ice machine. Pain racheted through her, she felt blood trickle down her neck, and rage roared through her. Time to die, jerkoff. She kicked the ice machine aside, reared back and exploded fire at him.

But all that came out was a hack and a small puff of white smoke.

He yelped and scooted across the floor as she frowned and tried again. Same result? What the hell?

She flung a metal storage rack aside and slammed her tail into the chef's gut, pinning him against the wall as a faint memory trickled into her mind. Wasn't there something in the annals about how dragons should always protect their necks in battle? Maybe she should have gone to class more often instead of running around town causing trouble.

He whimpered and tried to get his gun free of her tail, to no avail. She pressed harder and her frustration eased. She could still kick his hiney with her superior dragon strength. She smiled and leaned her face up against his. "Insult my mama, will you? We're going to have fun tonight . . ."

Something twitched between her legs and an espresso machine dropped to the floor in front of her.

Oh, no! Regret slammed into her. She'd forgotten about Mona! The ultimate failure in Guardianship would be to let something happen to the Goblet of Eternal Youth. Each moment she stayed endangered Mona.

She might be a failure as a woman and as a dragon, but God help her, she would *not* fail at being a Guardian. She flung the chef aside, grabbed Mona and spun around, bolting for the door. She lurched into wobbly flight as soon as her wings were clear.

It took her less than a minute to realize she was too injured to make it all the way home. Didn't that figure? She couldn't even rescue Mona competently.

THE DISH

Where authors give you
the inside scoop!

Dear Reader,

Do you think it's weird to have such an overpowering crush on a character that I have to give him his own book? Should I be seeking counseling? Eh, maybe. But I don't care. I love Finn and I don't care who knows it.

Every now and again, if a writer is really good and eats all her veggies, a character will walk into a scene fully formed, requiring almost no work; that's what Finn did for me. I was writing *Maybe Baby,* and had no idea where I was going with it (that's how I write, hence the need to dye my grays) and BOOM! There he was. All redheaded and bird-thieving and wisecracking; I just loved him. So when I had the opportunity to write a second book, I knew it had to be Finn's.

What made *The Comeback Kiss* (on sale now) so much fun to write was that I had this carefree, live-by-the-seat-of-your-pants guy in Finn, and I just had to send him back home again. There was so much fun stuff waiting for him in Lucy's Lake——his cantankerous uncle and goody-goody brother, and his regret personified in Tessa, the one woman he couldn't forget——that I couldn't resist slamming this slick guy into the one situation he couldn't scam his way out of. Plus, I love reunion stories. They make me all warm and fuzzy inside. Hope it does the same for you!

Happy reading!

Lani Diane Rich

www.lanidianerich.com

In Stephanie Rowe's *Date Me, Baby, One More Time* (on sale now), Justine Bennett is cursing her life. She's the Guardian of the Goblet of Eternal Youth, she hasn't left the house in ages, and it's been over two hundred years since she's had sex. But she's a survivor and here are a few tips from her Guardian handbook:

Survival Tip #1:
Get your priorities in order. See cute guy. See cute guy reach for the Goblet (yes, the one that has recently shape-shifted into an espresso machine). Kill cute guy immediately. Yeah, it's a thankless job, but that Guardian Oath you took pretty much limits your options. Not that the Goblet ever appreciates the sacrifice. Espresso machines can be so ungrateful.

Survival Tip #2:
Abandon all plans of having a personal life. You're married to the Goblet, end of story. (I know, I know, what's the point of staying young forever if you're locked in your New York City condo with no one but a cranky, over-sexed dragon to keep you company?)

Survival Tip #3:
Whatever you do, don't trust the gorgeous pretzel mogul standing outside your door. Why? Because he's the one ready to behead you and steal your legacy, all in the name of saving the men of his family from a deadly Curse that's going to kill him in less than a week.

Survival Tip #4:
Never, ever, ever, ever, ever have sex with the gorgeous pretzel mogul working his way into your soul. If you do, not only will you wind up being tortured in the Chamber of Unspeakable Horrors for all eternity, but you also may lose your heart, and he just might lose his head.

Stephanie

www.stephanierowe.com

Want to know more about romances at
Warner Books and Warner Forever?
Get the scoop online!

WARNER'S ROMANCE HOMEPAGE

Visit us at www.warnerforever.com for all the
latest news, reviews, and chapter excerpts!

NEW AND UPCOMING TITLES

Each month we feature our new titles
and reader favorites.

CONTESTS AND GIVEAWAYS

We give away galleys, autographed copies,
and all kinds of fun stuff.

AUTHOR INFO

You'll find bios, articles, and links to personal
Web sites for all your favorite authors—and
so much more!

THE BUZZ

Sign up for our monthly romance newsletter,
and be the first to read all about it!